A Soul
ENCOUNTER
A SUSPENSEFUL ROMANCE

CLARK VIEHWEG

Black Rose Writing | Texas

The author grants the final approval for this literary material.

First printing

This is a work of fiction. Names, characters, businesses, places, events, and incidents are either the products of the author's imagination or used in a fictitious manner. Any resemblance to actual persons, living or dead, or actual events is purely coincidental.

ISBN: 978-1-68513-116-6
PUBLISHED BY BLACK ROSE WRITING
www.blackrosewriting.com

Printed in the United States of America
Suggested Retail Price (SRP) $21.95

A Soul Encounter is printed in Georgia Pro

*As a planet-friendly publisher, Black Rose Writing does its best to eliminate unnecessary waste to reduce paper usage and energy costs, while never compromising the reading experience. As a result, the final word count vs. page count may not meet common expectations.

Dedicated to everyone searching for the true love in their lives.

Thanks to Kim for her editing. You made me look better than I am.

A Soul
ENCOUNTER

1
A WOMAN ON THE TRAIN

Eleven-year-old Roy Dalton didn't know his life was about to change that day. Several years would pass before the significance of that day's brief encounter would become apparent.

The day started badly for the young boy. His mother had scored some pink grapefruits. God only knows where she got them. And as often happened when Roy ate that citrus fruit, he got a grapefruit juice shower with breakfast.

He loved the sweet, tangy flavor, but digging the grapefruit meat out of the half of grapefruit his mother gave him to eat always proved challenging without spraying juice all over the kitchen. Today he got a juice shot in his right eye, which now, five hours later, was still burning. Because it was a Monday, which was wash day, his mother was busy on the back porch firing up an old coal-burning stove to heat wash water, so she wasn't in the kitchen to suggest he wash the juice from his eye. Instead, he smeared it all over the eye socket by trying to wipe it out with the bandana from around his neck.

The day was like any other: a hot, dry morning in Clifton, Idaho, a small town in the Rocky Mountains. The sun was brutal, the wind relentless, and the empty sky bluer than a robin's egg. The Dalton ranch straddled the railroad tracks two miles east of town, but the family home was in town a few houses from the post office. His mother refused to live out of town without neighbors close by if she needed some help.

Roy started driving a tractor at four, not unusual in small rural towns with farmers struggling to survive, and by the age of eight, he was driving an old beat-up Chevy two miles to the ranch to do chores and spend the day working. Usually, his mom made him lunch so he wouldn't have to leave work and drive home. But on wash days, she let him fix his own meal. Today, it was a slab of ham between two slices of mom's homemade bread.

In the late morning, he leaned against his horse, Jupiter, and with mixed emotions, listened to the oncoming train. He looked forward to stopping his fence-mending or irrigation chores to watch the train go by, but with one eye still stinging and a little blurry, watching the cars as they whizzed past wasn't as much fun as it usually was. Still, this was a passenger train, and they were always exciting. Through the train windows, he could see people eating and drinking, laughing, and having fun while traveling to some exciting far-away place.

Roy had two older brothers overseas and a younger sister living with his parents on fifteen hundred acres of rangeland and irrigated farm crops extending on both sides of the railroad tracks. Roy could never decide whether he lived on a ranch or a farm. His dad raised hay and grain for the range animals and sometimes planted sugar beets or peas. Roy believed he planted irrigation crops primarily to keep the boys busy.

His dad was laid up with a busted hip from a mean brindle steer that had pinned him against the corral fence. It was the middle of July, the summer of 1943, and his two older brothers were in the Army. Arnold was somewhere in Europe fighting the Germans or Italians, and Marlow was somewhere in the Pacific fighting the Japanese. The missing brothers and laid-up dad meant that all the ranch chores fell on Roy's eleven-year-old shoulders.

Their hundred and fifty steers were constantly pushing against the range fence as they tried to get to the greener grass. Besides keeping all the water holes clean from the windblown brush and tumbleweeds, Roy had to ride the eight miles of barbed wire fence daily. Most of the time, he had to stand up leaning posts, and sometimes he had to dig another hole and plant a new one. It seemed there was always broken barbed wire or wire just pushed off the post. The broken wire had to be mended from a roll of wire carried on Jupiter's saddle. Repairing broken barbed wire always resulted in a few skin cuts. Gloves were unheard of for the poor families at the north end of Cache Valley. Putting new staples on the wire pushed off the post wasn't so bad, but sometimes the wire got so stretched it was necessary to use a wire puller to tighten it up and make a loop on the fence post. If the wire slipped, it sliced up his hands.

This ranch work was man's work, but circumstances forced Roy to do a man's job. The ranch and farm were handwork, and parents expected kids raised in poor families to step up and do their share. With his dad lying on the living room couch in a body cast, it was up to Roy to do all the ranch work. Having never been over fifty miles from home, he didn't know any other life. He didn't mind the work; it was just that it was so damn hot in the summer and so blasted cold in the winter, and that freaking wind never stopped. Even that wasn't bad unless the wind blew hard enough to pick up grit from the soil that stung the skin and hurt the eyes when it assailed his face.

The Union Pacific north-south train ran through northern Cache Valley, splitting the Dalton ranch down the center, and it was Roy's daily practice to watch the noon passenger train called the New York Flyer as it rumbled past their fence. He liked the two daily freight trains all right. They were always interesting because the war was on, and the trains carried tanks, Army vehicles, and cannons mixed in with coal cars, oil tankers, and boxcars. Then there were always hobos sitting in open boxcars or riding on top of the coal cars. He always waved at those vagabonds, plus the engineer in the locomotive and the signalman in the caboose. They usually waved back as if they were watching the country float by.

Flat cars carried war material in big green Army boxes. He knew it was war material because stenciled in big black bold capital letters on the green wooden crates were the words US ARMY. Always interesting, these trains were the primary source of entertainment for the small town, and they offered a break in Roy's monotonous days. However, Roy's biggest absolute joy was the passenger trains.

Evening and nighttime passenger trains that passed their ranch were always a pleasure to watch, as the inside lights showed the passengers more clearly than the daytime train. Some passengers read books or papers, and some ate a meal. He could see passengers walking the aisle and chatting to other passengers on the train. Watching this light show as it flew by in the dark was almost magical. Each car looked like a jewel floating in space, carrying beautiful people towards heaven.

A poor boy like Roy never even dreamed that he might ride on such a train one day. His lot in life was work, work, and more work, seven days a week. His life was heat, freezing cold, and nasty winds. It was hunger. And it was tired, aching muscles. It was wearing patched hand-me-down clothes from his older brothers with worn boots too big for his feet and oversized sweat-stained overcoats that practically dragged on the ground in the winter. But if this is your life, and you know nothing different, you found happiness wherever possible. For Roy, it was the noon New York Flyer.

Roy liked his freight trains and watched them go by whenever convenient, but he always made it a point to watch for the noon Flyer. First was the name, The New York Flyer. He knew little about New York except that it was the biggest city in America and full of excitement. A New York train just had to be exciting. Then there was the name Flyer. For an overworked landlocked boy stuck in the desert, the very name Flyer evoked dreams of freedom and happiness. Happiness and pure joy. This train-watching time was a time to dream, to fly, to escape. The noon Flyer provided all these things, and Roy made it a point to get right next to the fence at noon whenever possible to see his train.

He had learned the train's name when his dad had driven to Pocatello for a part for their old pickup. Roy was only six and just beginning to take on a workload at the ranch. His father excused him from his daily chores that day and took him to the big city fifty miles away.

Pocatello in Idaho and Ogden in Utah were the two biggest railroad hubs west of the Mississippi River. It was the crossroads for trains traveling north and south or east and west. Big switching yards made it possible for trains to switch directions.

In Pocatello, Roy and his dad passed saloons where they could hear people laughing and having a good time. He saw blacksmith shops with fire and smoke from blazing forges and dry goods stores with people lounging around in front eating ice cream cones, all magical sites to the wide-eyed youngster. Hoping to find something he could use on their old worn-out Ford pickup; his dad drove to a garage that sold automobile parts. It just so happened that the garage was next to a train station, and the New York Flyer was stopped to take on water and coal. The train evoked a lot of talk from the locals, who gawked at passengers who got off to stretch their legs and view the town. While Pocatello has lots of attractions, the New York Flyer provided the best show in the city.

The name Flyer seemed appropriate as a big blue stripe two feet in width ran the train's entire length. The blue streak contrasted nicely with the stainless steel of the railroad cars. The blue line reminded Roy of a plane zooming along the ground. The railroad company emphasized this effect with little white blips on the blue streak that looked like wings. For Roy, watching the Flyer was the highlight of any day.

Experiencing the emotions of hope and envy, the poor people in Pocatello could only look with longing at the visitors dressed in fancy city clothes. It was probably on that trip to Pocatello that Roy fell in love with the Flyer. From then on, he tried to watch it as often as possible when it rolled through the Daltons' fields.

Back on the ranch, the steam engine's whistle was the first sign the Flyer was coming down the tracks. Roy always listened for the whistle as it blew for the county crossing six miles down the track in Oxford. He could always hear the whistle unless the wind was blowing too hard in the wrong direction. Without a watch, he depended upon the whistle to give him enough time to reach the fence to watch the train. Country boys learn how to tell time pretty accurately just by watching shadows on the ground, but this method is usually suitable only for ten to fifteen minutes of actual time. When you're busy mending fences or cleaning out water holes, you aren't always paying attention to the time. But that whistle always got Roy's attention when he could hear it.

Those old steam whistles were a lonely, sorrowful melancholy echo that sounded like yesterday and tomorrow all rolled into the present. In that sound, Roy saw pictures of New York and Hollywood. He saw the Liberty Bell and the mighty Mississippi River. The whistle sang songs picturing all the exciting and beautiful places Roy had read about or heard about from his teachers. It carried a promise of more exciting places and times. That old whistle held all the wishes and dreams of a lonely, hot, tired country boy, but the best thing about that whistle was that it carried hope.

He didn't have to ride Jupiter like the wind to catch his train today. It just so happened that he was working on that part of the fence right next to the railroad. It would have been perfect if his eye weren't giving him problems, but he still felt the excitement building that always came whenever the Flyer approached.

The big black locomotive kept growing as it approached, and as it grew nearer, Roy couldn't help but grin in happiness. His train was coming, bringing with it all his dreams of escape. He would see happy, contented people inside the train relaxing and having fun, drinking excellent, cool beverages, and talking about the exciting places they had been to or the beautiful places they were about to visit. But his fantasies did not prepare him for the eyes of the woman.

One passenger on the train, Sarah Peroni, was having a terrible day. It had only been a week since the soldiers in perfect uniforms full of ribbons and straight creases, boots all polished shiny black, and carrying their hats under their arms had knocked on her door with the news. Her husband of only six months, Dean Peroni, had been killed fighting the Germans in France.

It was wartime, and the government had rationed almost everything. Even with all her money, Sarah couldn't get decent stockings, and her clothes showed signs of significant wear. The only black dress she owned was a woolen shift with moth holes she had sewn shut, hoping the repairs were not too noticeable. Going back home to California from Washington, DC, where Sarah had worked as a nurse at the Walter Reed Hospital, seemed like a big step backward in life, but there was little choice. She couldn't continue seeing all the wounded men and their missing body parts. At least there were job openings at McDonald Airplane Company building warplanes, and she would be closer to her parents. Life seemed like such a burden. Even though she was one of the wealthiest persons on the train, Sarah was lonely, sad, and depressed. Her face was swollen from crying until she was all cried out. Her eyes were red with black rims all around them from a lack of sleep.

As the New York Flyer swept past the countryside, Sarah rested her grief-blotched face against the window and watched the country fly past. She was the poster child for dejection.

Nothing in her life was beautiful or exciting; she wasn't excited about getting a job in an airplane factory building warplanes. The war had taken her husband, her best friend, and her happiness. Working in a war-related industry had no appeal, but it was a way to serve her country, and she felt she owed it to Dean.

Only with great effort did she continue breathing. If she could just die right now, her troubles would be over. The landscape was attractive, with beautiful mountains in the background, but everything started looking the same after three days on the train. A conductor walked down the aisle, telling passengers the train would stop for water soon, but no one could get off the train, for the stop would be very brief. He made it sound like no big deal, nothing of significance.

There was a water tank for the railroad trains almost dead center in the Dalton ranch, although the New York Flyer rarely stopped there, unlike the freight trains. That day, the watermen didn't finish filling the New Your Flyer's locomotive water tank in Pocatello. Thus, this emergency stop for more water.

Looking out the window, Sarah tried to see something interesting. But she saw only a small boy in bib overalls wearing a tattered yellow straw cowboy hat with a faded red sweatband and a blue bandana around his neck and leaning against a beautiful bay horse. Curly brown hair seeped out below the hat, but the big grin on the boy's face caught her attention. Why should he be so damn happy when she was so miserable?

She couldn't help but notice the country behind the boy. While kind of bland, with no buildings, there was a beauty to the land, and it looked so peaceful. Behind the boy, cows were grazing in the wide-open spaces. The sky seemed so big and blue. She saw mountains in the background and some amazing orange and white cliffs. The grinning boy watching the train appeared to express the happiness missing in her life. If only.

The boy's pants had patches on the knees, yet holes still appeared here and there in the worn fabric. Only fifteen feet separated Sarah from the smiling boy, and with the train slowing down, she could see that his hands had been bleeding, and his work shoes seemed much too big. Obviously, from a poor family, she decided, yet the boy seemed mesmerized by the train. Then, with the train almost stopped, their eyes met for the briefest time, but that quick eye contact changed their lives forever.

She saw hope, dreams, happiness, and joy in the boy's face, but his eyes told a different story. Big gray eyes with flecks of yellow around the iris displayed longing and hunger, despair and loneliness, and fear. The sort of fear she saw in the eyes of the women sending their men to war. The fear of the unknown. Fear of being trapped. Fear of being trapped with no escape. His face radiated happiness, but his joyfulness never reached the eyes.

The woman's big brown eyes bore testimony to her grief and sadness. In her face, there was no hope, no future. Yet, as their eyes met, it appeared each could see into the soul of the other. It was as though they exchanged souls for just a moment, each bearing the loneliness and torture of the other. At that moment, the boy knew he was looking into the eyes of a war widow who had lost her true love. Likewise, the woman saw the boy's instant compassion in his eyes and wondered how someone so young and disadvantaged could see into her soul and feel her pain. That simple moment in time changed both lives.

The boy understood that money and privilege did not bring happiness and could not defeat sorrow or relieve the pain of a significant loss. In the boy, the woman saw he found pleasure in simple things, such as watching a passenger train, yet even in his longing and loneliness, he could still feel the hurt in others. This brief encounter would change both lives in ways neither could have imagined.

2
SARAH GETS A JOB

In 1941, Walker Bank in San Francisco was equal to most big eastern banks, including JP Morgan, Chase and Goldman Sachs. Hiram Walker, the founder, included in his group of business associates Leland Stanford, Charles Crocker and the rest of the robber barons. For the barons living on Nob Hill, every other place in California was downhill and down in the Garden City, known as San Jose, lived one of the state's largest orange grove owners, Roberto Peroni.

Roberto grew to dislike Amadeo Giannini, the founder of the Bank of America. Although childhood friends, Amadeo would not let the men who worked for the Peronis do business with his bank unless they all agreed to deposit their work checks directly into his bank every Friday. Some seasonal workers distrusted banks, and many detested the upstart Italian banker who rode roughshod over the field workers. Hence Roberto banked with the Walker Bank in Palo Alto, becoming, if not friends, business associates with the bank's owner.

Roberto had several children, many of whom went unrecognized by their father, but his favorite was his first son Dean. Hiram only had two children, both girls, one named Sarah and the other Maria. Inevitably, at one of the robber barons' feasts, Hiram invited Roberto and his family to attend. At that gathering, Sarah met Dean, and it was love at first sight. Whenever Dean's chores allowed him any free time, he went up to Atherton and the Walker homestead. And when Dean's number came up in the draft, the young lovers were married before they bussed him to Camp Pendleton for basic training.

Dean lived at the camp for ten weeks, where they allowed him only a one weekend furlough to spend with his new bride. After training camp, the Army sent Dean to Fort Belvoir in Fairfax County, Virginia, for 12 weeks of special training. Sarah moved to Washington, DC, to be with her new husband, and she took a job at the Walter Reed Hospital to do her part in the war effort. Then it was off to France for Dean, where he died six months later in a thunderous volley of machine-gun fire from the Germans.

While Dean went to Europe and the war, Sarah devoted her time to the hospital, where she nursed the battle-torn men. They hired Sarah as a nurse's aide, but after working eighteen-hour shifts for six months, she was as qualified as most formally trained nurses and many doctors. However, caring for the disabled, wounded, and depressed men took a toll on the young California girl, so when she got word of her husband's death and looking for a different life, she packed up and went home.

On the way home, a brief encounter with the boy and his striking, gray eyes that seemed so knowing changed the course of her life. She might have gone back to the house in Los Gatos her father-in-law had given the newlywed pair as a wedding present and become a hermit. Instead, drowning in a gloomy existence of self-pity and despair, she spent one week mourning at her parent's home in Atherton. Then the boy's eyes that were seared in her memory made Sarah see her sorrow in a different light, forcing a recognition that while her lot in life might be temporarily sad, it was not the longing and hopelessness she saw in those freaking gray eyes.

After spending a week with her parents reliving the sorrow, Sarah dumped her self-pity and moved to Long Beach, where she joined the war effort. Dean was gone, but the war roared on, and the government expected everyone with an ounce of patriotism to contribute. Shortly after finding a bungalow on the beach with six other girls, Sarah got a job at McDonald Aircraft building warplanes along with Rosie the Riveter.

Everything was rationed and in short supply except for work related to the war effort. Sarah worked long twelve-hour days, but she didn't mind the schedule. It kept her mind away from the sorrow and despair she experienced after learning about Dean's death.

As she settled into her new life, visions of the farm boy kept recurring in her dreams. To rid herself of these visions, she sought a detective to locate the boy and learn everything he could about the boy's life.

One of her roommates, a local girl named Cara, gave her the name of a private detective named Peter Hopp. Peter had a walk-in office just off Wilmington, near Long Beach, and near where Sarah worked at McDonald Aircraft.

Peter was a short, dumpy little man with a big black handlebar mustache that made him look like a circus clown in training. Bright brown eyes and colorful Hawaiian shirts added to the clown image. The one-room office held a battered, work scarred desk with one swivel chair behind it where Peter was sitting and two straight-back wooden chairs in front of it for clients. The only other furniture was a squat, gray, two-drawer filing cabinet. There was no window, and one dim light fixture hung on the ceiling. The door was open, and when Sarah walked into the gloomy room, she nearly turned around and walked back out, but she had only ten minutes to spend and didn't want to waste her trip.

"Mr. Hopp, my name is Sarah Walker Peroni, and I want you to find someone for me. Is that something you are prepared to do?" It was apparent from the tone of her voice that she held little faith in his abilities.

Peter was engrossed at the moment, so when Sarah spoke, her voice caught him momentarily off guard. Then, looking up, he saw this gorgeous woman wearing worker's coveralls. Although Peter could see the strain in her eyes, the woman was lovely, but her ill-fitting clothes did not spell success. He wondered if she could even afford his services.

"Well, I find missing people from time to time," he responded hesitantly. However, the tone of his voice suggested he didn't want to waste his time with someone who could not pay.

Sarah didn't miss the innuendo and almost walked out without another word, but she was short on time, for McDonald's only gave thirty minutes for lunch, and the trip each way to the investigator's office took ten minutes. "Look, there's this boy in Idaho, and I want to find out who he is. I'm prepared to pay for your time and expenses. Here's five hundred dollars to get started." Sarah pulled a roll of bills from her coveralls.

Seeing that much money made Peter regret his earlier tone. That was more money than he earned most months. Hell, it was more money than he had seen in several months.

"Miss Peroni, or is it missus? What do you know about this boy, and do you have any idea where he might be found?"

"It's Mrs. Peroni," she said with a catch in her voice. "Somewhere in Idaho between Pocatello and Ogden, Utah, is a little town with some orange-reddish cliffs in the background. I believe the town lies in a valley between mountains, and I know there is a water tank for the railroad near the town. In fact, the boy I want you to find works on a ranch near the water tower."

"May I know the nature of your inquiry? Why the interest in this particular boy?"

"No, you don't need to know that. But I can tell you; the boy has very gray eyes. He is approximately ten or possibly twelve years old. I believe he comes from a poor family."

Peter wasn't delighted with the scarce information. It wasn't much to go on, but business was slow, and five hundred dollars had a sweet sound.

"Can you tell me anything else about this boy?" While he didn't mind taking a brief vacation in Idaho, he was a professional and wanted to give the woman fair value for her money.

"No, only that he has a beautiful bay horse. When I saw him, his hands were bloody, and he was leaning on a fence post. Oh, there is one more thing. I do not want the boy or anyone in that town to know about my interest. No one is to know my name or the nature of your inquiry. Can you find this boy with no one knowing?"

Without meaning to, the desperation leaked through her voice, although why she was desperate to know about a young boy in Idaho remained a mystery, even to Sarah.

"Well, Mrs. Peroni, I'll do my best. You haven't given me much to go on, but if there is a town near some cliffs along the railroad tracks and a water tank nearby, I should be able to find the place. The boy might be a little more complicated, but there can't be that many ten or twelve-year-old gray-eyed boys with a beautiful bay horse in a sparsely populated area."

Displaying her wisdom and intelligence, Sarah handed over the five hundred dollars with this acknowledgment, "I think this should cover your expenses and pay for your time. If you return with the information I desire and need more money; we can discuss that when you return."

Peter recognized the desperation she displayed earlier and knew that anything less than success in his investigation would disappoint and probably mean no more money, regardless of his expenses.

"What exactly do you wish to know, madam?" he asked with respect now that he saw the money.

"I want his full name, address, and everything you can tell me about the boy and his family, and I don't want them to know about my inquiry. That is important."

"How do I contact you when you return? What is your address?"

"You don't need to know that, Mr. Hopp. I'll be back in two weeks for your report. That should give you plenty of time to find the information I seek."

"Okay, Mrs. Peroni, I'll see you in two weeks. Hopefully, with all the information you desire."

"Thank you, Mr. Hopp." The beautiful lady left the office, leaving it feeling like the drab, dreary little place it was when she entered.

3
SMOKY JOE

Freight trains were interesting because of the different railroad cars and the stuff they were hauling, such as military tanks, jeeps, and trucks. There were oil cars, coal cars, flat cars with interesting boxes, and boxcars, some with doors closed and locked, and other boxcars with their doors wide open. And, of course, every train had a caboose.

The railroad was the poor man's ticket to travel if you didn't get caught at the train stops by the railroad dicks. Roy's parents called these unticketed travelers hobos, and on every train, whether traveling north or south, there were hobos who tried keeping out of sight of the train engineers in front or the signalman riding in the caboose. Roy always waved at the engineers, the vagabonds, and the signalman, and usually, one or more waved back. Especially the hobos.

Sometimes hobos rode in the open boxcars with their legs dangling out of the door and hanging down the side, and sometimes they would be on top of the oil cars or the flatcars between boxes. It seemed to Roy that one in three freight trains stopped for water at the water tank in the middle of the ranch. So, while Roy saw no hobo get off when the train stopped, he was pretty sure they got off at times, perhaps from one of those midnight freighters.

The effects of the depression were still being felt in many parts of the country, especially far-off places like Clifton, Idaho. Highway 36, the major highway between Salt Lake City, Utah, and Boise, Idaho, ran through the tiny hamlet called Clifton. As a result, interesting people were constantly drifting through town. From April through October, the warmest months, gypsy caravans, hobos, traveling salespeople selling bibles, and Watkins peddlers selling vanilla extract and brooms trolled through the streets. In addition, every summer, one little man who sharpened knives and scissors and sold sewing machine needles came by in a tiny homemade camper.

One summer, a small circus came to town with trained horses, knife throwers, and lusty-looking women. The only thing Roy remembered about this event was the man with a bullwhip who could light a match from thirty feet away and start it blazing.

When a gypsy caravan rolled into town, mothers grabbed their children, locking them indoors because everybody knew gypsies stole children. No one understood why the gypsies would steal children, but everybody knew kidnapping children was their practice. The highway had wide, shallow borrow-pits along each side, and the caravan would park alongside the road for a couple of nights. Then, the men in bright, colorful shirts wandered around town looking for work before the procession moved on in search of a more favorable location.

Clifton folk usually extended warm hospitality to travelers through the area. They knew firsthand the hard, starving struggle to live in the days during and following a horrible depression. Yet somehow, and for reasons never explained, the gypsies always seemed to provoke some deep primal fear. Roy found these visitors exciting and always wanted to spend some time hanging around them, but his mother forbid him from making any contact, and, in a rare demonstration of rebellion, he ignored her orders and spent some time with the gypsies.

Vagabonds knocked on the kitchen door several times during the summer months, asking for a free meal. Always generous, Roy's mom gave them plenty of food and sometimes a place to sleep in the garage or storage shed. Later in life, Roy heard a story that vagabonds, hobos, and just plain hitchhikers left some secret mark on the property where others like them could find a free meal. Whether this story was true or fiction, plenty of men stopped by looking for a handout. Such a man was Smoky Joe.

Smoky Joe came by one July afternoon around five o'clock. Roy never knew if Joe had been hitchhiking or jumped off the train at the water tank down by the ranch. He said his name was Joe and offered to work for some food and a place to sleep.

Farmers and ranchers ate their dinner, the main meal of the day, at noon. Their supper was always homemade bread and milk, with homemade jam or fruit to sweeten the bread. For Joe, Roy's mom fixed him an actual plate of food rather than giving him our daily supper of bread and milk. Roy's dad made Joe comfortable in the toolshed. His mom had two or three days of work for Joe in her garden, so he stayed around a few days doing chores for her.

After his day's work, Roy would stop and talk with Joe to listen to his stories about traveling and how everything looked in other parts of the world. Joe had been all over the states, from Florida and Maine to California, and told interesting stories that intrigued the young boy.

Roy named him Smoky Joe during these talks, but only in his mind, not to Joe's face. He chose the name because Joe's well-cured skin smelled like the smoke from burn barrels. With no garbage pickup in the small town, almost every house around had a 55-gallon drum with the lid they cut out used for burning trash. Then, as debris accumulated, old magazines too slick to be used in the outhouse, soiled newspapers, and cardboard boxes unusable for toilet paper were also stuffed into the burn barrel. The smoke from this burn barrel had the same scent as Smoky Joe.

Roy imagined Joe got his scent from the barrels used for warmth that the hobos and tramps always seemed to have in their make-shift camps. He guessed the fire in the barrels might have also been another source of comfort. Perhaps just watching the flames brought out memories of better days.

Joe stuck in Roy's memory because he was the first black man Roy had ever seen. Roy knew the word negro and the more racist term employed by those folks disdainful of people of color, but his people in his small town never openly expressed such language and thoughts. Although not religious, Roy's parents studied the bible and often talked about bible stories in the evening before bedtime. With no television and a local radio station that did not entertain other than providing weather reports and crop prices, the family read and talked in the evening. According to the bible, the Samaritans were black people whom Jesus befriended, so black people were okay in the Dalton family. Jesus said so.

It is probably safe to say that Roy was essentially colorblind when it came to people. The only people he hated were the Japs and the Germans because both races intended to kill his brothers. It wasn't unusual in the small town to hear children playing games in which they dropped bombs on Tokyo or Germany. But Smoky Joe didn't fit into either hateful category, so he was okay. It is probably also safe to say that Joe picked up on the family's total acceptance of his skin color; in fact, they didn't even see his color, which must have impressed the traveling man. Roy undoubtedly thought Joe was a Samaritan and blessed by Jesus.

Clifton, Idaho, boasted three businesses during Roy's childhood. First, the town had the only gas station along

Highway 36 for thirty miles in either direction. This gas station along the highway also featured the area's only saloon, with pool tables and the town's post office. A mail truck dropped off the mail for the entire town here, and the saloon operator, who was the postmaster, put the mail in little numbered boxes for the town's residents. Roy's parents had box 13. Roy never knew whether the box number was plain meanness on behalf of the postmaster or an accident.

The second business was the local mechanic. Cars were constantly breaking down, meaning there was steady work for a mechanic. Farmers and ranchers also always needed a blacksmith to weld or make a replacement part for something broken, so the mechanic-blacksmith shop serviced everybody in the north end of Cache Valley.

Finally, there was the general store that sold practically anything a small town needed. There were candy bars, ice cream cones, twinkies, and bubble gum for the kids. For the ladies, the store stocked bread from the Wonder Bread truck that stopped once a week for those women who couldn't or wouldn't make their own bread. Some people in town didn't own farms or ranches, so the store stocked milk, eggs, and miscellaneous food items, such as condiments like ketchup, mayonnaise, and of course, select spices like salt and pepper. Roy's mom always bought her lard there.

Besides soda pop and other general store items, a rancher could buy horseshoes and horseshoe nails, screws and nails for boards, light bulbs, and fuses because they were always burning out. Nobody ever heard of circuit breakers, at least not in Clifton. A farmer could find a new pair of overalls, work shoes, dry socks, and garden hoses.

Most people traveling along the highway stopped in the small town at the gas station/pool hall/post office or the general store; therefore, it wasn't unusual for a Los Angeles detective named Peter Hopp to stop at the store to ask for directions and talk to the proprietor about the area. Small-town people, especially when Roy was small, loved to talk with visitors to the town to hear the news about other parts of the country, and Orson Pratt, the general store owner, was no exception.

Visitors asked many questions, and Orson didn't find it unusual to have somebody inquire about ranches in the area. Instead, he proudly talked about the Dalton ranch, the biggest ranch in Clifton. Yes, the Daltons had a large family and a boy about twelve named Roy who was doing all the ranch work as his father was laid up with a busted hip.

"Was the Dalton ranch next to the railroad tracks?" asked the stranger in town.

Surprised at the question, Orson answered, "Why yes, it is."

"And is there a water tank for the railroad engines near their ranch?" The stranger continued asking questions.

Orson looked at the stranger, a short dumpy man with a big handlebar mustache, but he seemed unassuming and friendly, so he saw no reason to wonder about the strange interview. "May I ask your interest in this ranch?" he asked. "I believe the water tank is almost in the middle of the ranch as it straddles the railroad on both sides."

"Oh, I'm sorry if I sounded a little pushy," the stranger answered with a disarming smile. "I saw a train stopped down in the valley by a water tank, so being curious, I drove down to get a better look. I saw this young boy with a beautiful bay horse and wondered if it belonged to the boy. Just curious, you know." The stranger again flashed his engaging smile. "We don't have any horses where I live," he continued as if this answer justified his curiosity.

"You must have seen Roy and his beloved horse Jupiter," Orson volunteered. Orson didn't seem inclined to wonder where the stranger lived or why he didn't have horses, for nearly every ranch and farm in the valley had at least one.

"If I wanted to send the boy a small gift, where would I send it?" the stranger asked. Seeing the questioning look in the proprietor's eyes, the stranger hastily continued, "I have a son about the same age and thought maybe I could send him one of my son's toys."

"Oh, well, you would have to get that from the post office down the street. It's in the saloon," Orson added with a scowl as if the saloon were an affront to his delicate sensibilities.

With a last smile and a "Thank you," the stranger left, and soon Orson forgot all about the smiling, dumpy little man.

4

THE REPORT

Sarah rode a bicycle to work these days since she lived only ten blocks from the McDonald assembly building and gas rationing made it impractical to drive. Nearly all the assembly workers were women, for most able-bodied men were in the armed services. A scattering of 4Fers worked here and there, and most of the supervisors were men with experience in aircraft manufacturing. Still, 95 percent of the people in the assembly buildings were women.

Many women lacked transportation, so McDonald provided shuttle busses around Long Beach and the surrounding towns. Sarah found it convenient to ride the shuttle downtown to visit her detective after the two weeks had expired. With gasoline rationed, it just made sense to leave her car in a garage she rented near her apartment on the beach. The shuttle vehicle was a green 1940 Chevrolet Army staff car that rattled over potholes in the road, but, at least, it saved on the small allotment of gasoline Sarah could buy.

Peter Hopp was in his shabby office when Sarah walked in. Today, he looked like the same dumpy circus clown with the handlebar mustache, although he wore an old suit that stretched tight around the middle and needed pressing. Peter must have bought it before gaining his last few pounds. Although it didn't register with Sarah during this visit, he wore the suit to impress the beautiful young lady. Noticing that the lady did not wear any rings on her fingers, Peter assumed she was no longer married. Perhaps her husband was killed in the war. He didn't know her work allowed no rings on the fingers because they were a safety hazard.

"Mr. Hopp, do you have the information I asked you to get?" No howdy-do or good to see you, just the question.

"Good afternoon, Mrs. Peroni. It's a delight to see you again. And yes, I have the information you asked me to get. I've written a report, and here is your copy," he responded, handing Sarah a folder with a few typewritten pages.

Sarah took the folder and sat down in one of the rickety wooden side chairs in front of the battered desk to take a quick glance at its contents. "Was the money satisfactory?" she asked.

"It was more than adequate, and in fact, I owe you some change. My rate is twenty-five dollars a day, plus expenses. I was only gone for five days, and my expenses amounted to one hundred and thirty-five dollars. Therefore, your change is two hundred and forty dollars, which I included with the report in your folder."

Flipping the pages in the report, Sarah saw two one-hundred-dollar bills and two twenty-dollar bills paper clipped to the back of the folder.

After glancing at the report, Sarah pulled the money from the paper clip and laid it on Peter's desk. "No, Mr. Hopp, the information is worth the five hundred I gave you initially. You keep the money. You earned the entire amount."

"That's mighty generous of you, Mrs. Peroni. Thank you very much. In these challenging times, every dollar helps, and this will help me considerably. I am in your debt, and should you ever need my help again, please get in touch." After this brief speech, you could see Peter's eyes watering, although he ducked his head so it would not be too noticeable.

Standing, Sarah made to leave. Then, holding out her hand so Peter could shake it, she said goodbye and went outside to read Peter's report.

Finding a nearby bench, she sat down to read. A slight breeze with a hint of the salty ocean air was blowing off the water while the sun played hide and seek behind shining, fluffy white clouds. Then, with great curiosity, she began reading Peter Hopp's report. As she opened the folder to read, Sarah could not help but see the boy's striking gray eyes and feel his warm empathy for her sadness.

My Dear Mrs. Peroni,

As you requested, I traveled to Idaho searching for your young boy and the place where he lives. I will not bore you with the mundane aspects of my search, but after consulting my Chevron road maps, I took a train to Ogden, Utah, to hire a car. It is about a two-hour drive to the orangish cliffs you saw from the train, and the small village is named Clifton, in honor of the cliffs just above the town. On Highway 36, at the northern end of Cache Valley, the village lies in a beautiful sheltered valley between two mountain ranges. Highway 36 is the main highway between Salt Lake City, Utah, and Boise, Idaho.

Clifton has about one hundred residents, including children. A gas station serves as the post office and pool hall, there's a general store that sells almost everything, and a blacksmith shop services all the small farms in the area.

Your young man's name is Roy Dalton. He lives in the town in a large, white, stucco house built by his father.

His two older brothers are in the Army, one in Europe and the other in the Philippines. He has one older sister.

Roy is eleven, turning twelve next month. Although young, he does a man's work running his family's ranch alone, as his father is laid up with a broken hip, and his older brothers are in the military. The youth appears to be uncommonly strong for a boy his age.

The beautiful bay horse you saw is named Jupiter and belongs to Roy. He rides the horse daily while he works the family ranch. The Dalton ranch is the biggest in the area, but the family is poor because the entire region is still recovering from the devastating depression. As a result, money is scarce, and when healthy, Roy's father often looks for work wherever he can find a job.

The local post office services the entire town and outlying farms and ranches by providing mailboxes assigned to the residents. The small six by six boxes were built into a wall and had glass doors featuring a combination lock. Roy's family has box number 13. My guess is they don't believe in bad luck.

This report I believe contains all the information you requested. I spent two days touring the area and visiting the Dalton ranch. While there, I watched Roy as the noon train called the New York Flyer went past the water tank you mentioned. Roy seemed riveted by the train as it passed by. Unfortunately, there isn't much entertainment in the area other than what the farmers and ranchers can manufacture independently.

I hope this answers your questions. As I mentioned, I spent some time in the area and can supply more details if you desire or are interested.

Sincerely,
Peter Hopp, Private Investigator

Sarah replaced the papers in her folder, stood up, and walked back to the bus stop. Her mind was on the smiling face of the happy young man with yearning eyes. She felt like she owed the boy something. He made her appreciate the life of abundance she enjoyed, and despite her significant loss, her wealth gave her freedom the young man might never experience. Perhaps there was a way she could help with that. It was something to think about as she boarded the shuttle back to work.

5
THE CHICKAREE

A year had passed since the brief encounter with the woman on the train, and Roy had almost forgotten the desperate sorrow he read in those dark, sad brown eyes. As he finished the evening chores, the evening passenger train went by with blazing windows showing people eating, drinking, and conversing with others. Some were laughing, and others were reading a book or newspaper. Yet, for some unknown reason, the train tonight reminded Roy of that train, which now seemed to have been years in the past, in which he saw the pretty woman wearing grief like a monk's robe.

Roy stopped at the post office to collect the family mail on the way home. To his great surprise, there was a small package addressed to him in the mail. Usually, if there was any mail, it was a letter addressed to his father requesting his service as a journeyman welder. At the moment, his dad was some place in Kansas, working on a railroad. It was a hard time, and the breadwinner went where he could find work. Roy had proven himself capable of managing the ranch, so everyone was comfortable leaving the ranch work to the young boy with a man's shoulders.

The Germans had severely wounded Arnold in a battle somewhere Roy couldn't pronounce. A bomb or grenade or mortar shell exploded and took off the bottom part of his right leg. Roy's mom was worried about his health, but thankful her son was still alive. Marlow was someplace in the Pacific Ocean, and the family had received no word from him in eight weeks. This lack of information had both of his parents nearly sick with fear for his safety, but their struggle for survival demanded constant work at home and on the ranch. Already in the small town of Clifton, two families had reports that their sons had been killed in action.

Roy could hardly wait to get home and open his package. It was a small package wrapped in brown paper with no return address. The post office mark over the postage stamps said Huntington Beach, California, a place Roy had never heard of or knew existed. However, people in small towns who received little mail found the postage stamps almost as intriguing as the contents of the letter or package. Roy was no exception as he stared at the stamps on his package all the way home from the post office.

Roy's mother and sister couldn't wait for Roy to open his package. Receiving a package from some strange place from someone with no return address was unheard of in the Dalton family. To his mother's best recollection, this was the first time anyone in the family had ever received a package in the mail. Everyone crowded around as Roy used his pocketknife to slit open the outer wrapper to reveal a beautifully polished wooden box with a brass hinge and a simple clasp. When Roy slid the clip and opened the box, everyone gasped. Inside was a magnificent silver pocket watch. Timepieces were rare in the small town, and no one owned anything resembling the watch now in Roy's hands. The watch had a cover on which was etched the image of a railroad steam locomotive. There was a small card with the box where someone with beautiful penmanship had written these simple words: FOR ROY, SO YOU CAN ALWAYS TELL WHEN THE TRAIN IS COMING. Then on the watch's backside were two large engraved letters, **R. D.**, for Roy Dalton.

The watch was pure silver and undoubtedly cost more than most of the town's people saw in a month. Roy gave the watch to his mother to fondle. She wondered who would send her son such an elaborate gift. But, in his heart and mind, Roy knew who had sent the present and was disappointed there was no way of expressing thanks. Roy's overalls did not have a watch pocket, and unwilling to carry such a beautiful item loose in his other pockets, where he always seemed to have a collection of nails or screws and other things that would scratch the silver, he had his mother keep it for him.

It was Friday night when the big boys in town liked to party. Unfortunately, the town did not have any girls the age of the older boys, so they almost always ended up in a camping spot just below the orange cliffs where they could build a fire and tell raunchy stories. On this night, the big boys decided to have a chickaree. Of course, this required chickens, and these boys knew just where to get the chickens and who they would use to get chickens for their party.

No one seemed to know where the name chickaree came from or if it was even a word in Webster's Dictionary or anywhere outside the small Clifton village. Tonight was Roy's first and only encounter with the name. Later in life, he suspected these older boys, fifteen and sixteen, might have invented the word to attract the younger kids they used to steal the chickens.

Roy had a friend about his age named Allen, who lived across the highway and down a bit. With his chores finished for the day, he was outside with Allen, working on an old car the two boys had purchased from a farmer for five dollars. The car didn't run but had pretty decent tires, a good body, meaning the fenders, although rusty and dented, were still attached, and none of the windows were missing, although a couple were cracked. They were busy under the hood changing the spark plugs when three older boys in town drove up in a two-year-old Ford, with Roy and Allen's other friend Billy, in the back seat.

One of the older boys, a kid named Alma, leaned out of the passenger window and yelled, "Hey, you guys want to go on a chickaree?"

Neither Roy nor Allen knew the first thing about chickarees, but they were not about to let these older boys know that. Whatever it was, it sounded great, and they were proud to be asked to join in the fun with these older boys. Imagine being invited to spend the night out with some older boys you looked up to with envy.

Allen had to ask his stepdad for permission, and Roy had to get his mom's okay. He was not sure his mom knew what a chickaree was either, but when he told her it was with Alma, Grant, and Blair, all boys she knew, she said okay. Alma was the bishop's son, a church leader, and if Alma was involved, it must be something worthwhile and harmless. Within a couple of minutes, Allen and Roy were in the car's backseat with Billy, feeling pretty smug hanging out with the big boys. Man, were they in for a surprise!

The older boys had a few bottles of ginger ale, which they shared as they drove around talking up the chickaree. Before long, they ended up in Dayton, another small village five miles to the south. The driver parked on the highway about fifty yards from some man's chicken coop. Being on the road was no considerable risk because, after dark, there just wasn't any traffic. Farmers all went to bed early to get up for the five AM milking. The older boys explained that Roy's job, along with Allen and Billy, was to sneak into the farmer's chicken coop and grab a few young roosters. Ideally, they wanted Roy and his friends to each grab two roosters, but one each would be okay. They said nothing about *stealing* the chickens. The big boys hinted that grabbing chickens was required to have a chickaree.

Roy and his friends came from families that hated the very idea of a thief, and none of the boys ever thought of themselves as thieves. Until that night, the only thing Roy had ever stolen was a pack of lifesavers when he was five, and his father, when he learned of the theft shortly after, made Roy return the candy and apologize to the store's owner. This experience was humiliating to the young five-year-old, which was his whole life of thievery. Roy never considered stealing anything after that.

Later in life, Roy realized that the big boys only invited him and his friends on this exciting adventure to do the stealing. He could never remember what those older boys told them to make them agree to do this deed, but eventually, they convinced the three young boys to do the job. The driver had to stay by the car, one boy had to watch for traffic, and the other guy was to keep an eye out for the farmer. Somehow, these older boys made it sound reasonable that the young boys should grab the chickens, and they did. Neither Roy nor his friends wanted to disappoint the older boys, and because they were all from good families, it seemed like it might be okay. And anyway, the bishop's son was the ringleader, and if he said grabbing the farmer's chickens was all right, then that must be the case.

Another thought running through Roy's mind was that every boy in the car lived on a ranch or farm that raised chickens. He knew that if his father were home, he would have been proud to donate six roosters to their chickaree, which was undoubtedly true for the parents of the other five boys in the car. It also occurred to Roy that stealing the chickens was part of the fun. Stealing and not getting caught.

The three thieves each got two roosters that had been roosting on a two-by-four in the chicken coop. The boys just went in the door and grabbed them. The roosters started squawking like crazy, making all kinds of rackets, so hoping they wouldn't get a load of buckshot from the farmer's shotgun, they took the chickens and ran like hell for the car.

The older boys were quite pleased with the chicken haul, a concession that made the younger boys feel good. Still, Roy worried about what his mom would think about him stealing chickens, but the thought foremost in his mind was how disappointed the lady on the train would be to know the young boy she sent an expensive silver pocket watch to was a thief.

After stealing the chickens, the boys drove to the Loading Place, a magnificent spot in the mountains above Clifton, about halfway between the town and the orange cliffs. The area was a relatively flat, tree-covered meadow surrounded by hills with a clean water creek running through it, and above all, it had privacy. The name came from the town's early settlement when the pioneers cut down trees for their buildings. The farmers drug trees off the mountainside with a team of horses to the loading place, where they were cut into lengths to be loaded onto wagons and hauled to the town.

Two of the older boys took the chickens to start the cleaning process. Alma, busy unloading his Dutch ovens and supplies from the car's trunk, asked Roy and Allen to fetch wood for their fire. Billy helped, and by the time they had their Boy Scout fire going, the chickens were cleaned and cut into pieces. Alma had the Dutch ovens ready and his secret spices for the coating. Roy wasn't sure what Alma put into the flour before coating each piece of chicken; however, he remembered he used a lot of melted butter in the hot Dutch ovens.

Before long, the smell of fried chicken filled the meadow, adding to the little group of thieves' hunger pangs and watering mouths. Farmers in the valley had bread and milk for supper, but growing boys were always hungry and could eat a small calf without breaking a sweat, so a whole chicken apiece was nothing.

Alma stayed by his pans, occasionally moving the top pieces to the bottom and turning them over. Roy was unsure how long Alma cooked the chickens, but it seemed like forever. Eventually, Alma declared the chicken ready, and so were the boys. Roy admitted later he had never eaten chicken so good before or after. His mom was an excellent cook and made fantastic fried chicken, but to this day, the gold standard against which he compared all other fried chicken was that Dutch oven chicken cooked by Alma on Roy's first and only chickaree.

Why that chicken tasted so good, besides the secret ingredients Alma used in his flour, probably had something to do with the excitement of eating stolen chickens with the big boys. Still, whenever memories of that evening arose, Roy felt a twinge of guilt about what the train lady might think of the young boy with whom she had shared an intimate, sacred moment and given a silver watch.

6

STARTING OVER

It was the summer of 1945, and the war in Europe had ended. However, the war with the Japanese was still ongoing, although the end was near. The only questions in every American's mind were how many more men had to die before the fighting was finally over and how much longer it could continue? No one, especially Sarah, knew what President Truman had in mind to end the war, but the workload in the airplane factory was slowing down, and she needed something to replace the hours she was no longer working.

Although highly trained and skilled as a nurse's aide, Sarah found hospital work too depressing. With so many wounded soldiers returning from both theaters of war, the demand for hospital workers never ended. She was still beautiful in her early twenties, but she'd been a widow for over two years. She felt like an older woman in her heart. The war does that to people, and Sarah was no exception.

She read a lot and dreamed of Dean and the life they might have had if the war had not intervened. Unfortunately, she didn't make any friends working at the McDonald Airplane factory, although nearly all of her coworkers had husbands, brothers, and friends in the military. There were even a couple of other war widows in her section, but Sarah found them too trivial and weak-minded. She enjoyed stimulating conversation with intelligent individuals, not twittering, giggling ladies discussing the latest fashion or lipstick shades while hoping for a new pair of nylon stockings—such nonsense.

On a Monday morning, reporting for work, a new supervisor responsible for her section confronted Sarah. Ralph, her old supervisor, had been promoted, and Dwayne, the new guy, at once made it known he expected beautiful war widows to appreciate his manhood in the most intimate way possible. Disgusted, Sarah turned and left the building without looking back or giving her job a second thought. And just like that, she turned her back on her job, the war, and everything she could leave behind related to her present life.

The government rationed gasoline, but with her looks and persuasive abilities, Sarah sweet-talked a gas station attendant with a fake 4F deferment into supplying her with twenty-five gallons of gas. She filled the tank on her forty-two Buick and had ten gallons stored in two five-gallon gas cans in the trunk. Then, stopping by her apartment, she packed everything she wanted and hit the road, driving east.

Sarah's parents wanted her to come for a visit, and Dean's parents were also eager for a visit, but tired of her life and everything in it, she was looking for something new, something fresh, something to excite her interests. Sadly, the war had sucked up America's able-bodied young men, except for the cheaters and those with legitimate deferments. Besides taking the young, the war had caused severe rationing of almost all tangible goods, such as tires, sugar, flour, and nylons, just to name a few items of interest to the general population. Tired of the war, the rationing, and everything related to her old life,

Sarah went east, driving aimlessly, seeking anything to help cleanse the stench of a life she no longer wanted.

Three days later, she found herself in Salt Lake City, Utah, home of the Mormons. Sarah stayed at the Hotel Utah in a luxurious suite and dined at the hotel restaurant. Although the war and rationing affected nearly everything, the Mormons, with their frugality and two-year supply rule, still had plenty of milk, butter, cheese, flour, and heavenly biscuits that Sarah swore were the best she had ever eaten. She stayed in Salt Lake for two weeks, enjoying being pampered by an attentive hotel staff of matronly ladies with sons and husbands serving in the war. Other than a lack of young men, the war seemed to have little impact on the hotel and its accommodations. Sarah almost enjoyed being alive for the first time in the past two years.

During her stay in the hotel, Sarah noticed a prominent display of pictures featuring Sun Valley, Idaho. While she was not privy to the Mormon church's interest in the Union Pacific Railroad servicing Sun Valley, the posters and information about the elegant lodge were intriguing. Prominently featured were pictures of famous dignitaries, movie stars, and her favorite author, Ernest Hemingway, who made Sun Valley his home. It was Hemingway's picture that turned the tide. Sarah retrieved her Buick and took the road to Sun Valley with no plans and expectations in mind.

Highway 36 went through a small Idaho village named Clifton, not too far from the Utah border. Here she had car problems with the engine overheating. Fortunately, the tiny village had a garage run by a world-class mechanic. Although lacking in schooling, as did many men his age, Lott, the mechanic, displayed above-average intelligence and a quick wit earning him high marks in Sarah's mind.

The problem with the Buick was a broken fan belt quickly replaced by Lott. While in the shop, the mechanic noticed one of the rear tires was nearly bald, and he suggested she have it replaced by the spare tire. While he was changing the tire, it occurred to Sarah that Clifton was the home of Roy Dalton, the young boy with an engaging smile and sad gray eyes that saw through her soul.

Sarah often thought about the young boy, and now, she found herself in the same small town, almost within arm's reach, yet she couldn't bear the thought of facing those eyes. The boy was much too perceptive, and she was afraid of what he might see in her today. Such nonsense, of course, yet Sarah couldn't ask Lott about the Daltons. Although young Roy tortured her in her dreams, she couldn't face the prospect of meeting him, even though her heart cried out for just such a meeting.

After Lott fixed her car and filled the Buick's gas tank, he told her as she was leaving to "keep smiling." What a lovely, strange way of saying goodbye. "Keep smiling." She would remember those words and how his blue eyes twinkled with some sort of magic. Sarah looked up at the orange-reddish and white cliffs high above and dreamed of sleeping beneath their majesty as she left the small village. What a ridiculous thought. Where in the world did that come from? It must be something in the water, was her last thought upon leaving town.

Sun Valley was everything Sarah hoped it would be. The striking Sawtooth Mountains, the lush valley, the beautiful Big Wood River, and Ketchum, a quaint little town with a unique, friendly feeling. The sky seemed filled with a million diamonds at night, and the air was so clean it felt scrubbed. Nothing about the town suggested California or Los Angeles and McDonald Aircraft. Although the area had several young men serving in the war, it never really felt like a war zone, unlike Huntington Beach and McDonald, which revolved around war activities.

Sarah parked herself in the gloriously spectacular Sun Valley Lodge while looking for a house. Finally, finally, this area was going to be her home. It just felt right. Since she learned of Dean's death, Sarah didn't feel the war for the first time. But first, she had to do some shopping. It was the middle of July, and there was a gift to buy for a special boy, someone who made her want to live, yet someone she was afraid to meet.

7

THE GENE AUTRY GUITAR

July 24th was a big day in Clifton, Idaho. It was Founders' Day, the day the saints first came to Salt Lake City, Utah. Settled by the Mormons, Clifton celebrated the day with Mormons throughout Utah, Nevada, and Idaho, wherever the Mormons settled. This celebration was their favorite holiday of the year; it even eclipsed Christmas.

Clifton was the central town along the mountain range between Dayton to the south and Oxford to the North. The small town had a blacksmith shop, a pool hall, a gas station and mechanic, and a general store, making it the focal point of every major celebration. The town had a parade featuring farmers with hay wagons decorated with colored ribbons, horse-drawn buggies, horse races, and even a tiny circus. Women had booths selling homemade ice cream, cookies, and fudge. The men had barbecues going with hamburgers, hotdogs, and grilled chicken.

Then there were the kid's games with gunny-sack races, greased pig chases, and pin-the-tail on the donkey. The people dressed like it was Sunday, except for the men running the cooking stations. The middle-grade schoolteacher, Horace Miller, had a booth selling homemade taffy. His ridiculous pricing turned out to be a disgrace to the teacher. He was selling candy bags, two for a nickel or three for a dime, so everybody changed their dimes into nickels. The parents had a pleasant laugh and wondered what in the world the man was doing teaching school.

Roy rode Jupiter in the horse race, hoping to win the five-dollar prize money put up by the Ford dealer in Preston, the nearest thing to a city having two whole city blocks of businesses, including a J. C. Penney's and a five and dime store. William McDermott raised horses and won the race easily on his prize thoroughbred stallion, aptly named Thunderbolt. Roy was disappointed, but Jupiter was no racehorse, simply a beautiful ranch horse.

The big celebration day is not a national holiday, and the US mail got delivered to the pool hall as usual. Disappointed at losing the horse race, Roy just kept riding over to the post office to see if there was any mail for the family. Neither brother was home from the war, and his parents lived to get news of their missing sons. To his delight and surprise, there was a small, thin package addressed to him from Sun Valley, Idaho. He didn't know anybody in Sun Valley, and it was almost unknown to the young man. To his disappointment, there was no name or return address outside the package, simply the Sun Valley postmark on the stamps.

Considered a rich man's place by the folks in Clifton, Sun Valley wasn't a usual topic of conversation in the small village of farmers and ranchers still struggling to overcome the effects of the great depression followed by the war and strict rationing. Roy's parents and the rest of the family were still at what passed as the town's park celebrating, and Roy was eager to open the package, but he was determined to wait and share the surprise with everyone else. After all, hardly anyone got packages in the mail unless you ordered something from Sears and Roebuck, and no one in town had the money for that kind of frivolous spending.

Dropping off his package at home, Roy rode Jupiter down to their ranch to do the evening chores. He raced through the milking and hog feeding, eager to get home and open his surprise. Roy was about to go back uptown for supper and share his package with the family when he noticed Brindle, a breechy mare, missing from the corral. Back on Jupiter, they raced around the ranch until finding where the bitch had broken the wire and escaped down to Deep Creek. This unexpected activity entailed another hour of searching and then chasing the damn horse back to the ranch. After repairing the fence, a tired and hungry young man finally made it home. The package was completely forgotten until he walked into the kitchen and found it resting in his supper bowl.

The family had all been waiting and playing a guessing game about what might be in the package and who might have sent it to Roy. They knew not a single person from Sun Valley or exactly where it was located. Finally, Roy's father went over to the Texaco service station and got an Idaho road map which showed where the package originated. They had heard that it was a skier's paradise, something no one in Clifton had the time or money to pursue.

Everyone crowded around the table as Roy, savoring the moment, slowly opened the package. Inside was a beautiful silk-covered box from a place called The Sheepskin Factory. With trembling fingers, Roy fumbled a little and opened the box to discover a handsome, handmade, soft leather wallet with the initials RD carved on the outside. And inside was a fifty-dollar bill. No Dalton had ever seen fifty dollars except Roy's father when he sold a few heads of beef cows. The message this time was more personal: '**Thank you FOR MAKING ME WANT TO LIVE again.**'

The Daltons sat stunned, mystified, and curious. Who on earth was sending Roy these extravagant presents and why? Roy knew who was sending these precious gifts; at least, he thought he knew. But he didn't know her name—only her sad, lonely, empty eyes. To him, she was the lady on the train. They had exchanged souls for the briefest of moments, and he could still feel her sadness at the loss of her husband. How she learned his name or where he lived, he did not know. Private investigators were not part of his universe, and the thought never crossed his mind. It was some kind of magic that he was reluctant to share, even with his family. How could he tell his mother that the gifts came from some woman he met on the train? She knew he had never been on a train in his life.

The general store sold popsicles that came in a paper wrap. The outside of the wrap had a promotion featuring a Gene Autry guitar. If someone collected 500 wrappers, they could mail them to an address in California and receive a Gene Autry guitar complete with instruction and a song book. Roy spent any free time scouring the borrow pits alongside the highway, looking for discarded popsicle wrappers. They were sticky, messy, gooey, and dirty, but he already had twenty-seven wrappers. Alternatively, you could get the same autographed Gene Autry guitar for only five dollars.

Roy raced over to the store to see if Orson Pratt would break his fifty-dollar bill into smaller denominations. He gave his parents forty dollars but kept ten for himself. He was going to own that guitar and to hell with popsicle wrappers. At the rate his stash was growing, it would take ten years to collect enough wrappers to get the guitar.

It took some doing and a lot of patience, but one day the postman delivered a large cardboard box to the post office addressed to Roy Dalton, Esq. The guitar had arrived.

Sure enough, there was a guitar inside with Gene Autry's name in cursive splashed across the soundbox. Included was a slim paper pamphlet showing how to finger the frets and form chords, along with five pages of Gene Autry's favorite songs. Roy was in heaven. Well, almost in heaven. He would have preferred a Roy Rogers guitar and songbook, and besides, he liked Roy's music better, but he would make Gene Autry do for the time being. The guitar was a piece of crap, but Roy didn't know that. It was almost impossible to tune, and it didn't stay tuned for over one or two songs. The autographed signature had worn off within days, and Roy spent more time tuning the blasted instrument than strumming chords. Yet, by God, he could make that piece of crap sound almost beautiful when everything worked properly. He didn't know it then, but his days on the ranch were numbered.

8
HOME AT LAST

When you are young and beautiful with money and live in Sun Valley, Idaho, one of the skiing capitals of the world, you skied. Sarah learned to ski. She could probably have qualified for the American Olympic ski team had she chosen to participate, but such competition seemed trivial after what she had witnessed and experienced. Instead, Sarah skied for the pleasure of feeling alive again. Her pleasures were the wind in her hair and the thrill of flying down steep slopes. Determined to make something of her life, Sarah took correspondence courses until she discovered she had a decorating talent, and her life as an interior decorator for the rich and famous began.

There was no shortage of the rich and famous in Sun Valley, and bored stay-at-home ladies with nothing else to do but redecorate their homes every two or three years provided Sarah with all the work she could manage. Before long, she had to buy a building to receive and store furniture along with drapery fabric, Persian rugs, decorator lamps, and coffee tables. She hired an assistant to keep up with the orders, eventually turning part of her new building into a second-hand store to sell the replaced furniture, pictures, rugs, and lamps.

She made the Sun Valley Lodge her temporary home while shopping for a house. Unable to find anything that excited her fancy, she settled on a riverfront lot and hired a builder to construct her new dream home. It wasn't the sort of house she would have lived in with Dean and raise a family, but for a beautiful young lady who was finding it easy to mingle, she wanted something private yet convenient enough to entertain friends and clients when she felt in the mood.

Sarah chose a rambling ranch-style house made of river rock with a large fireplace in both the entertaining room and the spacious, luxurious master bedroom. Although she never had friends stay over, Sarah still included a spacious guest room if someone like President Truman dropped by and needed a place to lay his head for the evening.

Skiing was a great sport to meet like-minded people, and Sarah was constantly in demand to join groups looking for someone to make a foursome. There was always a man wanting or needing a partner for the day, and Sarah's girlfriends, most of whom were married, were constantly trying to fix her up with someone. Over with the loss of her husband and finished with the grieving, Sarah was still a little hesitant to begin a new relationship. Plenty of rich, handsome men were smitten with the lovely, beautiful Ms. Peroni, but she declined every opportunity to further the relationship. Sarah couldn't understand her reluctance to begin a new romance. She was surrounded by many suitable bed partners or potential husbands, but she almost always went to bed alone at the end of the evening. Later, curled up in bed with a blazing fire and a good book, Sarah wondered if the fear of losing someone else she might love kept her from giving love another chance. However, that reason didn't feel quite right, and sleeping alone continued.

Another July rolled around, and Sarah had misgivings about sending Roy more presents. However, she still had Peter Hopp's number, so she rang him up, asking for an update on her favorite young man. A few days later, there was a call to report that Roy's new interest was the guitar. She learned about the pathetic Gene Autry guitar and Roy's determination to make the damn thing last, despite its misgivings. He had added more wood to stiffen the bridge, bought new strings, and glued pieces back together, yet he still made the little guitar sing.

Somehow, old Peter, being the detective he was, discovered that Roy had given forty dollars to his parents last year. It seems Orson, the store owner, told everybody in town about Roy's fifty-dollar bill and his giving forty dollars to his parents and buying himself the Gene Autry guitar with the rest.

Hearing the report, Sarah knew she could not abandon her mentally adopted young friend. Knowing he had shared most of the last present with his parents, she was determined to be more effective this year.

Sarah loved classical music. She knew who Gene Autry was, but she had never listened to him sing anything other than Rudolph the Red-Nosed Reindeer at Christmas time. So even though they plastered his picture all over Hollywood and most of Los Angeles, she didn't even recognize him as a singer, let alone as a man with a guitar made in his name. It was disgraceful to her that a famous man like that would allow his name to be marketed on a piece of crap, which Peter told her was the sum and substance of the Gene Autry guitar.

It was once again a call to Peter for his help in obtaining the next gift for young Roy Dalton. She wanted Peter to deliver it personally, although not directly to the Dalton home. Instead, he was to drop it off at the post office with instructions for how the postmaster would see that the gift reached its intended recipient.

9
THE BAND

This year, Roy would turn 15 when a young boy became a young man. The Army finally released Arnold from the hospital to return home with a wooden leg to replace the one ripped off by a German grenade. Such a long delay in being released after his injury was due to the lack of qualified nurses and doctors. Since Arnold's injury was not life-threatening, skilled medical personnel helped those with more severe conditions, leaving those like Arnold to wait until they had the time and resources to help him.

Mother Dalton was ecstatic to have at least one of her soldier boys home, even if he was no longer whole. Although weak and handicapped, Arnold could take over some of Roy's workload while their father worked out of state. Unable to lift much, he could drive the horses pulling the hay wagon while Roy loaded the hay. This simple addition almost cut the haying time in half.

On another hot, miserable July day when the temperature soared above the century mark, Roy was irrigating a field next to the railroad track when the noon Flyer came rumbling down the tracks. Roy stopped his chores temporarily while the train flew by, and he studied the people he could see sitting by the windows. Subconsciously, Roy always searched for another look at the beautiful, sad, and lonely woman. Of course, such miracles happen only once in a lifetime, as he well knew.

The running irrigation water made Roy thirsty, so climbing on Jupiter, he raced back to the watering trough and the hand water pump. The oppressive heat almost made him dizzy, so he stuck his head under the water in the trough. Then, feeling the need for a brief rest, Roy rode Jupiter across the rangeland to a small grove of trees where he could relax in the shade. The irrigation water would have to go its own way for a few minutes. It was simply too damn hot to stand in the sun for extended periods.

He was just settling down to rest when he heard a car honking on the road running by the ranch. The vehicle was a half-mile away, but the persistent honking meant somebody needed or wanted something. Reluctantly, Roy got back on Jupiter and rode over to the road and honking car.

The postmaster, Jack Woods, was driving his rusty green Studebaker with a bad muffler. He had two large packages for Roy. Unfortunately, they were two big, heavy boxes, and no way Roy could load them onto Jupiter. Asked why he brought the packages down to the ranch, Jack replied his instructions were to deliver them directly to Roy personally and to no one else.

"Who dropped these off at the post office?" Roy asked.

"I'm not sure, Roy. I was in the back eating lunch when Jane called me to come in from the kitchen. When I reached the post office room, the man who dropped them off had left, but Jane said he instructed me to bring the boxes directly to you. He even gave Jane five dollars to make sure I obeyed his instructions. I didn't want to burden you with these big boxes down here on the ranch, but I didn't know what else to do."

"That's okay, Jack; please take them back to the house in town and leave them with my mom."

"Well, okay, Roy, if that's what you want me to do." Jack was a small man, only five foot four and built like a jockey, although he had never ridden a horse, something practically unheard of in horse country. He dressed in Levi's and a long-sleeved, yellow woolen shirt. Roy wondered how the man could dress like that in this heat, but Jack seemed unaffected by it. Of course, he hadn't been working under the scorching sun all afternoon.

Like most men in town, Jack treated Roy like an adult, which he was in every way but age and size. Roy was already as strong as most of the men in town, and just last month, he had been over at the saloon getting the mail when the men drinking beer were engaged in an arm-wrestling contest. Roy watched for a minute and then volunteered to take on the champion. No one laughed at this suggestion, and no one seemed surprised when Roy whipped the winner in less than ten seconds.

After Jack left with Roy's packages, Roy raced through the day's chores and finished the irrigation for a few hours. While driving back to their house in town, Roy couldn't help but speculate on the contents of the two big boxes. One box looked suspiciously like a guitar case, but the other sizeable rectangular box was a complete mystery. By now, Roy was reasonably sure he knew who kept sending him gifts, and it bothered him not to say thank you to the dear lady. Raised to be polite and unable to express his gratitude troubled the young man, but there was no help for this troubling feeling.

When the family heard Roy's car in the driveway, they rushed into the living room where Jack had deposited the boxes. When Roy finally made it inside, his mother made him change out of his work clothes on the outside porch. Family members were not allowed in the living room wearing work clothes. Mother Dalton's rules about wearing chore clothes in the living room were not to be tested.

Dressed in his school clothes, Roy made it to the living room and the waiting family. Even though the packages were addressed to Roy, they all enjoyed watching the boxes being opened to reveal what might be inside. Entertainment in small rural towns was wherever you could find it, and watching someone open large, mysterious boxes came as close to excitement as residents in a small town were likely to experience for many more days or weeks.

Roy fished out a pocketknife from his jeans and carefully sliced open the box he thought was a guitar. Finally, a hard, beige shell guitar case came into view. Roy pulled the case from the box, laying it on the living room floor. Then he opened the case for all to see. The entire family gasped as an electric, blond Gibson, f-hole cutaway guitar, was revealed. No one had ever seen such a beautiful guitar. Such was his joy; Roy thought his heart would burst wide open. Who would have ever thought he would own such a marvelously beautiful instrument?

Now he couldn't wait to open the other sizeable rectangular box. Once again, the pocketknife flashed along the box's seams, cutting away the lid. This box held an amplifier for the guitar and the cords, plus several new songbooks featuring Eddy Arnold, Slim Whitman, Les Paul, and Roy Gallagher. Roy could not have been happier and made another life-changing decision at that moment. He would make the lady on the train proud of him, regardless of what it took.

At that moment, he decided to form a band. He did not know who would be in the band, but he knew the music they would play. He wanted to have the best country-western band in the entire country. Eddy Arnold, watch out. While Slim Whitman might be the yodeling star at the moment, just wait until the world hears Roy yodel. He had been riding the range on Jupiter for many years, yodeling just to pass the time. Walking the irrigation ditches at midnight, there was nothing to occupy his mind, so Roy yodeled. He mimicked Slim Whitman until he could sing higher, hold the notes longer, and do things with his voice no one had ever heard before. A new star was about to be born.

10
RIDING HIGH

The decoration business was going great. It was too good, if such a thing was possible. Sarah kept raising her rates until she commanded a fifty thousand dollar decorating fee, and she still had to turn business away. There was no shortage of wealthy, famous people for whom such a fee only meant they were getting the best decorator in the business.

Sarah lunched one day at the Pioneer Saloon with some ski buddies. Later, walking down Ketchum's Main Street towards her car, she passed an art gallery that sold artist supplies. Sarah had often had the gallery supply her with pictures for a home or office she was decorating, but she had never looked at the art supplies. Today, on a hunch, the decorator bought a sketch pad and a package of colored pencils.

Many of Sarah's clients had houses in Sun Valley either to live in during the winter for skiing or for the summer to escape the heat and humidity of their formal residences. As her reputation grew, these clients often flew Sarah to New York, Florida, or California to decorate their other houses. Sarah began sketching with nothing to occupy her mind on these business trips. To her surprise and delight, she discovered a natural talent for sketching. She started drawing the layouts of various rooms and furniture placement, but as her trips continued to grow, the drawings became sketches of new furniture designs.

Before long, Sarah had a sketch pad full of new furniture designs with a unique feel and look. She was buying a lot of high-end furniture from the Heritage Company in Birmingham, Alabama. Heritage made the most exclusive and high-end furniture available anywhere in America, and for Sarah's purposes, only the very best would do.

On a return trip from Florida, she stopped over for a couple of days in Birmingham to visit the Heritage factory. The owners recognized the name as soon as she introduced herself and welcomed her as one of their best customers. After the customary coffee and pleasantries, Sarah got right down to business. Opening her sketch pad, she showed Arch Woodling, the owner of Heritage, her drawings and asked if he would design and produce a furniture line for her only.

Arch looked at the unique and beautifully proportioned tables, chairs, and accessory pieces and readily agreed, but with one stipulation. He wanted to market her furniture to his other customers, giving Sarah a commission on each piece he produced for his buyers. Sarah was delighted to accept the proposition, and the Peroni line of exclusive furniture was born.

Within months, Sarah had draperies, rugs, lamps, and tableware carrying the Peroni label. Her decorating fee became $100,000 plus all expenses, and she still could not keep up with business. A short time later, as the Peroni label became known, Europeans came knocking on Sarah's Sun Valley door asking for her services. Oil Sheiks, princes, queens, and international bankers were among her clientele.

While decorating one of the Rockefeller apartments on Park Avenue, Sarah fell in love with their beautiful Murano chandeliers. The art of making world-class chandeliers and colored glass items has been handed down from father to son for many generations. Sarah flew to Italy and visited the Murano factory in Venice, where every item was handmade by experts. After much persuasion, the owners agreed to manufacture chandeliers according to Sarah's sketches.

After seeing Murano's beautiful colored glass vases, goblets, and artistic sculptures, Sarah determined to have her colored glass decorations made, but she visited a factory in Tennessee for this project. Once again, the sketchbook came out and resulted in an agreement to make colored glass items for only the famous designer. Before long, it became a tradition for Sarah to use colored glass in every interior decoration, usually hanging in front of a window. This colored glass became a Peroni trademark, recognizable by those in the know.

Sarah didn't need the money; she was already swimming in wealth without the time to spend what she already possessed. Still, the excitement of creating something different and seeing the satisfaction on her clients' faces when they viewed the finished product made her happy and seemed like enough to fill her lonely hours.

Young, beautiful, and wealthy, she was one of the most sought-after companions in the world. Hollywood stars and wealthy, influential, and respected men from around the globe sought an introduction to the famous widow Peroni. After months of fielding such propositions, Sarah ditched the widow label and became Sarah Peroni, the famous American designer/decorator.

It had been years since she made love with Dean, her long-deceased husband, and her sexual impulse did not wither and die. Still, she was unhappy with the men who sought her attention until Metrô, an Italian playboy, caught her fancy. Metrô came from a long line of fashion designers, and he knew how to dress well and address the ladies. While a long way from being the intellectual and thoughtful male Sarah would marry, she still let him seduce her, only to find out how much she missed having sex.

She let their affair run for over a week before calling it quits and moving on before it would be impossible to resist the charming young man. From then on, Sarah occasionally let the right men take her home or to a hotel when she found him companionable, handsome, and reasonably intelligent.

Sarah's love of classical music continued. She always rushed to get an opening night seat up front and, in the center, whenever a new opera or ballet opened at one of the premier venues in Venice, Sicily, Argentina, or Russia. However, as Sarah's reputation grew and her name became known in the classical world, she no longer had to clamor for a seat. Instead, she even stopped paying for her ticket. Having the famous, beautiful American lady attend opening night became a source of pride for the promoters, who lavishly treated Sarah to the best of everything they could provide.

Busy as her life became with filling every waking moment with clients' choices, opportunities for travel, and marriage proposals, Sarah never forgot her rendezvous in July when she decided to live again. Then, throughout the year, Sarah wondered how the poor ragged boy was getting along when she thought about him.

11
HIGH SCHOOL

Running down the center of northern Cache Valley is Bear River. Those towns on the west side of the river became known as Westside, while those on the east side of the river became known as Eastside. Preston, the most significant city in Franklin County, was home to the Eastside Warriors.

Along the west side of the river, the farmers and ranchers banded together to create the Westside High School, home of the Pirates. Five small communities of Clifton, Dayton, Oxford, Weston, and Corinne located their school in Dayton, roughly in the center. Without enough students to justify a high school by itself, the school district elected to make it a joint Junior-Senior High School.

Many parents with daughters were concerned about putting their twelve and thirteen-year-old daughters in the same building as the eighteen-year-old high school seniors, but they were outnumbered. There simply were not enough students to justify two separate schools.

So, Roy Dalton attended high school in Dayton, where they had different teachers for each subject, and to his great joy, he discovered Mr. Hill, the music teacher.

The school had a marching band, and Mr. Hill needed a trombone player, so he taught Roy to read music and play the sliding trombone. In the marching band, Roy met most of the students who would become members of his band, which he had already named. The Tumbleweeds.

Carol Jensen played the alto saxophone, producing one of the sweetest sounds Roy could imagine. John Sant was a pianist who began taking lessons at the tender age of four and, ten years later, was an extremely accomplished musician. Ted Balls played a wicked trumpet, and Billy Taylor had his own set of drums. Over the succeeding years, other members would join the band, but Roy figured these would do to start if he could only talk them into joining the Tumbleweeds.

Roy's workload and ranch chores didn't allow for participation in any high school activities requiring after-school practices such as competitive sports, making him an outsider. This task was made easier by the big bully, Earl Ward. Earl was a senior and a star on the school football team. Earl was a big boy weighing 250 pounds, standing six feet tall. A three-year letterman in football, he was popular with the in-crowd.

A few weeks into the fall semester, Earl bullied Roy, who, at five eight and only 140 pounds, didn't stack up as much of a threat to the bigger senior. The taunting and snide insinuations continued for a few more weeks until the day Roy snapped.

Although not part of the big boy clique, Roy was popular with the girls. He was handsome, intelligent, and easygoing, which translated into pussy material to the bigger, older Earl. This situation continued until something happened in physical education, PE, a misnomer of the highest order. This required course was nothing more than sloppy play, which the football coach/civics teacher didn't control.

Television was almost unheard of in Cache Valley. Then, a television station in Salt Lake, a city one hundred miles south, started broadcasting black and white programs that could be picked up with rabbit ears if adequately adjusted. The picture was snowy, blurred, and barely adequate sound, yet some of the wealthier farmers in the valley had to have this latest gadget. One of the most popular programs was professional wrestling, shown every evening.

Roy's family did not own a television set. Roy had never watched professional wrestling, so when the football coach suggested the students wrestle during PE, Roy was clueless. However, when Earl, being a star on the football team, one of the coach's favorite students, wanted to wrestle Roy, the coach agreed, although Roy was much smaller than the coach's star player.

The coach knew nothing about wrestling, but he knew that allowing Earl to wrestle Roy was wrong. Still, what could be the harm? Maybe Roy would be banged up a little, wear a few strawberries on his skin for a few days, but it was just PE, and sometimes kids got hurt.

Earl did not know the trouble he faced. Overconfident, arrogant, and snickering with the other football players in the class, Earl jumped onto the mat, taunting Roy, the pussy, to get a move on and get on the mat. Earl had straight black hair and dark brown eyes that sometimes appeared black when he was in an evil mood. Standing bare-chested on the mat, Earl flexed his muscles to intimidate his chosen opponent. During the past several weeks, Roy had been waiting for this moment. Working to keep the grin off his face, Roy took off his T-shirt and strolled onto the mat.

Earl had watched some wrestling matches on television, so he knew what to do and what holds you needed to take your opponent down. Ten feet apart, the two boys faced each other, and the coach blew his whistle.

Gunning for his smaller opponent expecting to inflict maximum damage, Earl practically leaped across the mat, knowing precisely what he wanted to do. Roy waited for the bigger boy to come for him. Wrestling steers, hauling hay, milking fifteen heads of cows twice a day, and digging post holes toughen a person. Earl came from a more privileged family, exempt from the daily chores so he could play sports. As Earl reached for Roy, intending to put him in a headlock, Roy quickly grabbed Earl's arm and twisted, forcing it behind Earl's back. Fueled by weeks of humiliation and anger, Roy twisted Earl's arm even harder until he popped Earl's shoulder out of the joint.

The scream jolted the coach out of his slumber. The entire class stood gawking at the big bully as he lay sobbing on the mat. How did this small high school junior best the star football player who was almost twice his size?

Without a clue about putting a shoulder back in the socket, the coach loaded his crying football player into his car for the fifteen-minute drive to Preston and the only doctor in the county.

Roy put his T-shirt back on and went into the locker room to change back into his street clothes, and went on his way to band practice. That day ended Earl's bullying.

12
SARAH, THE LONELY DECORATOR

Sarah's business interests kept her busy, but she lived a lonely life. She found the wealthy, privileged men who sought her company to be shallow, vain, arrogant, and dull. Thinking of attracting more eligible men into her life, she dumped the widow part of her name, becoming Sarah Peroni, the decorator. There was no longer any reference to her long-dead husband.

Traveling the world decorating houses, apartments, and business establishments for the affluent, she grew weary of the constant movement and limited herself to taking only ten contracts per year. At one hundred thousand dollars per contract, she had the income to support an entire staff, including a full-time secretary. Margie Wilderson became her girl Friday, responsible for managing everything, including Sarah's social life.

Sarah was never a smoker and a light drinker, limiting herself to a glass of champagne or an excellent Cabernet Sauvignon. On a trip to France at the Chateau Lafite Rothschild, Sarah met with Marie Laurencin, who insisted on having the famous American decorate her villa. The two women became instant friends, and

Marie was so impressed with the beautiful young American and the job she performed decorating the estate she awarded Sarah ten cases of their best wine. With no place to store such a valuable wine, Sarah had an exceptional wine cellar added to her Sun Valley house. Reluctant to share this rare treat with just anybody, it became something of a challenge to her friends and suitors to be invited to share a bottle.

Her new schedule and support staff allowed Sarah more free time to enjoy her home and take part in local activities. She met Ernest Hemingway, with whom she became friends after the famous writer discovered he could not entice the widow into his bed.

One morning after her shower, Sarah decided she had enough of the coarse bath towels. So, she flew to Egypt on a whim, searching for the world's best cotton. Satisfied that she had found what she was looking for, Sarah commissioned a factory to create a unique line of linens and towels. They discretely monogrammed her initials SWP into one corner of each towel, sheet, and pillowcase. Margie sent a flyer to each of Sarah's customers, informing them of the new cotton product. The line became an instant success.

Once Sarah discovered how easy it was to create her product line, she visited Thailand for silk for scarves and bedspreads. Then it was on to India for rugs and drapery. Within two years, everyone seemed to want a Peroni scarf or woven carpet. Sarah had the Midas touch, where everything she touched turned into gold. If only her personal life could find the same success.

However, the more men she met, the more dissatisfied she became with the other sex until Sarah stopped having dates entirely. The men wanted to marry her for their enhanced reputation, to get access to her money, or to get the gorgeous woman into bed. Dean was a distant memory, and her social life felt empty. She satisfied herself with classical music and entertaining books or attending the opening of an occasional opera or ballet.

Sarah did not forget about the young boy with very gray eyes and his beautiful bay horse. Each July, she mailed five hundred dollars to box 13 in Clifton, Idaho. It was her thinking that any more would disrupt the boy's life. She could and wanted to send more, but was afraid of the consequences. Instead, Sarah instructed Peter to make an annual pilgrimage to the small town and report on the boy's activities.

By now, Roy was a young man, and it delighted Sarah to learn how he had taken to the Gibson and seemed able to find practice time. The war had ended, and both of his brothers returned safely, although one brother was missing a leg. Peter reported that with the price of beef rising, Roy's father could stay home and work on the ranch, giving Roy time for his music.

GIs returned home by the thousands, and most were looking for girlfriends or wives. Or both. To avoid being constantly hit upon, Sarah retreated to her home in Sun Valley whenever her schedule allowed. When she was in one of the big cities visiting clients, her friends knew better than to fix her up with a date. She became known as untouchable. Although breathtakingly beautiful and a delight to be with or around, would-be suitors were warned to stay the distance.

Sarah had resigned herself to a life of loneliness. She accepted she had her chance for love, only to have the war rob her of happiness. Ah well, she could dream.

13
THE TUMBLEWEEDS

Once he became proficient on the trombone, Roy invited his four potential band members to come by his house for a visit. He told them he wanted to start up a band, but all four seemed reluctant to make such a commitment. Sure, he could play a decent trombone, but he was no Glen Miller. Still, they came by to hear his pitch.

The older Dalton brothers raised chickens before going off to the war, and without their help, the family could not continue raising chickens except for their own use. Most of the chicken coop became empty, so Roy threw up a partition and created a practice studio away from their house. Mother Dalton loved her bright gray-eyed boy but grew weary of the constant practicing and his yodeling. Although beautiful to hear, the yodeling was a little loud for comfort. The entire family was happy to have Roy and his music stay in the chicken coop.

The four recruits showed up after school late one spring afternoon. Roy took them into his studio, which still smelled a little like chicken shit, but he assured them he was working on a solution to end the smell. Roy had scrounged a few folding metal chairs from the old limestone grade school building built in 1879 that had been demolished to make way for something more serviceable.

First, Roy told the group of his plans for a band that he wanted to name the Tumbleweeds. He explained that while he could play the trombone, which they already knew, his preferred instrument was the guitar. They didn't know about his guitar and were even more reluctant to join a band with a guitar player. They all knew that his trombone playing, while adequate, was not stellar, and they assumed his guitar playing to be in the same category. Seeing the reluctance on their faces, Roy knew the time for show and tell had arrived.

All four would-be new band members gasped when Roy brought out his beautiful blond Gibson and plugged it into the amplifier. They all knew Roy's family was poor and how hard Roy had worked on the ranch. They also knew this guitar represented more money than many families lived on for an entire year.

Surprised as they were at the guitar, to say it astonished them when Roy began playing would be an understatement. They had never seen or heard such playing in their lives. Already sold, when Roy started singing *Chime Bells* and began yodeling, the four young classmates began clapping, hooting, and hollering like their lungs were on fire. They all knew Eddy Arnold's singing and Slim Whitman's yodeling. Country music was about all their local radio stations played. But they did not know Roy had such talent. No one outside of his family had ever heard him sing. Being a loner with no real friends to share in his passion, Roy's talent had gone unnoticed.

The Tumbleweeds band became a reality that afternoon in the Dalton chicken coop.

Stored in one corner of the chicken coop were boxes of egg cartons from the time Arnold and Marlow raised chickens. The new band members pitched in and helped paint the walls before stapling egg cartons on the walls and ceiling. The Mormon women formed the Relief Society group, which helped grieving families when someone died. The ladies made quilts throughout the year, which they sold at an annual bazaar. These handmade quilts were beautiful, and the band bought two to hang in their chicken coop practice room.

The first five hundred dollars that arrived in the mail for Roy Dalton went for Jensen speakers and Macintosh amplifiers. They bought a better set of drums for Billy Taylor and an old piano for John in the years that followed. Band practice began three times a week for the first six months and then every day after school and nearly every Saturday. Roy hired Mr. Hill, their music teacher, to help arrange the tunes they played. By the end of the first year, the band was ready for its debut.

The junior prom is one of the featured dances during the high school year, and the junior class always tries to hire the best band available. They had engaged The Lightning Boys for this year's prom and were looking forward to hearing them perform. The band had an excellent reputation, and some students had heard them perform over in Preston. Unfortunately, the band's leader came down with smallpox a week before the prom date, and the band had to cancel. Several students knew about the Tumbleweeds, but no one had ever heard them play, yet with no other choice, they agreed to pay the band one hundred dollars to play at the prom.

No one outside of the band knew quite what to expect, so when Roy hit the first chord on his Gibson, the entire crowd knew they were in for a special treat. First, the band started with some fast tunes to get the crowd warmed up; then, they played a slow romantic song featuring Carol and her saxophone. The next song featured Ted's trumpet, followed by a tune with John on the piano. Finally, everybody relaxed and was having a good time enjoying the delightfully surprising band.

Then, the time had come for *Chime Bells*.

After the first stanza in which Roy sang in a clear tenor voice, he began yodeling. Until that moment, there had been no singing, only instruments. No one outside the band had heard Roy sing, and of course, they did not know he could yodel. Instead, the song began with an E chord strummed on Roy's Gibson, and with that sound, nearly everyone knew something special was taking place. Almost everyone listened to KPST, the local radio station in Preston, and was familiar with Slim Whitman's version of *Chime Bells*. When Roy's voice hit high C above middle C, you could hear the bells ring in his voice and from the strings of his guitar. His singing and yodeling brought the house down.

That night made the band's reputation, and Roy became the most talked-about singer in the valley.

Eric Hobson, who managed KPST, heard about the performance and invited the band to play on the radio. They accepted the invitation, and this exposure led to engagements for every function in the valley needing or wanting a band. They played at weddings, dances, and nearly every big celebration throughout Cache Valley. Before long, their fee became two hundred and fifty dollars for a performance, and they were still turning down engagements.

Roy was an all-American boy, a genuine, vigorous young man with normal hormones. There was never any question about his sexuality, but his mother caught him masturbating at twelve. Mother Dalton was a Godfearing Christian woman, even if they didn't go to church every Sunday, and she lit into young Roy with a vengeance. She called him a nasty boy playing with the devil. What he was doing was wicked and was never to be repeated.

Roy was confused but respectful of his parents at his age, especially his mom, but he was careful never to let her catch him playing with his penis again.

14
PAINTING

Twenty-six and one of the most beautiful women in the world, not to mention one of the wealthiest, Sarah grew weary of her busy life. She scaled down her assignments, accepting only those jobs with a unique appeal. She engaged a contractor to construct an addition to her studio lit by one of the most stunning chandeliers imaginable to display her furniture and other exclusive products for her customers.

Sarah had her house wired with speakers in every room so she could listen to her favorite classical music no matter where she might be at the moment. Sitting in her enormous room in front of the fireplace with a sketch pad in her lap, she listened to her favorite recordings while sketching new furniture layouts.

Next to the Pioneer Saloon on the corner of Sun Valley Road and Main Street stood the First Citizens Bank. The bank was housed in a large, two-story brick building built in 1884. It featured a Ben Franklin stove in the middle of the first floor to heat the bank during the cold winter months. Hanging on the knotty pinewood walls were paintings by a local artist, Arlene Barbier.

Arlene specialized in landscapes featuring the fantastic local scenery. While waiting for a buyer, the paintings added a touch of class to the rustic bank interior. Arlene was in the bank one day when Sarah came in to make a deposit. A small petite woman only five foot two inches tall, Arlene still had a full figure and, on this day, was wearing a flowery sundress cut low in front to display a full bosom and a high hem to show off her shapely legs.

Arlene's painting featuring the picturesque Sawtooth Mountains hanging on the wall attracted Sarah, who stood admiring the work when Arlene came and stood by her side. "Do you want to buy the painting, Sarah?" she asked in greeting.

"Oh, hi, Arlene. No, I was just admiring your talent. You seem to capture the feel of those beautiful mountains perfectly."

"Thank you for noticing. So many people just look at paintings as though they were just another picture."

"I know it takes talent to make a picture stand out, and your paintings all display an incredible talent."

"My word. Such a compliment coming from one of the most talented women I know."

"A compliment well earned, dear lady."

"Sarah, I have been to your showroom admiring the beautiful Peroni furniture, chandeliers, and rugs. I wonder if you would allow me to hang some of my pictures on your walls. I'll pay you a commission for every painting that sells."

"Arlene, I'd love to hang your pictures in my showroom. They might give it a little class, but there is no way I'll take your money. Instead, I would like you to provide me with private painting lessons."

"Well, that is a high compliment, but let me first say that your showroom needs no more class. You have taken care of that without my pictures. But may I ask, what is your interest in painting?"

"You were probably unaware, but I have been sketching pictures of the furniture I created for some time now. Plus, I always make sketches of the rooms I will decorate to get a feel for what to do with the space."

"No, I didn't know about your sketching, Sarah, and if you are serious, I will find it a pleasure to teach you how to paint."

Over the next few months, Sarah spent two hours twice a week at Arlene's studio, learning how to paint. She had a natural talent and already had a feel for spacing, color, and proportion from her sketching activities. Before long, her work was nearly on a par with the teacher.

Unwilling to be a copycat by duplicating Arlene's style, Sarah made it a point to visit the Metropolitan during her next New York visit, where she could study the masters. The museum featured a Van Gogh, one of his sunflower paintings. Also included in the museum were some Rubens, a Rembrandt, a Cezanne, and a Monet. Sarah returned home satiated at last and determined to create her own style.

The nearby town of Hailey was next to Sun Valley's regional airport. A nearby rancher raised thoroughbred Arabian horses, and Sarah loved the beauties at first glance. She wanted to paint Roy's bay stallion but lacked a clear picture of the horse in her mind, so she spent several hours sketching the black Arabian. Sarah drew the horse in every imaginable pose before she began the painting.

This work of art began by painting the canvas with a flat black base. Then, as she added images in color, she scraped off a little here and there, exposing the black undercoating. White highlights were added, giving the painting extra depth. She completed painting the picture of a wild black stallion with several coats of a special homemade varnish she learned to make from Arlene.

Sarah painted the magnificent creature at a full gallop, his tail flying straight back and his mane standing up in a curl. The head was turned slightly towards the viewer as though he could see someone watching him. There was an eager glint in his eyes, as though he was in heaven and having fun racing down a beautiful green meadow. It was a stunning picture that grabbed and pulled the viewer into the scene. With this work of art, a new artist was born.

Unhappy with the lighting in her house, Sarah commissioned a contractor to build a studio above her bedroom, accessible by a broad curved staircase. Windows to supply light throughout the day surrounded the room.

The Sun Valley Artists' Association, which brought world-class entertainment to the privileged residents, engaged Andres Segovia for a concert at the Sun Valley concert hall. Sarah attended and found the classical guitar soothing and comfortable listening. Before long, Sarah filled her home with Segovia's music while she painted in her studio.

15
WRITING MUSIC

With their KPST exposure, the demand for the Tumbleweed band seemed unquenchable, so Roy raised their rates once again to quell the demand for their services. However, Roy still had chores to perform, and the band members were all students with lives besides music. Still, they practiced several times a week while performing at least one night each weekend, and sometimes they had two or three gigs in a row.

The KPST radio station recorded the band while they played live on the air so that the announcer could play one or two of the band's numbers almost daily. Inevitably, the band's reputation reached the station manager of KSL in Salt Lake City, Utah.

KSL was a 50,000-watt clear channel radio station. In the evening, when the e-layer in the ionosphere reflects radio waves, listeners can hear the station throughout the western United States. Station manager Larry Perkins listened to the band on KPST on a visit to Preston. Impressed, he invited the band to come and play one night on KSL in the big city. Fortunately, this offer was too good for the band to pass on.

On the night they played in Salt Lake City, the e-layer was particularly strong, and the radio station reached Nashville, Tennessee, and the ears of Malcolm Wisely, a local music producer in Tennessee's capital city. Malcolm helped create the Nashville sound, which put the city at the forefront of country-western music. Home of the Grand Old Opry, Nashville prided itself on the music legends around town, men like Eddy Arnold and Slim Whitman, and female stars like Patsy Cline and Kitty Wells.

As Malcolm listened to The Tumbleweed's music, in his musical bones he felt this band could be huge, with some better arrangements, original music, and proper promotion. He called KSL and spoke to Larry Perkins, requesting information about the band while the band was still playing. Malcolm did not know the band members were a group of high school students.

Larry talked with Malcolm for several minutes, and the two men outlined a plan to present to Roy and the others about the band's future, a plan Larry explained to them after they finished their one-hour live radio show.

When everyone was ready to listen, Larry explained they would need to make a record and compose some original music for the band to make it to the big time. He told them about his call from Malcolm in Tennessee and how the man would supply someone to help arrange their music if they would go to Nashville.

The band members had a year of high school to complete. They lived in an impoverished area barely above the poverty level, and finishing high school, something denied to their parents, was ingrained in their parent's wishes for the children.

Larry agreed with their request to continue their schooling and volunteered to be the band manager as soon as they were ready to get serious about going professional.

When they started the band, it was mostly to have some fun with their music and perhaps pick up a little spending money if they could ever get an engagement. However, the reality of having more engagements than they could manage, plus the possibility of going to Nashville and making records, seemed like a dream come true. Visions of future fame and glory and wealth danced in the Tumbleweed's heads as they drove home from Salt Lake.

Carol had an idea for a new original song, and Roy was also determined to write music. As they parted for the evening, they each felt on the break of something good, perhaps a life away from poverty and hard work.

Looking for inspiration, Roy went to Hart's music store in Preston. They had some new classical records, including a recording by a guitar player named Andres Segovia. Interested in hearing other guitar players, Roy bought the album and listened to an acoustic guitar for the first time. He loved his Gibson and wouldn't trade it for the world, but there was something about the sound of a pure acoustic guitar that caught his attention. He often played the Gibson without the amplifier, and while his guitar had an acoustic body that gave it a unique sound, it didn't sound like Segovia's guitar.

Roy went to Logan, Utah, forty miles away, to find an assortment of acoustic guitars. After strumming on the entire selection, he bought one for eighty-five dollars that sounded like the one Segovia had played on the album he purchased earlier. Over the next few months, Roy practiced on the acoustic, learning to play with his fingers instead of using a pick. He mimicked the sound of other classical guitar players on albums he bought until becoming just as proficient on his new acoustic as he was on his favorite instrument, the beautiful blond Gibson.

Larry Perkins, the manager of KSL in Salt Lake City, made a weekly trip to Idaho, visiting the band, listening to their practices, and making suggestions for arrangements and new songs they might consider playing. He asked about any new material they might be composing on each trip. Carol told him and her bandmates she was working on a new song but had some problems with the words. She felt the tune was right, but somehow the words escaped her at the moment. Finally, after a few weeks of getting nowhere, she agreed to play the song for her bandmates and let them help her with the words.

Roy thought about a song that stuck in his mind and decided to compose something romantic, using the acoustic guitar for accompaniment. He worked on the music for almost a month before allowing his bandmates to hear it for the first time. This session would also be when he introduced his new full-bodied acoustic guitar to his friends.

To say his friends were astonished at his accomplishment when he played a Sor composition to warm up his fingers would be an understatement. Finished warming up, Roy began singing his new love song, bringing tears to his friend's eyes. This ode to the lady on the train was the song that would later make the band. He titled his love song *A Brief Encounter*, about a poor, lonely boy who meets a beautiful, sad lady on a train. Their eyes met, and in that instant, they briefly exchanged souls.

When he struck the final chord, the chicken coop practice room was silent for several moments; then, his bandmates began clapping. After an interlude, they all set about making suggestions for an arrangement that, later in Nashville, when they started recording their first album, the experts could only suggest adding a base plus a fiddle player.

Of course, his bandmates all wanted to know the inspiration for such a beautiful ballad. The only thing Roy would admit to was that he found the inspiration while standing next to Jupiter. Over the next few years, Roy often thought about the beautiful, sad lady, wondering what had become of her. He fantasized about meeting her, but in his mind, he was still a ragged eleven-year-old boy, and she was lonely, sad, and much older than his eleven, almost twelve years.

When Larry Perkins first heard their new song, he too had tears in his eyes, and he knew their future would be solid if they stayed together and continued writing music like what he had just heard.

16
THE ARTIST

Sarah decided she loved painting pictures more than the decorating business. As a result, she accepted fewer offers for new decorating assignments. However, with the war ending and the American economy recovering rapidly, city after city built concert halls, and they all wanted Sarah Peroni to decorate their lobby. As a result, Margie would drop by Sarah's house with the details when a particular new assignment came through the doors that her agent thought would interest the boss.

Sarah still traveled the world for opening night at the world's premier opera houses, although these days, she flew in her own private Lockheed JesStar L-329. Lonely beyond despair, she desperately wanted to find a husband before growing older. Like many women, Sarah longed to be a mother and raise a couple of children. In her mind, she would have one boy and one girl. And it didn't matter in which order they came.

Unfortunately, every man who interested her was already married. In whatever social milieu she found herself in, whether at a social event or when visiting friends in either New York or Los Angeles, eligible bachelors her age were rich, spoiled, and twits, interested only in getting laid and partying. Preferably at the same time. They seemed incapable of discussing anything except baseball, football, gambling, and the movies. She could not find an actual brain in the entire field, and her social strata didn't mix with anyone who might possess an IQ above 110.

Peter Hopp was engaged in conducting an annual pilgrimage to Clifton and reporting on the boy guitarist. She heard from Peter about the band and Roy's growing proficiency on the Gibson. While Peter practically raved about the young man's talent, Sarah was a terrible snob, refusing to believe that an electric guitar made music. And she was confident that country-western music fell way outside the spectrum of anything worth devouring her precious listening time. Peter never mentioned Roy's singing; he may never have heard Roy yodel.

Before long, Sarah's studio was full of paintings. She specialized in animal pictures. There were pictures of birds, such as a pine hen sitting on a tree branch or a snow rabbit hiding under a sage bush, but it wasn't all pictures of fuzzy animals appealing to kids and homemakers. She painted black bears fishing in the river and wolf packs in the snow, hunting for dinner. She also painted unusual animals, such as a weasel in the winter with its snowy white hair or rattlesnakes sunning themselves on a rock.

Sarah never painted the violence of nature or images of animals feasting on some kill. Instead, whenever she finished a painting, she set it aside for a week. Then, after looking at it with fresh eyes, if it didn't evoke warm feelings, she covered it with a black primer and started something new.

Two years later, her paintings were in such great demand by the big galleries in New York that Sarah commanded twenty-five thousand dollars for an average picture. About a year after she started painting, Sarah loaned *The Black Stallion* to a friend who wanted to showcase some of Sun Valley's local talent for an artist's exhibition held outdoors at the Sun Valley ice skating rink. Because almost everybody knew about her decorating skills, for there were barely any mansions left in the valley that didn't boast some piece of Peroni furniture, it came as a surprise to most that she was an accomplished artist in another arena. When the owner of the Pioneer Saloon saw the Black Stallion, he offered Sarah five thousand dollars for the picture on the spot. She turned down the five, then ten, and ultimately twenty-five thousand dollars for the fantastic picture. This one she determined to keep for herself. There is only, and always, one first of anything, and your first picture is something special. Right up there with your first romantic kiss, something almost everybody remembers, although most forget those that follow almost immediately.

17
THE WEEDS

This year was when Roy turned eighteen and graduated from high school. It was also the last gift from the mystery lady. Having received the annual reports from Peter, Sarah knew about the Tumbleweeds and their success. Knowing little about country music other than what she heard from others, Sarah listened to The Grand Ole Opry one Saturday night to understand what Roy might be doing. On the radio that night, Sarah heard a harmonica for the first time in her life and added it to Roy's collection of instruments. Still not a fan of country-western music, she wanted to support her "friend" in any way possible.

In the middle of July, Roy received a small package in the mail with what had become the traditional note.

> *Dear ROY,*
> *You're a young man now, and this will be my final gift. You have probably guessed that I have received regular reports about your progress. Congratulations on the band. I am pleased that you like the Gibson guitar. Maybe this harmonica can add to your musical collection.*
> *Good luck,*

Your friend, the Lady on the Train.

The small package contained a gold-plated M HONER harmonica in the key of G. What surprised Roy was that he had been considering adding a harmonica to his collection of musical instruments. During the band's performance, at some point, Roy would play his trombone on a slow dance tune. Then, for a romantic ballad, he might pick up his acoustic guitar to accompany his singing, followed by a pure classical guitar song such as *Leyenda* by Albeniz. The harmonica would make a significant addition if he could learn how to play the blasted thing.

In August, Larry Perkins came by with the news about going to Nashville. Malcolm Wisely, the Nashville producer, had arranged for the band to practice with a professional musical arranger and record an album. They were due in Nashville in three weeks.

Roy could number the days he would still be a rancher. His brother Arnold studied to become an engineer at Utah State Agricultural College in Logan, Utah. After returning home from fighting in the Pacific, Marlow married a beautiful local girl named Frann and built a home on the ranch. His goal was to take over the ranch from his parents in the future. With the war now over, Cache Valley began prospering, and with the price of beef rising, Roy's father could stay home and work full time on the ranch, freeing Roy from his daily chores.

Roy had composed three more songs during the past two years, and Carol finished two others independently. With six original musical pieces and an entire repertoire of classic country western music, the band headed to Nashville with their new manager, Larry Perkins.

Malcolm introduced the band to his chosen arranger, a beefy, old, southern gentleman named Horace Walpole. Horace must have weighed three hundred pounds, but he moved gracefully, appearing light on his feet, as many heavy people do. With a

Colonel Sanders white beard and jolly bright green eyes, Horace was an instant hit with the band.

After listening to several of the band's songs, Malcolm recommended adding a bass player and someone to play the fiddle. Arlo Mendenhall and Pug McDonald joined the band. Arlo played a beautiful instrument with a sweet violin sound, while Pug had a five-foot bass instrument that looked like polished obsidian.

After three more weeks, the band was ready to record its first album. Larry and Malcolm thought the name Tumbleweeds sounded too much like a hick band from the sticks. They recommended calling the band simply The Weeds. Roy and the others had no objection, so THE WEEDS became the band's name.

Roy wanted to name the album *THE LADY ON THE TRAIN*. The album's feature song was Roy's ballad *A Brief Encounter*, which made some sense given the album's name. They released the album two weeks later, and the band became famous overnight. Within 45 days, the album went gold, their first million record album, and *A Brief Encounter* became the number one single on every musical chart in the country. Listeners could not get enough of *A Brief Encounter* or Roy's yodeling on *Chime Bells*, both becoming 45 single record standards.

The Grand Ole Opry booked them for a one-hour show, which started a stampede for requests for the band's appearance. Requests for performances swamped Larry, who began booking the band in small thousand-seat concert halls, which proved to be too small, so soon they were playing to audiences of five and then ten thousand people. They toured the United States for a year, playing in almost every city with over one hundred thousand residents.

Requests for radio and television interviews came in by the hundreds. In addition, there were requests for photoshoots and public appearances that forced Larry to hire an assistant to help with all the bookings. He found a delightful young lady in Cincinnati named Joann Concord with experience as a travel agent. The band needed hotels, meals, transportation for the players, and their instruments, including amplifiers, speakers, and microphones. Joann was perfect for the job. A petite blond with an oval-shaped face, Joann looked like a forest elfin you might encounter in a Jean Anderson children's book. She reminded people of a young Audrey Hepburn.

While on tour, the band worked on new music. Roy and Carol composed new pieces for their next album on buses and airplanes. They kept Joann busy trying to find practice studios where the band could work on the new songs. Horace Walpole, their arranger, would meet them in various cities to help with the arrangements. Before their first tour ended, the band was ready for their second album, *TIMELESS*. The album's cover was a picture of Roy's silver watch with the **R. D.** initials clearly visible.

Now, Roy wanted to experience sex like every other young person on planet earth, and keeping his impulses in check took every ounce of self-control he possessed. There was no concert where women didn't throw their house keys, hotel keys, and notes on the stage looking for a hookup. But Roy had one rule for Malcolm and his assistant Joann: they always were to book him a private room. He didn't want to watch his friends make love in the same room. He was afraid of losing control and joining in the fun.

18
CONVERSION

During her many visits to New York decorating famous Park Avenue apartments, Sarah became friends with many art gallery owners and managers. For example, the Shining Jewel on 5ᵗʰ Avenue featured a dozen local artists Sarah admired and used in decorating. Aharon Benowitz, the gallery manager, admired the beautiful young decorator. When Sarah brought in two of her paintings to see if the gallery would hang them, acceptance was immediate. Not only was Aharon smitten with Sarah, he genuinely loved her animal paintings.

Sarah was so delighted to find a professional in the art world who would sponsor her work, she was practically flying down the street when an album cover in the front window of a music store caught her eye. At first, Sarah thought she might be mistaken, but stopping for a closer look, she could see the silver watch with the initials *R. D.* stamped on the watch's cover. The album's name was *Timeless* by some band called The Weeds. Peter had told Sarah that Roy's band was the Tumbleweeds. Could they have changed their name? Was this Roy's band? She did not know of the band's success, as she was not into country-western music. Unfortunately, there were no longer any reports from her detective.

Going up to the counter, Sarah asked, "May I have a look at that album displayed in your window? The one called Timeless."

"Yes, certainly. You have excellent taste. That album is the band's second, and it's dynamite."

"You said this is their second album?" Sarah asked in confusion.

"You must not follow the country-western music scene. The Weeds are the biggest thing in country music these days. Many of their singles have even been number one on the popular music charts."

"Would you have their first album?" Sarah asked.

"Oh, my yes. The band named their first album The Lady on the Train. Before we knew how big that band was going to become, we didn't stock a large number, and then when it went gold, we couldn't get any more for the longest time. We still can hardly keep up with the demand for either album. It's right over here. Let me show you."

The junior clerk led Sarah over to a bin stocked with country-western albums, with Weed albums taking up six inches of rack space. This number of albums prompted Sarah to comment on the large number of them.

"It looks like you have quite a stock of these on hand now."

"By next week, we will sell them all. Hopefully, our next shipment will arrive before we run out."

Sarah picked up The Lady on the Train and turned the album over to look at the back cover. There was a large picture of the band and a smaller picture featuring Roy playing his Gibson.

Sarah gasped, turned white, and nearly dropped the album onto the floor.

Noticing the woman's reaction, the clerk asked, "Lady, are you okay?"

Catching her breath and smiling at the young man, she responded, "Yes, thank you. I never saw a picture of Roy Dalton before. He's... really quite handsome, isn't he?"

"Oh, my lord. You should see him in concert," he gushed. "The girls go crazy. Hell, if I were a girl or had different hormones, I'd make a run at him. He is absolutely fabulous."

"I don't suppose you would know if he is married?" Sarah asked the clerk.

"Not that anyone knows. I don't believe he even has a girlfriend. The band has been on the road ever since releasing their first album. I saw him play in The Garden a few months ago, and, man, can he play that guitar. But his singing is out of this world. Until you hear him yodel, you have never heard pure music."

"I thought yodeling was something the Swiss did in their Alps or something, not actual music."

"Madam, that might have been the case before Roy came on the scene, but not anymore. *Chime Bells* is on their first album, and I get goosebumps just thinking about that song."

Sarah continued to scan the listing of songs until *A Brief Encounter* caught her eyes. "This song, *A Brief Encounter*, do you have the words?"

"They print the words to all the vocals on the dust cover inside the album jacket. *A Brief Encounter* is the album's signature song, written by Roy himself."

"And I suppose you heard him sing this song?" Sarah asked.

"Yes, ma'am, and he had me bawling like a baby. Everyone had tears in their eyes. That song is a real tearjerker. It is the only song where he plays the acoustic guitar for accompaniment."

"You mean he plays an acoustic guitar beside his Gibson, pointing to the picture on the album cover, the one here in the picture?" she asked.

"Oh, he plays a wicked classical guitar. His shows always have one pure acoustic piece backed by the band."

"He sounds pretty versatile," she commented.

"Yes, mam. He also plays the trombone and harmonica on some songs."

"I did not know he was so talented," said the lady.

Sarah opened the band's first album, including *A Brief Encounter*, and began reading the words. Before finishing the last stanza, she was crying. Something Sarah had not done since Dean died, and she met a young, poor boy wearing raggedy patched pants and bloody hands while on the train. Okay, only one of them was on the train, and the boy was across the fence leaning against a beautiful bay horse, but somehow, they met and saw into each other's souls. Now, look at what he had become. Sarah couldn't help but wonder if her gifts had anything to do with his success. She hoped that was the case.

"I'll take both albums," she said to the astonished clerk. People seldom cry when reading the lyrics of a song.

"You can't go wrong with Roy and The Weeds," he responded.

The clerk went to put the albums into a bag, but Sarah stopped him. She wanted to look some more at Roy's picture, but she didn't say this to the clerk, only, "I'll just take them like this," she said as she was leaving the store.

19
PLAYING AT THE MET

The Weeds were not just an American sensation; they had caught on across the Atlantic. Larry wanted to arrange and book a European tour for the band. He wanted the band to leave as soon as they completed their second tour in America, but Roy wanted to finish a new album before starting their next tour. In addition, Carol had met a man she wanted to marry, and Billy wanted to take a break from the drums for a few months. The band members all made enough money to retire if they chose, but Roy and the others loved performing, and Roy didn't mind not having a home.

Meeting with Larry and Horace, Roy asked their thoughts about replacing Carol and Billy. Larry didn't have anybody in mind, but Horace knew many people in the music business and started making calls. The following week, the band had several candidates from which to choose. There was no shortage of people who would love to be part of the hottest country-western band in the world. After holding auditions for two days, the band decided on Les Aranson to play the saxophone. He was not Carol, but he played a soft, romantic alto that made you want to hug somebody. Jackson Wood played the drums like he had been practicing on them his whole life, which wasn't that far-fetched.

While the band rehearsed the third album with their new members, Larry was busy scheduling the European tour engagements. He had arranged about half of the tour when he got a call from Elizabeth Horsman, chairperson for the New York Metropolitan Opera house. A former Diva past her singing career, Elizabeth wanted to schedule The Weeds for an impromptu concert. The Opera company had just lost the lead singer, Dame Joan Sutherland, who was expected to make her New York debut in *Luci di Lammenromoore*. Unfortunately, one passenger was diagnosed with a highly contagious disease on the ship carrying her to America, causing it to be quarantined. As a result, it would be two weeks before Joan could rehearse with their orchestra, and Elizabeth wanted The Weeds to perform in her place. This invitation was as close as it got to an easy decision for Larry. This one time, he would not let Roy say no. The Met chooses few to play in its sacred hall, and Larry was not about to let this opportunity pass.

The band was in turmoil as they decided which songs to perform. They selected two classical guitar pieces by Roy since it was a classical forum. Larry sent copies of all the music they would perform to the Philharmonic Orchestra for practice, and then the day before their show, the band rehearsed with the full orchestra.

When the big day arrived, the band outfitted themselves in tuxedos made of black Antico Setificio Fiorentino silk. Naturally, everyone was eager to show classical music buffs that country bumpkins could also occasionally pass for the upper class. When the band took the stage in their tuxes, with brilliant white shirts and bright blue cummerbunds, the audience rose and gave a respectful welcome, not the screaming crowds the band usually experienced. But then, this was the Met.

They opened with Roy playing a Tarrega piece on the acoustic. The audience appreciated the music giving Roy and the band decent applause when the song ended. They followed this with two more instrumentals, and then they played *A Brief Encounter.*

Opera patrons have seen some sad scenes and heard heart-wrenching songs from many of the world's most revered vocalists, but when Roy sang his ballad about a poor ragged boy and a beautiful lonely widow, it moved the entire crowd to tears. Then, without a dry eye in the house, Roy struck the opening chords to *Chime Bells,* and when the yodeling began, the audience gasped and then began what, for a staid opera crowd, was pandemonium.

It is doubtful that many of the upper crust members of the audience had ever heard anyone yodel, but it is a guaranteed fact that they had listened to no one sing like Roy sang that evening. With a classical tenor voice backed with years of practice, Roy gained a thousand new listeners that night. His extremely high glissando atonal sweep brought all the opera patrons to their feet, clapping and shouting like cowboys at a Teresa Brewer concert.

After receiving that rousing response, the band relaxed and performed many of their big hits and favorite songs. The mark of a successful evening in concert or the theater was curtain calls. On this night, the band played three encore tunes and could have played more, except they had practiced no more songs with the full orchestra. The evening closed with a song Eddy Arnold made famous, *Cattle Call,* except there was not another person on earth who could yodel like Roy.

The band left the stage to a standing ovation, and Roy was the new darling of the Metropolitan opera crowd.

20
MISSED OPPORTUNITY

The airplane ride home took forever. Sarah was eager to listen to Roy and The Weeds. It was ridiculous, but she couldn't wait to hear Roy sing *A Brief Encounter*. After reading the words in the dustcover, she knew it was about their meeting. An improbable, impossible meeting, somewhere in space between a sad, lonely woman and a poor lonely, overworked boy in ragged clothes. She was equally sure that her gifts helped spur Roy's interest in the guitar and a music career.

Her private plane landed at the Sun Valley Airport, and Margie, her assistant, had her car parked near the apron for easy access. Home at last, she changed into a loose-fitting cotton jumpsuit, and then after opening one of her precious bottles of Rothschild's cabernet, she put The Lady on The Train on the record player and settled back to hear The Weeds.

Sarah was never a fan of country music, and the first three songs on the album did nothing to change her mind. The guitar music was pleasant, and the instrumentals were okay, but Mozart or Beethoven it wasn't. Then Roy started strumming his classical guitar, playing the slow ballad *A Brief Encounter*, and when his voice entered the song, Sarah completely lost control of her emotions. First, listening to his sweet tenor voice describing his joy at seeing the train and his lonely, desperate life, she bawled like a three-year-old child who dropped their first ice cream cone in the dirt. Then, when he felt the heartache of the beautiful lady on the train, Sarah thought she could not cry any harder.

She had never paid attention to yodeling before, and she had heard of no one who could produce such a sound. Yet when Roy started with *Chime Bells*, Sarah felt lifted into the arms of angels.

Oh my God, what a voice and talent to evoke such beautiful, painful memories. She remembered how the empathy in his eyes gave her the courage and will to live again. Sarah called a telephone number on the jacket cover to learn about concert dates and was surprised to learn they were playing at the Met in New York next week.

As a frequent patron of the opera hall, they recognized her name, and someone connected Sarah with the house manager, a big portly lady named Estell Workman, who always wore large flowery print dresses to hide her big body.

"This is Estell. How can I help you?" Her voice was warm and soft, much like her body.

"Estell, this is Sarah Peroni, and I just learned about your upcoming concert with a band called The Weeds."

"Well, yes. It isn't your typical opera fare, but our soprano got delayed, and we needed something to fill the time. One of our members heard the band play and recommended them to the committee. He played some of their songs for us to hear. Okay, some people call it music, but some of it was pretty pleasant. So, what's your interest, Sarah?"

"I just listened to their first album and thought it was impressive. Later, I discovered you booked them for a concert next week; I wondered if I could get a ticket?"

"Oh, Sarah honey, (she called all the regulars honey-easier than remembering names, although that wasn't a problem with

Sarah), I'm so sorry, but we have over two hundred names on our waiting list."

Hoping for a positive answer, Sarah asked, "But don't you always save a few seats for the special guests?"

"Oh, honey. I would have a front-row seat reserved for special guests just like you, but I even gave up my seat for some senator. I'll be watching from backstage. If we get a cancellation for one of our good seats, I'll move your name to the top of the list. But I have to tell you. As popular as this group appears to be, I wouldn't hold my breath."

"Okay, thanks, Estell. Will you have them back?"

"Can't answer that until after the concert, and we see how the members react. This band engagement was a quick fill-in. We needed a respectable band available on short notice. The Weeds are just completing a new album and heading for a tour in Europe. We lucked out getting them. Apparently, they're pretty popular."

"Well, thanks for the information. Goodbye, Estell."

"I'm so sorry, Sarah. I wish I could help. Goodbye."

Sarah called the Weed's contact number looking for information on their European tour. Many of the dates were already set, but nothing matched the openings on her calendar. So, she decided to wait a few days and try again. She missed the band at the Met, but hopefully, she would catch them someplace overseas. Unfortunately, it would be many more long years before Sarah got to see Roy and The Weeds.

21
DISASTER IN ROME

Madrid, Lisbon, Paris, London, Oslo, and Stockholm were all significant events with sold-out auditoriums. Europe was slowly recovering from WWII and was ready to celebrate. European people everywhere welcomed the Americans, and almost everyone knew about The Weeds. Unfortunately, disaster struck when they were playing in Rome.

While driving to their second concert, a run-away bus whose driver died of a stroke struck their limousine. Everyone in the band suffered an injury, but Roy was riding in the limo's backseat where the bus rammed into their vehicle. After pulling him from the wreckage, they rushed an unconscious Roy to the nearest hospital, Nuovo Regina Margherita, which was one of Rome's finest.

Roy was in a coma for six days, after which he began a long slow recovery to complete consciousness. Both arms and legs were broken, along with several ribs. Lying in a traction bed with all appendages swinging in the air, all Roy could do was move his head from side to side and talk. It would be another two weeks before he could speak an entire sentence coherently. They feared he would never sing again if he could not speak correctly.

Joann Concord, Larry's assistant, stayed at the hospital around the clock to receive updates on the various band members and Roy. She reported doctors were concerned about Roy making a full recovery and resuming his life as a bandleader. Weed fans worldwide were in shock and praying for their star to make a full recovery.

Another month went by before they cut away the casts, freeing Roy to move for the first time in six weeks. Then, of course, he was too weak to stand and could barely hold a glass of water, but at least he sounded like his old self whenever he spoke. Realizing his predicament and hearing the doctors talk about the possibility of not performing again sent Roy into a depression where he rarely spoke to anyone.

They released Roy from the hospital, but a physical therapy regimen was necessary to recover complete motor control of his body. While on a road trip before becoming famous, the Tumbleweeds were touring in a VW bus and played at a bar in Moab, Utah. Roy fell in love with the southwestern United States and sought that area to begin his recovery. With Larry's help, he rented a mansion outside the town to recover. Larry hired a physical therapist named Anita to help get his body into shape.

He rented the mansion because it came with a large indoor swimming pool that Anita put him into daily to exercise his legs. Then she started working his arms with the elastic exercise ropes. Roy could walk by himself within another six weeks and do modified pushups with his arms. As his health and body recovered, so did his spirits, but he still didn't try singing or playing any musical instrument.

Anita was an uninhibited Australian who went naked into the pool when she exercised Roy's legs. Then, harboring a crush on the handsome, famous country singer, she playfully teased him with her naked body, trying to interest him in another kind of exercise. While Roy's body was wasted, the accident did nothing to inhibit the flow of hormones in his blood, and the naked

Aussie finally overcame his reluctance to engage in sexual activity before marriage. Coming from a small town with Christian values and a family that taught virtue, for Roy to let down his guard was a big deal.

Anita was a plain-looking, muscular girl with a friendly smile and dark brown eyes that exuded a cute puppy-dog look. With short blond hair and a size 44-D chest, it wasn't hard to get the handsome love-starved singer into her body. Getting him to propose marriage was another matter entirely.

After their first physical engagement, Roy was almost sick with guilt, but Anita assured him it was just sex. Nothing personal. She wasn't expecting him to marry her, although secretly, she hoped just the opposite. Naïve Roy bought into the lie quickly as his hormones continued to override his brain. As Roy's strength improved and his body recovered, their sexual workouts became increasingly regular until they became a daily and twice-daily affair. The virtuous Roy could not get enough of this sex stuff. Instead, he grew to find life enjoyable and worth living again. Roy finally picked up his Gibson and began playing.

It took a few weeks before he felt comfortable playing, and before long, Roy picked up the acoustic and fingered the chords to *A Brief Encounter*. His voice cracked and sounded weak. Still, he persisted through the entire song until finally, in disgust, he laid the guitar back in its case as Roy wondered if he would ever sing again.

As his leg strength improved, Roy and Anita began taking walks in the beautiful red countryside surrounding his rented mansion. Before long, he was running up hills and felt his breath control return. Finally, it was time to bid the big-breasted Anita so long and thanks. While she had nursed him back to health, he compensated her with more than his willing sex organ.

With his health restored, Roy began taking day trips to the fantastic surrounding national parks. Arches National Monument, Canyonlands National Park, and the Grand Canyon.

However, Roy's favorite place to spend time alone was The Dead Horse Point. When Roy read the story about how this beautiful place earned its name, he cried.

Roy read about the Point's history, where in the late 1800s, ten cowboys chased a herd of wild horses out onto a lonely outcropping high in the desert above the Colorado River. This outcropping was a broad plateau, with no water accessible only by crossing narrow mountain ledges with steep cliffs on each side. Out on the point, the only way back was by crossing these narrow ledges. Thinking of returning in a few days when the horses were tired and thirsty, the cowboys blocked off the horse's return. Unfortunately, with no water on the plateau, the horses all died before the cowboys returned.

Roy discovered Dead Horse Point in his reading, and after investigating, it became his favorite go-to location. The plateau ends high above the Colorado River, which can be seen winding through the canyons far below like a rattlesnake slithering through tall grass. There is a hundred and eighty-degree view of sweeping panoramas in which you can see valleys and mountains over a hundred miles away. But looking down the cliffs at a sparkling Colorado far below with no way to reach the beautiful water, Roy couldn't help but think of the wretched thirsty horses plight.

Sitting on the edge of the cliff with his legs hanging over the edge, Roy wrote about his favorite horse, Jupiter, and the good times they had together. This exercise got his creative juices flowing again, and he continued writing songs for a new album. Soon, an entire blank songbook had been filled with new material. Finally, he appropriately named the new album *Vistas*, a valid country-western album about riding horses and chasing the wind.

Finished with exorcising the demons from his soul, Roy sat at the cliff's edge and began singing *Chime Bells*. The first time sounded terrible, and Roy wondered if he would ever sing and yodel again. Still, Roy tried again and again. The next day he returned and began yodeling until his throat was raw. The singer rested his voice for a day and then resumed practicing his voice. It took a little over a month, but his singing was as good as it had ever been to Roy's ear. Perhaps it was his imagination, but he thought his voice had a little more depth and emotion. Possibly, he felt his near-death and miraculous recovery and long rehabilitation had something to do with the sound of his voice. Of course, he reckoned it could all be in his head.

Roy called Larry about getting the band back together. Anita kept the manager informed of Roy's progress until she and Roy parted ways, and Larry had been waiting for this call for over a year.

22
LIFE GOES ON

Sarah was at her home in Sun Valley when she got the devastating news about Roy. For some unfathomable reason, grief nearly overcame her. She had never met the man. Only recently had she heard him sing and his band play. Sarah never even knew what he looked like until finding that album cover in New York. But, somehow, she felt even worse than when receiving word that Dean had died.

Sarah's only connection with the man happened long ago and lasted seconds. It felt like a very brief encounter when he was a poor lonely boy seeking happiness by watching the trains go by, and she, a lonely, heartbroken widow, was going back to her parents. Their encounter wasn't even real. More like an imaginary meeting, but then that wasn't right either. Dammit. What was wrong with her and this silly fetish with a man she didn't know and only exchanged thoughts or souls with once somewhere in time, in some hidden mental location, and only God knows where that was?

The only thing Sarah knew was that Roy was in a coma, and no one knew what lay ahead. Later, she learned he had woken up but that his injuries were extensive, and they did not expect him to perform again. Sarah experienced sadness again, for she had never heard and seen Roy perform. To manage her regrets, Sarah returned to painting with a vengeance.

Looking at *The Black Stallion* hanging above the fireplace in her upstairs studio, Sarah painted a picture of Roy as she imagined him to look riding on his beautiful bay horse. She took Roy's image from the album cover, changing it to fit her fantasy of a young boy in ragged pants flying through a lovely green meadow on the horse's back. The horse was in full gallop, with his tail flying straight back and his mane flowing back into the boy. The boy with Roy's face had such a look of happiness, with his straw hat hanging down his back and his curly brown hair blowing in the wind. Sarah's eyes were almost too damp to see the result when she finally finished the picture.

Sarah agonized over a title for the picture for days, struggling to find the perfect name. Finally, she settled on a name that evoked deep feelings for someone she had never met in the flesh. She named the work *Lost in Time*. Because almost no one ever came to Sarah's studio, the picture of Roy on Jupiter remained private, her tribute to their brief encounter.

Shortly after she finished her picture of Roy, Arlene, the woman who taught Sarah to paint, came by Sarah's home for a visit. Because Sarah was upstairs in her studio working on another painting, Arlene had to ring the bell several times before Sarah reluctantly put down her paintbrush and went to see who was at the door.

"Oh, hi, Arlene, sorry to keep you waiting. I was in the studio upstairs, working on a new picture. Come in, please."

"Hi, Sarah." Arlene came in, and the two women hugged each other. "Hope I'm not disturbing our most famous artist too much."

"No, it's okay, Arlene. And your modesty prevents you from acknowledging your own accomplishments. Your paintings grace many more walls than mine. Would you like to visit my studio? I don't believe you have been by to visit since I had it constructed."

"I would love to see where you create such masterpieces."

Arlene followed Sarah up a beautifully wide curved teak staircase into the spacious glassed-in studio.

"Oh my," she gasped. "I did not know your studio was so grand and with such fantastic lighting. And what is that picture next to *The Black Stallion*? That one I have seen, but this new work, *Lost in Time,* is such a beautiful piece, and what a great name. The boy seems so happy, Sarah, yet there is something in his eyes. A smile of happiness is on his face, but his eyes look sad. How did you ever create that effect? Somehow, the title seems to fit."

"That one I only recently finished. I'm afraid it's a long story."

"It seems like such a strange combination of images—a poor boy in ragged pants, yet such happiness. But the sadness in his eyes. What is it that is lost in time, Sarah? Is it our ability to experience such happiness in our lives? And what is that source of sadness in the boy's eyes?"

"I saw that boy and his horse from a window on a train I was on one time. The image stuck in my mind. I had only recently learned about my husband's death, and seeing such happiness made me want to experience that same feeling."

"Oh, my dear. I'm so sorry about your loss. I never knew you lost a husband. I suppose it was the war?"

"Yes. Maybe our ability to experience the happiness you see on the boy's face in the picture dies with our youth. That ability might get lost in time."

"Sarah, is that country music I hear playing in the background? I thought you were a classical music buff."

"Yes, that is music from a band called The Weeds. Yeah, I know. How country can you get? The band leader and featured singer is a man named Roy Dalton. That is his face you see riding on the bay stallion in the picture."

"But the picture is of a young boy, not a man. And how did you ever learn his name if you only saw him from a window on a train?"

"I warned you, Arlene, that it is a long story."

"You have sufficiently piqued my interest, dear lady. Now you have got to tell me the story."

"Okay, but we better open a bottle of wine for this story, but if I bawl, please forgive me. That picture always brings tears to my eyes as I remember the occasion."

"I see a box of Kleenex handy. I may cry along with you. And let us get that wine."

Sarah went to her wine cellar and fetched one of her precious Cabernets. When they each had their glasses filled, she began. "I fell in love with Dean, my husband, when we were both teenagers. We got married just before he left for the Army. America had just joined the war, and Dean was one of the first ones drafted. So, we moved to Washington, DC, where he was sent for special training, and then he was off to the war. I was notified about his death a few months later."

"That had to be devastating, Sarah, losing the love of your life and husband at such a young age."

"It was. I was a total wreck and left Washington to go back to California to see my parents and work in an airplane factory."

"That was the train ride you mentioned?"

"Yes, the train stopped for water at a small village tucked in the Idaho mountains. As the train was coming to a stop, my head was against the window. My eyes were red and puffy from crying, and my heart was broken. Then, looking out the window, I saw this poor boy in ragged pants and a tattered straw hat standing by a beautiful bay horse. The boy's hands were bloody, but he had such a look of happiness on his face. Our eyes met briefly, but for only a moment. In his eyes, I saw loneliness and sadness that matched my own, and it seemed like we exchanged souls for just a moment. I know this sounds weird, but that is how it felt. I was in his body, feeling the pain in his bloody hands and the sadness of his life. A boy was doing a man's work with no future. And I felt him in my body experiencing my grief and sadness, yet I could also feel the happiness I saw in his face."

"Such a strange encounter. Do you think the boy felt this exchange like you did?"

"I know he did. It was in his eyes. As he experienced my sorrow, he realized I had just lost my husband and was grieving. The look of compassion that flashed in his eyes almost made me feel ashamed. Yes, I had lost my husband, but I had wealth, looks, talent, and a future. This boy appeared to be lost with no way out of his life of work and loneliness, but he found happiness in watching a train go past. It made me ashamed to think that I was suffering, but my grief would pass while his unhappiness would last forever. This strange encounter made me want to live again and find happiness. It jolted me out of my sorrow."

"You say his name is Roy Dalton, and he is the lead singer of a country band. That doesn't sound like the life you just described."

"I hired a detective to learn about the boy and his family. Then, I started sending him gifts with a bit of money. The money meant nothing to me, but it was a fortune to Roy. He bought a cheap Gene Autry guitar with his first gift and taught himself to play. After I learned about this, I had my detective buy him a real guitar for his next gift. The gifts ended when he turned eighteen, and I lost track of him for a few years."

"Did Roy know who was sending him these gifts?"

"Not that I ever learned. My detective was very discrete. I didn't want the boy to know who I was. I wanted to keep my identity a secret."

"So, what's with the music I'm hearing?"

"I told you I lost track of Roy after he left high school. I thought at eighteen he was old enough to make it on his own. It wasn't until I was in New York last year and walking past a music store and saw a picture on the cover of an album in the window. I recognized the picture. Well, not the picture, but the object in the picture."

"You tell me you just discovered this picture walking by a window?"

"Yes. It was a picture of a pocket watch. The very first gift I sent to Roy. I figured him being a poor boy, he wouldn't own a watch, so I bought a silver pocket watch and had his initials engraved on the cover, R. D. A picture of this watch was on the outside of a music album called Timeless. I bought this watch personally, so I knew it belonged to Roy. Then I went into the store, bought the album, and discovered what happened to Roy Dalton. Hell, he is more famous than I am, and that's saying something."

"Well, that is a fascinating story, but it doesn't explain the picture you painted of him riding his horse. Did you ever go meet him?"

"No, and that is the rest of the story. It turns out that the album in the window was the band's second album. The band's first album was called The Lady on the Train. Sounds familiar, doesn't it? And he titled the lead song *A Brief Encounter*, just in case I might miss the album's title. I'm sure he was reaching out to me. Here, let me play that song for you."

Sarah went downstairs and returned just as Roy struck the beginning chords to *A Brief Encounter* on the acoustic guitar. When the song ended, both ladies were in tears.

"My God, Sarah. I know that song. It's beautiful. It was number one on the music charts worldwide a few years ago. And such a voice. I didn't know it was a love song about my best friend. But, of course, he never knew who the lady on the train was, did he? Did you two ever meet?"

"No, last year he played at the Met, and I was dying to go see him, but it was too late to get a ticket when I learned about the engagement. I pulled every string I had to get into the concert, but I had no luck. They made a recording of the band's performance at the Met. The concert opened with Roy playing a solo classical guitar on an acoustic. That was the music I was playing when you rang my bell. After the Met, the band went on a tour of Europe and was recently involved in a terrible car crash. The limousine Roy and the band rode in was crushed by an out-of-control bus. Roy took the worst hit and was in a coma. He recently woke up, but he is never expected to perform again."

"Oh, that is so sad. I'm sorry, Sarah. Thanks for telling me the story. I wish I had met this, Roy Dalton. He must have been one hell of a man. Did he ever get married?"

"I don't believe so. According to everything I know about him, he is still a virgin, which I doubt, but the country music magazines mention nothing serious with anybody."

"Now, the title of your picture makes more sense. An opportunity lost in time."

"Something like that. It has many meanings, but I love the feeling of happiness on the boy's face. I hope Roy got to experience some of that during his life of fame and fortune. Oh, Arlene. I almost forgot. Here's the first album I mentioned, the one with Roy's picture on the back cover."

"My God, darling. He looks fabulous. Is that the guitar you bought?"

"I think so. You can see it's a Gibson, which is what my detective told me he purchased."

"So, he named the first album after you. Then when that didn't bring you out, he put your gift on the second album's cover, calling it Timeless. And you named your picture *Lost in Time*. There's something poetic and mystical there."

"I know. In some strange way, I felt connected to Roy and thought we might be together somehow. I know this sounds crazy when I must be at least ten years his senior. And that pains me. I never got to thank him personally for my life. It's a gift I will always treasure."

"Who knows, Sarah? If he lives, you might still meet one day."

"I have prayed for that day, Arlene. But I'm afraid it may be too late. They say he may never walk again."

"I have learned one thing, dear friend: life is full of surprises. One day, you may get your wish. You just never know. Why don't you go see him, Sarah?"

"Oh, God, Arlene. You can't imagine how I have beaten myself up. I could have flown to Europe and seen him in half a dozen cities, but none of his concerts fit my travel plans, so I waited for the band to return to the states. It seemed silly to fly overseas just to hear a country music band. And now I can't find him. There is no word about his location. They released him from the hospital, and he disappeared. The band broke up and is scattered. I called his agent, but he either knows nothing or is reluctant to give information to another groupie."

"Well, this is a sad story. I hope one day you get to meet this guy."

"Yeah, me too. I don't suppose it hurts to dream. It seems so damn silly now. But back then, I was such a music snob. If it wasn't something classical by some long-dead composer, I didn't want to hear it. Country music was something only hillbillies listened to while drinking moonshine and screwing their sister. Excuse the language. But that was me being a snob. I could have met him years ago if I had ever listened to anything but classical. And now, dear Arlene, you have got to hear Roy yodel."

23
TOGETHER AGAIN

Larry kept track of the band members while waiting to hear about Roy's progress. With Anita's frequent progress reports, he knew that the day would come when Roy picked up his guitar and started playing again.

Finally, Larry got everyone back except Pug, their bass player. Pug played in another band and had a contract he couldn't get out of without severe penalties. Larry called Malcolm Wisely, their Nashville producer, for help, and he soon found a lady bass player named Kathryn Wilson. Not only did the lady play a wicked bass, but she sang like an angel. Tall, nearly six feet, and thin, Kathryn had long black hair that hung down past her waist. Blessed with an oval face with classic Greek sculpturing, she soon became one of the band's favorite musicians, often singing solo songs written by Roy. She would straddle her bass and swish her long hair in rhythm with the music as she sang, making her quite popular with the band's audiences.

Without Carol, who helped write some of the band's original music, Roy had to compose new music by himself, a chore he loved doing, for it helped focus his mind. Horace Walpole returned, the band's original music arranger, and helped Roy arrange the songs for Vista, the band's new album.

Roy rented hotel suites in Nashville for the band to live in and practice the new songs while waiting for a recording studio to open. While the band rehearsed, Larry was busy working on a new tour. Of course, nobody wanted to return to Europe right away, but Japan was calling, along with Hong Kong, Singapore, and Australia. So, thinking of Anita, his Australian PT lady, Roy voted they resume playing concerts, including Australia. Since none of the band members had ever been down under, they all readily agreed, and the band's new tour was ready to kick off, starting with a return date to the Grand Ole Opry.

Jupiter, the album's signature song, became number one on the pop charts. Not since *Horse with No Name* had a ballad about a horse garnered so much attention. Pictured on the album's cover was an artist's rendition of Roy's beautiful bay horse standing on a precipice at Dead Horse Point and overlooking the Colorado River and the sweeping vista below the ledge. Jupiter seemed intent on viewing the scene as though searching for a way to reach the river. It was a spectacular picture evoking solid emotions for those who knew the story of Dead Horse Point. Roy never specifically wrote songs about horses dying of thirst, but the entire album was a tribute to those long-dead horses.

With word about Roy's recovery and the band's new album hitting the airways, ticket requests for their first engagement at the Opry became the hottest thing in Nashville. Unless you were connected or extraordinarily lucky, finding a ticket was impossible. Malcolm had the concert played on speakers outside on the streets, which nearly caused the city to shut down the roads. Thousands were standing and waiting for the show to begin. Everyone wanted to know if Roy could still perform.

The show opened with Roy singing *Chime Bells*. Knowing that people would wonder about his voice, Roy chose that song as an opening to dispel any doubts about his recovery. The crowd was already excited about seeing the band and listening to hear if Roy could still sing. When Roy began yodeling, the crowd went wild. He had the entire town rocking and screaming with delight. Radio stations worldwide covered the event live, so Weed fans heard their favorite country singer for the first time in over a year. Television was getting big in the early 1950s, and those fortunate to have clear reception saw a tall, handsome man with curly brown hair, gray eyes, and classic good looks sing like the performance was a heavenly opus to all living souls. Weed fans worldwide were brought to tears when they heard Roy's last long treble notes ring high in the air.

The band at once went into their new album, Vistas, and Roy's tribute to his faithful horse Jupiter brought the house down again. To say the album and concert were an enormous success would underplay their actual impact. Roy and The Weeds were back.

24
MISSED AGAIN

Several days after Arlene's visit, Sarah was in her studio finishing a painting of a pileated woodpecker on a pine tree snag outside of her studio. With a distinctive red thatch on top of its head, this bird made the snag a daily stop on the bird's morning territorial run. Flying from one snag to another, the red-topped bird pecked out a call to let the world know that this tree was in its territory. The beautiful bird made a stunning picture, and Sarah was admiring the result when her telephone rang.

"Hello, this is Sarah."

"Sarah, this is Boris Austin from America's National Churchill Museum on the Westminster College campus in Fulton, Missouri. I got your name from a mutual acquaintance and would like you to consider decorating our museum."

"Wow. Such an honor; I suppose you know I am a huge Winston fan?"

"Yes, and that is the second reason we want your services. Your reputation for classy, sophisticated interior decorating is unsurpassed, and we wanted somebody in love with Mr. Churchill to decorate our museum. We feel the man deserves the best America can offer, which means you."

"Well, I am deeply honored and would consider it a privilege to decorate your museum. When will you and it be ready for my services?"

"We are ready now. We have been researching decorating talent for the past two weeks, looking for the right person until someone suggested your name. After doing our research, we concluded you were the perfect person for our job."

"I am just finishing a project here in my Sun Valley studio. I can fly to Kansas City early next week if that is acceptable. Can you recommend accommodations?"

"There is no need for that, my dear. There is a fully furnished house on the campus we reserve for visiting dignitaries, and you certainly qualify. I believe you should find it will serve you nicely."

"In that case, I look forward to seeing you, Mr. Austin. Shall we choose a place and time to meet?"

"Of course."

And just like that, Sarah's next three weeks were taken up with her exciting new project. She became fully immersed in work, which was the only way Sarah did things, believing that it takes concentration and patience to create something beautiful. In all the new action, she missed the notice about the Weed's reunion and Roy's miraculous recovery.

Boris invited Sarah to dinner on her last night in town. It was supposed to be a casual affair, but Boris lost his wife in an automobile accident two years earlier and was also single. He made no secret of his interest in the attractive widow.

Boris took care of his body and health and was still fit at forty-eight. Dressed in a charcoal gray suit and pink tie, he wore a matching handkerchief in the breast pocket. He looked dapper when he picked up Sarah, who wore a black Coco Chanel cocktail dress with spaghetti straps and fashionable high-heeled shoes. She looked like her usual fabulous, sexy, beautiful self. Both people seemed a bit overdressed for a simple casual evening, but both were out to make an impression. It had been a long time for Sarah to find an available man interesting, and although Boris was almost fifteen years her senior, the man was attractive.

Boris took Sarah to The Golden Spoon, a local favorite that served the best Chinese food in Missouri. At least, that is what their menu advertised, and to Sarah, it didn't seem like an exaggeration. After dinner, Sarah had Egg Pudding and Arnold the Almond Jelly for dessert. They enjoyed their after-meal coffee when a local high school boy came into the restaurant with his date. He was carrying a portable radio, playing music that Sarah thought sounded familiar. Then, of course, the restaurant manager at once made the boy turn off his radio, but Sarah had to know what was playing.

Getting up from the table, she excused herself and went over to the young boy, who prepared for his date in dress pants and a long-sleeved white shirt and tie. His girlfriend wore a blue and white sundress that showed off her tanned legs and deep cleavage.

"Hello," Sarah said to the boy. "I apologize for intruding on your evening, but I could not help but hear the music you were playing as you came in. Would you mind telling me what that song was on the radio when you entered?"

"Oh, sure, you must be a fan. That's the new Weed album. They're playing live right now at the Grand Ole Opry."

"I thought Roy Dalton was injured and could no longer perform."

"Yeah, he was in an accident in Italy, but I guess he fully recovered. You should have heard their opening song. Roy sang *Chime Bells*, and it took almost ten minutes before the audience would let the band continue. There was so much applause, hollering, whistling, and people crying. Boy, it was magic."

"May I borrow your radio to go outside and listen for a minute? I promise to give it right back."

"No problem. I'll go with you. Karen," he said, speaking to his date. "I'll be right back," and he escorted Sarah out onto the sidewalk.

The band was in the middle of *Jupiter* when Scotty, the young man, turned on the radio.

"That's a song on their new album called Jupiter," the boy told Sarah. "I heard it on the radio earlier. It's a song about Roy's horse. The whole album is dynamite. That Roy Dalton is my hero."

Their minute turned out to be more like ten as Sarah and the boy had trouble leaving the music to return to the restaurant. Finally, feeling guilty, Sarah thanked the boy, and they both returned to the restaurant.

Sarah went over to the manager and told him to serve the young couple whatever they would like, and she would pay for their dinner. Then, as they had finished with their meal, Boris was ready to leave, so Sarah gave the manager a hundred-dollar bill and told him to keep the change.

Boris tried to interest his beautiful companion in an after-dinner cocktail on the drive back to the house where she was staying. It had been his impression that his lovely companion was at least interested in pursuing some kind of relationship, but she seemed withdrawn and sad. He could not understand the reason. Sure, he saw her and the young boy leave the restaurant, and they were gone much longer than he thought reasonable. Then she returned, spoke to the manager, and handed him something. The entire scene made such little sense.

"Sarah, have I offended you? You almost seem sad, and I thought we might spend a little more time together."

"I'm sorry, Boris. You have been an excellent, gracious companion. It was rude of me to leave you alone for so long. There was something on the radio the boy was playing. It brought back some memories that I had nearly forgotten. I'm afraid I wouldn't be good company for an extended evening. I'm sorry.

Perhaps we will meet again. I love your museum and will be happy to come back for a visit after you have completed setting up all the displays. I must see how they look with the decorating."

"Yes, I would like that, Sarah. Please call me when you are ready to visit, and I will make all the arrangements."

Sarah found a radio back in her lodging, but the Opry show was over. She flipped around the dial and found a western country station playing music by The Weeds. Damn, she missed him again. Someday, she vowed, I am going to meet that young man. Flopping on her bed, Sarah listened to country music until she fell asleep.

25
AUSTRALIA

Larry and Joann, his assistant, had the band flying out to Japan the week following their Opry concert for three performances in Tokyo, followed by a week for everybody to do a little sightseeing. No one had visited Japan previously. Then, it would be on to Shanghai and Singapore before ending the tour in Australia.

They sold out all three concerts in Tokyo and played to highly enthusiastic audiences. Country Western music was catching on in the war-torn country that could seemingly not get enough of anything American. The tall, dark-haired Kathryn with a siren's voice was almost as big a hit as Roy. In a country that had been under the yolk of ruthless military men and where women were practically second-class citizens, seeing a woman perform with a male band was exciting by itself. She sang like an angel, which only made her seem more special.

Roy visited Kobe to try their famous beef. Coming from a ranch that raised beef cattle, he found it hard to believe there was better beef anywhere. The war had diminished the supply to near exhaustion, but Ito Kannabe, their Japanese tour manager, found a place to serve the curious Americans.

With Roy's first bite of Kobe beef, he almost died from pure pleasure. In fact, in his mind, this was even better than sex with

Anita, and that was saying something. The delicious meat almost melted in his mouth with a hearty flavor that made any meat he had eaten before seem like charred cardboard. Roy couldn't wait to get back home and tell his dad about this fantastic meat. He did not know the labor and attention it took to produce this tender and flavorful meat.

After visiting Mount Fuji, Larry insisted on taking the band to see some famous Kyoto Zen Gardens. Most of the band members, including Roy, had never heard of a Zen Garden. Still, after spending several hours in the peaceful surroundings soaking up the serenity, they all had to admit this was the highlight of their stay in Japan.

Shanghai and Singapore went by in a blur. Both cities were still in war recovery mode, but they welcomed the band with enthusiasm. These concerts were the band's first experience where the officials would not allow the groupies to assemble by the stage exit. After their concert, Roy always hated this part and would not let himself take part. While he was no longer a virgin, sex still meant something to the Idaho country boy. Still, it seemed like some kind of a letdown when the band departed for more fun and left him standing in a vacant parking lot.

Sydney was a whole different welcoming story. During WWII, Winston Churchill would not send any men to Australia to help fight the Japanese. America, however, sent nearly a quarter of a million men to help the Australians. The American troops were better paid than the Australian soldiers, meaning these interlopers had more money to squander, making the Americans a hit with the local women. When the band landed in 1953, the Australians were in love with America and everything American, especially country-western music. The Weeds were the country's favorite singing group, topping even the so-called popular music.

And, of course, Roy could speak almost like a native after living with Anita for nearly a year. During his performances, Roy spoke with an Australian accent that, while admittedly was not great, still endeared him to the locals who loved that he even tried.

After Sydney, the band played concerts in Melbourne and Perth. It was a huge surprise to see several hundred aboriginal people at the Melbourne concert. While in Melbourne, they learned that this area had been the primary home of these people for over forty thousand years and even predated the tremendous Egyptian dynasties.

After completing their Australian concerts, the band flew home for a few weeks' vacation while Roy returned to Melbourne. He was curious about the aboriginal people and wanted to visit their homeland. Richard Thornton, their Australian tour manager, introduced Roy to a person named Koora, who agreed to take the tall American for a walk-about.

Koora stood five foot one and weighed upwards of one hundred and ten pounds. His soot-black skin seemed even blacker than coal. When he smiled, he revealed a mouthful of sparkling white teeth. He wore his long dark hair in braids interwoven with white seashells. Roy was told which vehicle to rent. Koora suggested a vehicle that looked like a modified Jeep. Koora also ordered Roy to buy extra gas cans filled with fuel, and then the pair took off with Koora directing. They drove for several hours until a weary Roy called it a day. Koora found them a camping spot for the night. He instructed Roy to sleep with his clothes on if they had to leave in a hurry.

They were not too far from a river and swamp, and Koora informed Roy that crocodiles sometimes hunted this far from the water. Although unfamiliar with the beast or its habits and tired from a long day of driving, Roy went to sleep instantly.

Around three a.m., Roy felt a hand gently shake him awake.

"Time to go, mister. We will have company soon."

He was paying the native for his skills, so Roy listened and hastily packed his ground cloth and sleeping bag. Within seconds, the pair was in the Jeep driving on a dirt road and going to where Koora pointed.

"What sort of company were we expecting, Koora?"

"Four big crocs were creeping up from the swamp. They have an advanced sense of smell and acute hearing, and they see better than humans. I'm not sure what attracted them, perhaps our scent. So, it was best to get out of Dodge. Isn't that what you Yankees say?"

"Koora, where on earth did you get that expression? Get out of Dodge?"

"In the movies, Yank. I love those John Wayne flicks."

"Jesus. You probably say klicks instead of miles, too, right?"

"Nah, we ain't got the metrics yet. But it's probably coming. It is a better system."

"How did you get your education, Koora? You seemed very well informed and speak fantastic English."

"Just lucky, Yank. Okay, turn here," he said and pointed out the way he wanted them to travel.

They drove for another hour before coming to the spot where Koora told Roy to park the Jeep.

"We walk from here."

"What about the Jeep and the gasoline? We just leave that here in the open?"

"No problem, mister. Everything will be safe. No one ever comes here but my people."

Koora dumped his clothing except for a pair of brown denim shorts. Then, bare-chested and barefooted, he started walking, encouraging Roy to come along and to bring only a canteen of water with him.

They walked for several hours, with almost no conversation. Occasionally, Koora would ask, "How are you doing, Yank?"

Roy would grunt back, "Just peachy, Koora, just peachy."

In the middle of the afternoon, they came to a small encampment of aboriginal people.

"This is my home, Yank. I grew up here in this village."

Roy looked around at the nearly barren landscape. A community water well lined with black rocks covered by a small thatched roof from which hung a rope and a water bucket. Villagers would throw the bucket down the well, and they pulled on the rope to bring the filled bucket to the top of the well after it filled up. This well was their only source of water.

The houses were all constructed of mud bricks, undoubtedly made from the soil surrounding them and the precious well water.

"My people have lived here for several hundred years," Koora told Roy. "We could not live near the water source because of the animals. Mostly the snakes. Australia has maybe the most poisonous snakes in the world. And, of course, the crocodiles and other deadly creatures live near the water. Out here, there is nothing to attract other deadly creatures. Even the white man finds this place uninviting."

"I suppose," said a humbled Roy, comparing Koora's home to his beautiful hometown in Idaho, "the white man was just another dangerous beast."

"For perhaps a hundred years or more, he was the most dangerous of all," Koora said, without a single trace of emotion.

Roy wondered if their roles were reversed, could he ever sound that dispassionate?

He met Koora's family and the other villagers. Before coming here, Roy imagined he would have called them a tribe, but now that term seemed demeaning.

Roy had his walkabout and got a feeling of Australia few westerners ever experience. A grateful, humble American with love for some black people with whom he could barely communicate, bid his companion goodbye. But first, he insisted on contributing substantially to Koora's village to purchase a water pump and maybe a few other western conveniences they could tolerate without disrupting a lifestyle that had lasted longer than America had existed.

Taking a last look at Australia as his Pan American Boeing 377, called the Clipper, passed over the final bit of land, Roy gave a silent thanks to Anita. Without her enthusiastic talk about her homeland, he might never have had Larry book this tour.

Roy settled back in his seat as an attractive flight attendant brought him a flute of champagne. He barely noticed his hostess; his mind was on the next Weeds album. Roy already had it named, even though he had yet to write a single line or note. Thinking about a civilization forty thousand years old, he named the album SOMEWHERE IN TIME.

26
FRUSTRATION

Angry at herself for being so focused that she missed the Weed's reunion and Roy's recovery, Sarah returned to her Sun Valley studio. But, determined never to let such an opportunity escape her in the future, she planned how she would meet this tall, handsome singer she had helped create.

Reading about the band's trip to Australia, Sarah knew she could not expect to make that trip and attend a concert there without connections, which she lacked, so she took matters into her own hands.

Sun Valley was home to the Sun Valley Artists Society. Movie stars, such as Clint Eastwood and Lee Marvin, plus such luminaries as Ernest Hemingway and Averell Harriman, had their homes there. The famous Sun Valley Lodge had pictures of Marilyn Monroe, Lucille Ball, Errol Flynn, Gary Cooper, and many other Hollywood stars hanging on the walls. Then photos of the rich and famous, such as the Kennedy family and several European princes, dukes, and diplomats, were all pictured having fun on the ski slopes.

Being the home to many celebrities and those just plain rich, the Sun Valley Artists Society held a summer concert series catering to their rich and famous patrons. World champion ice skaters put on shows at the famous Sun Valley ice skating rink open all twelve months of the year. Concert pianists, opera singers, and guitarists, such as Andrés Segovia gave concerts in the Sun Valley concert hall. The Artists Society booked the most famous stars it could entice to perform at Sun Valley throughout the year. Free lodging at the now world-famous Sun Valley Ski Resort, plus all the skiing, hiking, bicycling, horseback riding, swimming in the famous oval swimming pool, or just relaxing on vacation in a beautiful location, was enough to entice world-class performers. Of course, the chance to run into a few movie stars or essential government officials or dine next to Clint Eastwood didn't hurt either.

As a member of the Society, Sarah tried to get the rest of the Society committee members to invite The Weeds to perform for the locals. Unfortunately, most of the local intelligentsia had never heard of The Weeds. Even learning that the band had performed at the Met did not persuade them that this type of entertainment was suitable for their affluent society. Even though Ketchum was the epitome of small-town America, the Society felt that country music and art simply did not mix.

A frustrated Sarah searched the music world magazines and bulletins looking for news of Roy and The Weeds. Instead, she read about their Australian tour and the band returning home without Roy, who was on something called a walkabout. Nothing she read said anything about a new tour or any scheduled concerts.

The weeks went by, and Sarah busied herself with several new painting projects. She played the new album Vistas while she painted and thought about Roy and his horse. Although admiring the album cover, Sarah wished she had painted the rider and horse pictured. In her heart, Sarah knew she would have done a better job, but, of course, Roy did not know who she was or what she could do.

Sarah rarely went to their public library other than on meeting days, even though it had one of the most significant budgets in the entire country and sponsored most of the local society's entertainment. The Artists Society met in one of the library's reading rooms, and as Sarah walked by a picture book featuring the national parks, she stopped to take a quick look at the book. To her surprise, she looked at a picture she recognized; it was the same scene pictured on the album cover of Vistas.

This book was how she discovered the story about Dead Horse Point, and now she knew the inspiration behind Roy's latest songs. Taking the book home, she wanted to paint something the story and picture inspired, but she couldn't get her head around the exact composition. Instead, she concentrated on painting animals in various settings. Although she wished to duplicate the cover of Vistas, the artist in her would not compromise and copy another's work.

Frustrated at first, she finally settled on painting the entire scene. She painted a picture of the cowboys chasing wild horses across the narrow canyon ridges onto the overlook where they would all perish. It was a beautiful scene with an azure blue sky and wild horses of nearly every color: pintos, palominos, bays, dapple grays, plus pure black and a few white horses for contrast. The horses' tails and manes were flying in the breeze. Cowboys riding horses with saddles were whooping and smiling as the wild horses ran down the narrow ledge. Leather cords around their chins held the cowboy's large, floppy ten-gallon hats in place.

Sarah captured the wide-open vista below Dead Horse Point in brilliant red, orange, and gold. It was a stunning picture with the sun glistening on the Colorado River far below. Incredible unless you knew the story, and then there was a poignancy that could bring tears to your eyes. She titled the painting *Joy and Sorrow*. The viewer had to be familiar with the story to understand the picture's name.

27
GOING SOLO

Before returning to the States, Roy felt like taking a break from the band and performing solo. With the band's success, Roy didn't need more money. His walk-about with Koora and meeting people with a forty-thousand year history could change a person's perspective in life. His plane stopped in Hawaii on the return home, but as Roy walked around the airport with its corridors open to the palm trees and beautiful flowers, he loved the feel and decided to stay in the Islands to write the words and music for Somewhere in Time.

Throughout the airport were colorful brochures describing the Islands and their attractions. The old plantation town of Lahaina on Maui attracted his interest, as did Haleakala, the ancient volcano. So, changing his ticket, Roy bought a one-way flight to Maui, where he rented a seaside cottage to listen to the ocean and feel the tropical breezes. The setting felt like some kind of spiritual connection to the ancient people of Australia. This ocean and the island of Maui were here when those old aboriginal Australians were roaming the outback. His beach and the ocean waves sounded the same today as they did then. For Roy, it was his turn to get lost somewhere in time.

It was the whale season in Maui when the giant humpbacks came to feed and give birth. Roy could sit with a pair of binoculars on an overlook in Maalaea Bay and watch the whales jump out of the water like they were playing. Fascinated by the giants, Roy found a place near the Whaler, a Maui tribute to the whales, to listen to their songs from a recording made by cetologists. Intuitively, he knew these giant creatures roamed the oceans, singing their songs at the same time as those ancient aboriginal people sat chanting around their fires.

At some point in the island's history, a large tree had washed ashore close to the cottage where Roy was staying. All that remained was a part of the trunk, and Roy could not tell what tree species the trunk came from, but it still made a great place to sit and listen to the ocean and write a song for the whales. To Roy, the whales were a species that appeared to have been misplaced somewhere in time, along with many other treasures.

Thinking about all he knew about whales, which admittedly was not much, he remembered reading about whale oil lamps and that certain natives in Alaska hunted whales for their flesh. The whales were their primary source of food.

Roy wrote words and music based on the chants of the Aboriginals and another song inspired by the whales singing. The ideas for Somewhere in Time kept coming while Roy sat on his log listening to the ocean.

Somewhere in time, we lost the way to communicate with nature,
We lost the ears to hear whales sing, somewhere in time,
We lost our way to happiness, somewhere in time,
Somewhere in time, the echoes of a lost love ring,
We lost this magic, somewhere in time.

Once, people built large, magnificent monuments.
Somewhere in time, we lost the ability to hear nature's music,
Ancient heroes walked the earth, somewhere in time,
Somewhere in time, we lost the lyrics to life's music,
All of that was lost, somewhere in time.

The words seemed to flow quickly, and the melody not so much. Only after listening to the whales' songs did the music merge into the lyrics. It wasn't genuine country-western music, but Roy loved how it felt in his soul. Then, as he wrote and hummed, he could feel the music pulse in his body, and he almost ached for his acoustic guitar. Then, sitting on his log humming, Roy recognized the beat to his melody: it sounded like the chanting of the Aboriginals.

A call to Larry Perkins was in order. Roy was determined to make a solo album without his band; however, he wanted Larry to keep the band members happy and informed until he returned to resume their concerts.

"What in the hell do you mean, you're going to do a solo album?" Larry did not sound happy.

"Larry, I did my walkabout and spent some time with the Australian Aboriginals. Did you know their civilization goes back forty thousand years?"

"No. Really? What has that got to do with you going solo?"

"It's just that I feel like paying homage to their civilization and culture. Then, I have also listened to whales sing, and watching those giants splash out of the ocean is breathtaking, Larry. Their songs sound like the native chants I heard in Australia. I've written most of the lyrics and some of the music. I'm going to Honolulu to see about a recording studio. I'm not abandoning the band, but I don't think this album fits into the

Weed's repertoire. You can book some concerts for about six months out if you want and if the band is willing."

"Do you want us to promote your single?" Larry sounded resigned but willing to move forward.

"That would be fantastic, Larry. As soon as we lay down a few tracks, I'll send you some copies to give you a feel for what I'm doing."

"It cannot be a Weed album. How about something like Dalton and the Whales? I'm going to use some of the whale singing as background. There will also be some Aboriginal chants, but I have to find a choral group willing to do the chanting."

"Are you sure you want to do this, Roy? It could wreck your appeal to your country base."

"I'm aware of the risks, but it's something I want to do. Hopefully, this will only enhance my resume with the popular music crowd."

"Okay, I'll wait for your package and start looking at cities for a few concerts. Do you have any preferences?"

"Yes. You mentioned a request from Sun Valley, Idaho, for a concert. I believe I would like to play there. It's close to our homes in Cache Valley, and isn't that where Hemingway lives?"

"Well, I believe so, but what? Do you want to sing for Hemingway?"

"Not particularly. But he is one of my favorite authors, and I would like to meet him. So if playing a gig in Sun Valley can promote a meeting with him, then yes, I'll do a concert there."

"Okay, Roy. I'll see what we can arrange. Good luck in Honolulu."

"Thanks, Larry. I appreciate all that you have done for me and The Weeds. See you in a few weeks."

Hot damn. I might get to meet Hemingway. And with that thought, Roy resumed humming tunes and writing music.

28
HAPPINESS

Happiness can be so elusive. Yet we ever strive to be happy. We plan to be satisfied. We want to be happy, but often our wants go unfulfilled. Now, Sarah was truly happy for the first time in a long time. She had just returned from a meeting with the Artists Society Committee, who had finally agreed to ask The Weeds to play a concert at the Sun Valley Auditorium. Sometimes, the little triumphs bring happiness, not the big, glorious weddings with hundreds of guests. Significant events can be more tiring and stressful than a time of joy. Today, Sarah could barely remember her marriage to Dean. She must have been happy then, but her memories felt rushed and stressed. Getting The Weeds to Sun Valley had been Sarah's dream for a couple of years, and the strait-laced committee members finally caved. This success was a time to celebrate and feel the joy in her body. Roy was coming to Sun Valley. Hopefully.

Several weeks would pass before Sarah learned The Weeds had accepted their invitation to play in Sun Valley, but the date was uncertain. Then, finally, their manager supplied a window when the band might be available, but the date depended on the return of the lead singer and bandleader Roy Dalton.

Return? Where in the hell was he? She read about the band's success in Australia, but there was no mention of Roy. *He didn't run off and get married, did he?* This thought soured her happiness for reasons she found challenging to admit to herself. She wanted Roy for herself, dammit. *Was that too much to ask? Dammit, she practically made the man.*

Okay, Sarah knew she was acting irrationally. Hell, Roy didn't even know if she was still alive. For all he knew, the woman who sent him those gifts in the past had remarried and had a family by now. Or perhaps she had died during the war. Their brief encounter had happened many years ago. Did he remember their brief, shared moment as she did? Did their encounter leave him feeling the same emotional tug she experienced?

Sarah knew she was not behaving rationally. Hell, when she remembered that ragged-looking young boy, with those bloody hands and soft gray eyes, showing such joy on his face, she felt guilty. Of course, Sarah could not expect someone that age to share her feelings, but Sarah knew differently in her heart. They had exchanged souls for a moment, and somehow, she knew he felt the same way about her. He could not have married another woman, dammit. He belonged to her.

Another few weeks went by before Sarah discovered Roy had a single album about to be released. The name of his new album nearly caused her to faint- SOMEWHERE IN TIME. So, he named an album Timeless, and she had a painting called *Lost in Time?* To Sarah, this synchronicity was all she needed to know to believe her connection to Roy was real. Why else would he have a title so close to her painting of him unless there was a connection? *No*, she decided, wherever Roy was, he was not with some floozy and about to get married.

As soon as the album SOMEWHERE IN TIME became available, Sarah bought it to play in her studio while looking at her paintings. This new album had a large picture of Roy in Hawaii. Tanned like a seafaring captain, he flashed a dazzling smile with white teeth that almost didn't look real. Instead, they looked the color of white seagulls with the sun glistening on their feathers. And those gorgeous gray eyes showed the compassion she felt all those years ago. My God, he was a handsome man!

Sarah tried to imagine the emotions behind the words and music while playing the album. It wasn't like anything she had ever heard before. Roy played a soft acoustic guitar to accompany his singing, plus a drum beat resembling the rhythm of chants heard in certain tracks. As the album progressed, Sarah felt herself being drawn into an alien history of humanity she'd never experienced. The whale's songs seemed to flow into Roy's music, almost as though he were singing along with the pods in the ocean. And the chanting. Discovering that there had been human beings living on this planet forty thousand years ago made her feel almost proud to be alive. The music on this album celebrated life, and the title was perfect. We all exist, *SOMEWHERE IN TIME*.

Sarah looked for Arlene, who taught her how to paint, as she drove uptown from her riverfront home. Arlene had seemed so drawn to Roy's singing and Sarah wanted to share this new album with her friend and to make sure the two of them had front row seats for the Sun Valley concert whenever it took place.

In her studio painting, Arlene welcomed her former student with a smile and hug.

"Sarah, how perfectly delightful. You look happy, darling. What's the occasion that brings you to my humble home? I know you don't need painting lessons."

"Oh, Arlene, I'm not much of a guest. I should ask how you're doing and tell you how fabulous you look, even with paint daubs on your smock."

"Okay, we've done the greeting bit, and I'm surprised and happy to see you, but you didn't answer my question. So what's the occasion?"

"Well, I'm almost embarrassed to tell you for fear you might laugh at me, but Roy Dalton has a new solo album, which I just played in my studio. I was hoping you could come over to my house and listen to it with me while sipping on a little wine. I'm eager to see if the album affects you how it did me."

"That's an invitation I cannot refuse. You've made me curious. But what would cause you to insist on me listening to your Roy Dalton? Although I like his singing, and he's a handsome one."

"Oh, before I forget, Arlene. The Weeds are back together and will perform right here in Sun Valley. They agreed to a concert in the next few months. Apparently, Roy went solo after the band toured Australia. He did a walk-about, whatever that is, and listened to the Aboriginals chant. It's on the album. He also listened to the whales sing. That's also on the album. Anyway, I'm on the art committee and will get us both front-row seats for the concert. You will come, won't you?"

"Of course, darling. Let me get out of the smock, and we'll listen to your man sing. And I know you've got a great cabernet we can drink while we hear the whales sing."

"He isn't my man yet, Arlene, but dammit, I'm going to change that as soon as I get my hands on him."

"And how do you know he isn't already married, Sarah?"

"I don't know, Arlene. It's just something that I feel. It sounds crazy, but it feels like something destined us to be together."

"Well, I will not say you're crazy, darling, but you are. Okay, maybe there is something to this soul-sharing business. Let's go hear the album."

Arlene followed Sarah back to Sarah's home by the river in her car so Sarah wouldn't have to drive her back. Then, both ladies went up to the studio where the horse paintings hung. Sarah brought up a couple of wine glasses and the bottle with an opener. Once everything was in place, Sarah started the music.

They drank in silence while the music played, and by the time the last chant ended, they had finished the wine.

A subdued Arlene spoke in a voice that sounded almost reverential. "My God, darling, that album makes me feel ancient."

"I know. I feel the same way. Somehow, it connects us to the past. I can feel it in my bones."

"Well, if he is anything like his picture, you'll have to fight me for him, Sarah. Lordy, but that man can sing and play."

Ignoring her friend's remark, Sarah said, "I hope he plays one or two of these songs at our concert. But, of course, it's a Weed concert, so he might not do these solo songs with the band. I guess we'll have to wait and see."

"I think that in any concert, Sarah, they let each musician show their stuff, including the drummer. Even in classical music, the composer seems to arrange it so that during one of their long compositions, every section of the orchestra gets time to show off a little."

"You're right, Arlene. I'm just excited to meet this talented man."

"How can you be in love with a man you never met, Sarah?"

"But we met Arlene. Maybe only briefly, but we met. And anyway, who said I'm in love with him just because I love his music?"

"It shows in your face, darling. The way you speak about him, the look in your eyes. It's love, all right."

"Oh God, Arlene. What if he doesn't want to be with me?"

"What? Are you out of your mind? You are not only the most beautiful, gorgeous, stunning, talented person in the world; you are also rich beyond count. Hell, I'd be after you if I were a man. How many marriage proposals do you get on an average day?"

Sarah laughed. "Well, it's fallen off a bit lately. It's down to around thirty-five or forty."

"It's good to hear you laugh, Sarah. When this handsome lad shows his face here in Sun Valley, I will help you tie him in knots so strong he could never escape."

"I'm going to count on that, Arlene. I'm not sure I could ever laugh again if Roy rejects me."

"That won't happen, Sarah. No man who writes about time and a brief encounter with such emotion will ever reject the source of his own happiness, and that is you."

"Well, we did meet, *somewhere* in time."

29
THE LIMELITE SALOON

The solo album with the famous Roy Dalton was a hit when the first radio station in Hawaii played the opening song. The next station to play the new album was KKDA in Dallas, Texas, and from there, it was the BIG 98 in Nashville. Although the album was not country-western music, Roy was such a big name in the country genre that the station played his album to an enthusiastic audience who called the station in such large numbers that their calls flooded the exchange. Requests for performances began flooding the Weed production crew and Larry Perkins, who contacted Roy for his thoughts about doing a few solo shows.

Roy wasn't crazy about performing without the band, but Larry promised him that the band was ready to begin rehearsals as soon as he was ready. If Roy wanted to do a few solo gigs, that would be all right with him and the band.

"You know, Roy, we have a few cities lined up for another brief Weed tour, starting in Seattle next month. You probably need a couple of weeks with the band to get your timing right and practice some of your new music, which I'm sure you want to play. But the next couple of weeks are open if you want to do a few solo shows."

"Larry, we played in the Limelite Saloon in Aspen, Colorado, back in the days when we were still the Tumbleweeds. I loved that old saloon, and it felt right for me. Please see if you can book me in there for a few performances."

"That's a pretty small nightclub if I remember correctly. Maybe a hundred or hundred fifty seats. Are you sure you want to perform for a crowd that small? They won't be able to pay you as much as you're worth."

"Larry, it isn't about money. I just love the feel of that place. It's intimate, just the feeling I want. I want to sit on a stool and interface with the audience. Large auditoriums are grand, and the energy is fantastic, but something about a smaller audience gives me a sense of fulfillment."

"Sure, okay, Roy. I'll get back to you as soon as I know anything."

"Thanks, Larry. And find us a place for the band and me to practice. Say two weeks from now."

"You got it, Roy. Talk to you soon."

Two days later, Roy was camped out in Aspen's historic Hotel Jerome. The hotel displayed copies of Zane Grey's novels, which he set in the country around Aspen 50 years ago, and some of Luke Short's stories. Luke still lived in Aspen, although he no longer wrote books. As a boy, Roy read both authors and loved their stories. Returning to Aspen brought him the feeling of country-western hospitality, and the scenery was spectacular.

Near his hotel, Roy could see the large, tailing hills from the old Smuggler mine, once the most significant producing silver mine in the world. The mine harvested trees from all the surrounding mountains for shoring, and the forests were just now showing signs of revival.

Another aspect of Aspen that Roy loved was the stories about the lost gold mines in the area. A favorite of his was the story about an old prospector who came into town twice every summer, bringing a load of gold on his mule. His mule carried high-grade ore, and everybody wanted to know where the old prospector had his mine. On his last night in town, the old prospector threw a big party, spending his money like there was no tomorrow, which for him might not be that far away.

After the night's celebration, the old prospector loaded up his mule and returned to his mine. Some locals followed him for a few days, but the canny old prospector led these boys all over the mountains until they tired of following him before he went home. He repeated this scenario over and over for a few years until one year; the old man never came back to town. Speculation ran wild, but no one knew what happened to the old guy, and no one ever found his gold mine.

Walking down Big Valley Drive, Roy passed a woman's tailoring shop, which displayed three large quartz rocks with gold streaks running down the sides. A sign in the window claimed these were some rocks from the old prospector's lost mine, but Roy didn't go inside to investigate. Instead, he wanted to check out the Limelite for his show tonight.

The Limelite Saloon was a yellow limestone building with blue awnings and a big redwood arch over the front door. The stately building looked like it could have been a courthouse at one time before they added the awnings and arch. Overall, it looked inviting, and Roy went inside to see if the layout had changed since he played there with the Tumbleweeds. Bob Gibson was just finishing up a set singing "Yellow Bird" while playing an electric Gibson when he entered. Bob had a gravely baritone voice with a pleasant timbre, although it sounded a little mushy to Roy's ears like he had some gum in his jaw.

The Limelite had a sizeable U-shaped bar inside the door, with two tables deep along both walls. The legal limit for patrons was 120, but it wasn't unusual for the crowd to exceed 150. A stage was on the back wall opposite the front door. A convenient back door behind the stage allowed musicians to carry in their speakers' amplification and musical instruments closer to the stage. When Bob finished his set to a rousing round of applause from an appreciative audience, a matronly woman took the stage, much to Roy's surprise.

Roy noticed the signs around town announcing the Aspen Music Festival, but he thought little about it, absorbed in thinking about his upcoming performance. When Martha Sloan took the stage, everything fell into place. Martha was in her mid-sixties, but she looked about forty-five. Before she began her set, Martha took a minute to welcome all the musicians to the music festival. According to Martha, who was Norwegian, musicians worldwide concentrated in Aspen for two weeks to play and study with masters of every instrument and vocal genre, from opera to folk. Martha herself was an international folk singer who performed in several languages, singing the folk songs of different nationalities.

Martha played the lute, plucking the strings like a classical guitarist to accompany her singing, often playing polyphony music with two simultaneous melodies. With her soft contralto voice, she had the audience eating out of her hand or mouth in her case. She opened her set with an Italian folk song, followed by one from Germany and then her home country, Norway. As the set continued, Roy felt transported to a different time and place while the talented Ms. Sloan held the audience enthralled. When the set ended, Roy wondered how this group of international musicians in the audience would react to his brand of country-western music. But he need not have been concerned.

There was a half-hour intermission after Martha's set before Roy took the stage, and he used the time to chat with Martha and Bob Gibson backstage, yeah, named just like Roy's guitar. Both performers knew of Roy's work with The Weeds and seemed pleased to spend a little time with the famous American composer and singer. Finally, it was time for Roy to take the stage in his first solo performance since he sang in churches as a teenager.

Roy had both the Gibson and acoustic guitars on stage and opened his set with the acoustic, singing the ballad *A Brief Encounter*. Then, after bringing the audience to tears, he picked up the Gibson and went right into *Chime Bells*. By the time the last high-pitched bell rang in Roy's voice, mimicked by the highest E-chord possible to play on the cutaway, the entire crowd of international musicians was on their feet, stomping and applauding like a crowd of teenagers at an Elvis concert.

After the crowd settled back down, Roy talked about the Australian Aborigines and their chanting. Next, he went into one song from his new solo album, beating the bass strings in the chanting rhythm while playing the harmonica that made sounds almost like the Aboriginal's chanting. He then played a piece about the whales, nearly matching their melody and sound on his guitar and harmonica. Like Martha before him, Roy's music set him apart from anything most of the musicians in the audience had ever experienced. Two of his most appreciative listeners were Bob Gibson and Martha Sloan.

Roy played at the Limelite for a week before leaving to join the band in Nashville, where they met to practice with Horace Walpole, their arranger. Roy wanted Horace to help arrange the music in his new album into sounds for the entire band. After that, it was time to take the road. Sun Valley was now only a few weeks away.

30
IMPATIENCE

The committee had arranged the concert date with The Weeds, but that wouldn't take place for another six weeks. Sarah found it difficult to concentrate on anything until then, as her mind kept conjuring up different scenarios for her meeting with the handsome, talented, and famous Roy Dalton. Sarah felt like a caged animal. That she was beautiful, wealthy, talented, and famous herself didn't matter. She never saw herself in terms other than just another human being on planet earth, struggling to make sense of life and finding pleasure in living. The thought of meeting this strange man who jumped into her body as a young boy was almost frightening. What would happen when they met in person? Would he even recognize her? Would he be able to read her like a book as he had as a child? Would he be in a relationship with another woman? God, she had to get control of her thoughts.

Thinking of ways to settle her mind, Sarah decided it was time to visit Boris Austin in Fulton to see how Churchill's Museum looked with her decorating now that they had finished with the displays. She called him on the number he had given her previously.

"Hello, this is Boris." My, but he sounded formal. For a minute, she was almost ready to hang up without speaking.

"Boris, this is Sarah Peroni. I'm calling to take you up on that offer to visit your museum now that they have finished with all the displays."

"Sarah, how wonderful. When were you planning on visiting?" He did sound thrilled that she had called.

"I just finished with a project here in Sun Valley and could leave anytime. I have a plane, so I needn't worry about flight schedules. Is the cottage available, or should I get a hotel?"

"Yes. The cottage is available, but Sarah, I have a large home with a perfect guest room. You are welcome to stay here with me."

That suggestion sounded a little pushy to Sarah. She found him attractive; he was good company, and she knew he wanted to pursue a relationship, but staying in his house didn't seem like a good plan. Instead, she wanted the freedom to decide if they would make love and when. Besides, Roy was coming to town, and she didn't want to be involved with another man until she discovered what might happen when they met.

"I'm sorry, Boris, but I would be more comfortable in my place. Can you make the arrangements?"

"Oh, you bet. And I'll be happy to make sure you have transportation and the cottage. Do you have a date in mind?"

He didn't seem happy to Sarah, but his voice still sounded pleasant.

"I thought I would leave tomorrow if that was not too soon." *But, my God, maybe I sound too eager.*

"No, it's perfect. If you give me your schedule, I'll have a limousine waiting at the airport."

During her flight to Missouri, Sarah agonized over her meeting with Boris. Should she go to bed with him or not? There was no question in Sarah's mind that having sex was something Boris wanted, and she also found him attractive. Still, Sarah wondered if going to bed with Boris would be a betrayal to Roy, a man she had never met in person and who may not even want her or be available. He may already have the woman of his life. Hell, she was a mess. Still, a part of her romantic self would not let go of an image of them together, no matter how improbable. So why was she rushing to see Boris? Was she afraid that Roy would be unavailable, and she may as well settle for a respectable man she found attractive? Oh, God, why was she putting herself through this torment? She would find out the truth about Roy in just a few weeks. Surely, she could wait that long after all these years.

It took almost four hours for Sarah's plane to reach Jefferson City, the waiting limousine, and a smiling Boris Austin.

Boris left the door to the limousine open as he rushed to the steps of Sarah's plane, "Sarah, my God, but you look beautiful and welcome to Missouri." Then, with a wolfish smile, Boris grabbed a hesitant Sarah in a bear hug.

Boris struck a romantic picture by wearing a fawn-colored top-coat with a Russian-looking fur hat. It was the middle of February, and his swarthy good looks and tanned face spoke wonders for sun lamps and ego. Wearing a stylish red Christian Dior overcoat with black fur trim, Sarah looked like she stepped out of a fashion plate magazine ad featuring beautiful women.

Pulling away from Boris's tight embrace, Sarah said, "Hello, Boris. It's good to be back in the land of Mark Twain."

"Ah, yes. Twelve feet of water."

"Pardon, did you say twelve feet of water?" Sarah looked confused.

A smug Boris replied, "Yep, twelve feet of water. That's what Mark Twain means. It's steamboat slang for 'twelve feet of water.' You may not know that Twain was a licensed steamboat pilot for four years. The Civil War ended civilian traffic on the river, so he went out west to Virginia City and started writing stories using Mark Twain as his pen name."

"My Boris, but you are a fountain of knowledge. Not only is Missouri home to the Churchill Museum, but it is the home of America's greatest writer, so some believe. Although I'm partial to Hemingway, who lives in my hometown."

"Well," Boris commented, "Mark and Earnest, two great names." Boris took Sarah's elbow, led the way to the limousine, and doffed his hat in a sweeping gesture with a bow. "Your carriage awaits, my dear."

Sarah slid into the back seat as Boris shut the door and went around to the other side of the limousine. Then, getting in the car, he slid over the seat next to Sarah, a move that made her uncomfortable. To ease the strain on her nerves, Sarah commented, "It's too bad we are so far from the Mississippi. I would love to go for a steamboat ride."

"It's only a little over two hours by car over US-40, my dear. Let me take you there while you are visiting our beautiful state."

Leaning against the door to put a little space between herself and Boris, Sarah said, "That would be nice, Boris. Let's see how my visit goes. I may have to rush back to Sun Valley. It's the height of ski season, and we often get unexpected high-ranking guests like US Senators, State Governors, and of course, there are always plenty of movie stars and foreign dignitaries. Our Artists Committee, of which I am a member, must entertain certain guests of honor, and I help when that happens. We never know when someone will show up who deserves the red carpet treatment."

"I certainly understand that. We have much the same situation here in Fulton. Let's hope you don't get summoned before we get to take you on that steamboat ride."

Sarah continued to hug the door, and sensing his guest's unease, Boris kept his distance.

"I have a little surprise for you, Sarah. Hope you don't mind."

"Oh!" A slight frown creased her smooth features. Sarah disliked surprises.

Attuned to Sarah's mood, Boris hastily added, "It's nothing grand, my dear, just a few friends from the museum whom you already know. I thought we might have a little welcoming party at the museum."

Knowing Boris meant well, Sarah was quick to respond. "That sounds appealing. Would it be possible for me to freshen up first at the cottage?"

"Oh, certainly. We'll stop there first to unload your luggage. The party won't start before we get there," he said with a wink and a broad smile.

When the limousine drove into the driveway of the guest cottage, Sarah noticed several cars parked along the drive, lights were glowing from every window, and she could see people were moving about inside, holding drinks in their hands.

"I thought the party was at the museum," Sarah commented in a honey voice laced with daggers.

"Oh, sorry, my dear. I said the party wouldn't start without us. I'm sorry if I gave you the wrong impression."

While Boris was handsome, pleasant, and attentive, his *my dear* was getting on Sarah's nerves. She hated the phrase and didn't consider herself anyone's dear. Besides, Sarah thought his earlier remarks were slightly misleading, if not deceitful. Sarah mentioned freshening up from her trip before being entertained, and Boris responded that she would have time for at least a visit to the bathroom. This lack of consideration did not bode well for a happy stay in Churchill land.

The limo driver jumped from the car, opened the door first for Sarah, and then ran around the car to get the door for Boris. As Boris escorted Sarah into the house, the driver carried her luggage.

Despite what Boris proclaimed earlier, when they entered the door, the welcome party was already in full swing, with people laughing, drinking, and talking in loud liquor-fueled voices.

Putting on a fake smile for the partiers, Sarah directed the driver to the bedroom, where he deposited her luggage before retreating. He could sense the woman's displeasure. Then, throwing a bit of a snit, Sarah took her time in the bathroom to freshen up and change from her traveling clothes to something more in line with the party atmosphere.

When she strolled from the bedroom wearing a white sheath dress that did little to hide her curvy body, she wore a genuine smile that dazzled the guests. Boris was hovering near the bedroom door when she entered the room, and he was quick to take possession of her elbow and shepherded her around the room like a proud husband showing off his wife. Sarah began the trip looking forward to seeing Boris and perhaps even getting intimate, but his sly deceitfulness and possessive attitude quickly turned her against any relationship. She was nobody's damn trophy wife and resented being treated like one.

Boris was too full of himself and too proud of his conquest to notice the chill in her attitude. He assumed it was simply a matter of the lady being overwhelmed by the large crowd. As the evening progressed, he thought she would grow more comfortable. He never realized that Sarah did not like being presented as "his woman." That might have happened had he chosen to be the gracious host she met on her earlier visit. Still, Boris incorrectly assumed the only reason she returned to Fulton was to have a relationship with him, which was not that unreasonable.

As the party wound down, Sarah started becoming anxious. She knew Boris expected to spend the night with her at the cottage, even though she had previously explained she wanted her own lodging, thinking they could get to know each other a little better before going to the next step in their relationship.

She need not have been concerned. Boris ultimately picked up on her chilly attitude and was smart enough to reason why, although he was confused. He believed she visited specifically to sleep with him. Tomorrow was another day, and he would try hard to avoid being overly possessive.

31
REUNION

When Roy joined the rest of the band in Nashville, it was almost as though they had never been separated. They were all eager to hear about Roy's adventures in Australia with the Aboriginal people and his whale stories while living in Hawaii. Roy truly loved the other players in the band and enjoyed regaling them with his adventure stories. While telling his stories, Roy augmented the narrative by playing bits of his new album on a guitar and repeating the chanting and whale singing. While sorry that they missed out on these adventures, they all adored Roy and were genuinely happy for him and eager to learn their new songs. Nashville and the world were waiting for their next album and performances.

The Grand Ole Opry began in 1925, about ten years after national radio broadcasting began. The new Opry House was built in 1935 and has since housed the longest-running radio broadcast in history. Located just off Highway 155, the Opry House was only a couple hundred yards from the Cumberland River, one of the major waterways in the southeastern United States. It wasn't unusual for visitors in the Opry's early days to arrive by boat.

Famous for the many significant stars who have graced its iconic stage over the years, no one had a more significant impact on its stage than Roy Dalton and The Weeds. When word went out that The Weeds would open their new tour at the Opry House, there was a great rush for tickets. While he knew that the lady from the train would never appear at the show, Roy still insisted on keeping one seat vacant near front and center, just in case. He didn't know her name or if she were even alive, but every performance was, in some meaningful way, a tribute to the generosity she displayed to a poor farm boy. The vacant seat was Roy's reminder to be grateful for the blessings in his life. After spending time with one of the oldest civilizations on earth, Roy felt blessed to live and do something that brought him such joy and happiness. The vacant seat was a small price for such a great reward.

Of course, there was no way the train lady would know a seat was reserved for her. Still, Roy kept the seat vacant. But, having witnessed and been the recipient of several miracles in his life, he knew such strange and unlikely events could happen. It was a measure of respect for Roy that no one in the band or Larry, their manager, ever questioned him about the unsold seat. When the band first started performing, Roy only said it was for his friend when asked about the unsold seat. One look into his eyes, and no one asked which friend, or who, was this friend that no one ever saw?

The new tour was called *Our Ancient Lives*, with the new album cover using the same name, featuring a picture of the Australian Aboriginals dancing around a fire under a full moon. It was a striking cover with a star-studded sky in dark blue over the dancers cast in orange by the glowing fire and the big yellow moon just over the horizon. The opening song for both the concerts and the album was Roy and his harmonica playing *Songs of The Whale* while the band chanted refrains Roy learned while doing his walkabout. Then, the band swung into *Chime*

Bells without a break to let the audience know Roy could still perform and to get the crowd involved with the show. When Roy and his guitar hit the final high C, ringing like a silver church bell, the Opry crowd belonged to Dalton and The Weeds.

Broadcast live worldwide; Our Ancient Lives became the latest must-have album for county music lovers and Weed fans everywhere. The concert ended on a high note with another yodeling song by Roy, a new song added just for this concert at the Opry. The song, *I See the Moon,* was based on an old song Roy's mother used to sing. He never learned where the music originated, but Roy changed the words and changed the tune to fit his style. After several encores, they finished the evening, almost an hour later, with another new song written by Roy. *You Never Walk Alone* became the latest pop song of the decade. The Opry fans bid the band farewell with tears in every eye and a standing ovation that could have ruptured the ears.

While leaving the stage, Roy glanced backward at the empty front-row seat as he wondered what had happened to the lady on the train?

32
DAMNATION

After she escaped from the advances Boris made last evening, Sarah wasn't sure what she would do if he continued to make the moves towards making love? Yes, he was attractive and was a decent, if not a great, companion and might be a superb lover, but was he what she wanted? It had been a long time since Sarah had made love with any man. Sure, there had been lovers over the years since Dean died, but nothing serious on her part. Dozens more had tried, and some men she slept with wanted more than a brief affair, but she had found no one to make her heart sing as Dean did.

As Sarah began getting dressed for her day with Boris, she wondered what to wear. Anything that accentuated her already full figure would appear provocative, yet she owned nothing that would hide her figure. Hiding her figure had never been a problem before. Instead, she settled on a dark blue pantsuit with a loose fit, hoping the silky material would not give the wrong impression.

They agreed to meet for a late breakfast, and Boris showed up precisely at ten am with a broad smile and carrying a box of Dutch chocolates and two dozen red and white roses. The gesture was sweet and thoughtful, although it showed an interest far from that of a genial host. Doing her best to appear friendly yet cool to further advances, Sarah found a vase for the flowers in the pantry. Then, thanking Boris with a brushed kiss on his cheek, Sarah headed for the door, showing that she was ready for a restaurant and breakfast. No fooling around, at least, not now.

Boris drove them to a nearby mall with a Marie Callender's restaurant. Breakfast was relaxed and pleasant as Boris seemed content to let their relationship develop at its own pace without pressure from him. They discussed plans for the day, and Sarah was eager to see how the museum looked now that all the displays were in place.

The day was going as Sarah had hoped, with a pleasant host eager to show off his museum and their work to incorporate as much of Churchill's memorabilia as they could acquire. The museum staff had done an excellent job arranging items like Churchill's bust next to drapery folds incorporated in Sarah's decorating arrangements. Both Sarah and Boris thought the museum looked great and did a good job representing the man they believed saved England during the big war.

It was midafternoon when they finally left the museum, and Boris suggested a nearby coffee shop to grab a sandwich and a cup of coffee. Tired of standing and walking, the idea appealed to Sarah, especially as the coffee shop was only a short distance away. Whatever plans Boris might have had in mind for the rest of the day were blown away as they reached the coffee shop with several newspaper vending machines arranged in a row just outside of their doors.

In particular, *Country Time* ran a large ten-point Rozha One font headline; DALTON PLAYS THE OPRY. Intrigued, Sarah stopped to read the words directly below the headline, where she discovered that Roy and The Weeds were doing a concert at the Grand Old Opry in Nashville at this very moment. The paper proudly announced that the show would be broadcast live to practically everywhere in the world. Damnation, and here she was, stuck in Missouri without a radio.

Turning to Boris, Sarah mentioned her love for the band and suggested they find someplace to listen to the concert. Boris, of course, was more than happy to oblige his guest, for he still thought there was a chance for a more meaningful relationship. Neither one had a portable radio, and the only one Boris could think of was the car radio.

Forgetting her tired feet, Sarah almost ran back to Boris's car, eager not to miss any more of the concert than necessary. She need not have bothered because the paper had made a mistake, and the show was not scheduled to begin for another hour. After an unnecessary apology to Boris for the hurried trip back to his car, they drove back to the coffee shop and their promised coffee and sandwich. It was all Sarah could do throughout their light lunch to focus on her conversation with Boris while her mind kept drifting back to the concert. She knew that Roy's voice was okay, for she had heard him perform recently after his Australian adventure. Still, she was curious about how the band would treat his new material.

Fortified with a bottle of wine and two paper cups, Boris was gallant and ensured they were back in his car in time for the concert. When they introduced the band, it was all Sarah could do to keep from squirming in her seat and when Roy started playing the opening song on his harmonica; she felt goosebumps running up her arms. "*My God,*" she thought, "*I'm acting like a lovesick teenager.*" This thought was followed by another that was equally disturbing, "*And who am I supposed to be in love with? Certainly not someone I've never met.*"

They talked little during the performance. Boris seemed content to sit and watch Sarah, who seemed almost to swoon whenever Roy sang solo. He did not know about the relationship between the singer and his companion, nor did he think to ask. It was inconceivable that this beautiful, talented artist could be associated with a country singer. Boris concluded that Sarah simply loved listening to the singer without giving it much thought. Although not a fan of country music, he had to admit that the man had a good voice and his singing was pleasing to the ears.

When the final encore ended, Sarah felt drained. Thinking about the singer and her response to the concert she had just listened to, Sarah began fretting about his appearance in Sun Valley. She felt giddy just thinking about meeting this handsome singer with a golden voice. Sarah had achieved fame in her own life and gained a reputation as an interior decorator and artist. But her level of fame was no match for Roy's and his band. Sarah could not even imagine standing in front of thousands of people, let alone singing.

While Boris talked about stopping at a lovely lounge for a drink before dinner, Sarah barely heard his voice and had difficulty concentrating on his words. She finally understood he wanted a cocktail before dinner, which was okay with her. Sarah could use a drink to settle her nerves. One thing was clear: she could not go ahead in a relationship with Boris while her emotions were raw and unclear. It would have to wait until after the Sun Valley concert.

33
A LONG WAIT

When Roy returned to his hotel room following the concert, the usual concert groupies were waiting for him to make a selection. He was about to take a couple of girls to his room when the desk clerk waved him to the counter.

"Mr. Dalton, your manager gave me this letter for you. He said it was delivered to your practice studio. It was unclear just how it came to the studio, for there was no address on the envelope, as you can see."

Roy took the envelope and glanced at the address block. The envelope was addressed:

Mr. Roy Dalton (The Weeds)
Nashville, Tennessee

Apparently, the Nashville post office was familiar with Roy and The Weeds and knew where they practiced. Many of the band members and the band's staff received letters while the band was camping in the city. The letter was from his mother, and Roy couldn't wait to get to his room and see what she had to say. It must be bad news; she rarely wrote to her son while he was on the road. Roy usually called his mother every two weeks to check in on the family and supply updates on his health and schedule. Tonight, there would be no girls. Mom's letter would be read in private.

Dear Roy,

Well, son, we are sure happy you are healthy again and singing. We listen on the radio whenever your concerts are being broadcast. Mr. Perkins helps keep us informed about where you will perform and where we might listen to you sing. We can now get Salt Lake and Logan on the radio, so it isn't just KPST in Preston anymore. One of the stations almost always carries your performances when they are broadcast, and once in a while, all three stations will have the show.

Arnold graduates this year from college. He's going to be an engineer. Can you believe this? And Marlow is running the ranch along with your father. No one rides Jupiter anymore. He's just too old.

Everybody here is doing good, and I have to tell you, and this is why I'm writing instead of waiting for your call; everybody is going to Sun Valley for your concert. I mean everybody. The school district is loaning a couple of buses, and we're having a party on the bus to your show. It seems like everybody in Cache Valley wants to see and hear you perform live, all those people who used to listen to you when you kids were called The Tumble Weeds.

We just thought you might like to know that practically the whole damn valley is coming to see you, son, so I just wanted to give you a head's up in case you wanted to do a little get-together. And of course, the family is eager to see and hear you and hope you can spare a little time for us after the concert.

This show will be our first concert, and everybody is really excited. Marlow and Frann can't come with us because Frann is expecting soon, and somebody has to stay home and do the chores.

Anyway, that's the news. Put on a good show for the home folks. I know that's a stupid thing to say, but what's a mother for if not to make silly suggestions?

All my and your dad's love,

Mom

Well, hell. So, the whole town was coming to hear him sing. He initially balked at playing Sun Valley because the auditorium only held five thousand people. Only five thousand. Jesus! There was a time when he played and sang for less than fifty. Now, unless the venue could seat at least twenty thousand, the band was not interested. But after reading his mom's letter, Roy felt better about playing near his home. It felt kind of good to perform for his little town. He could remember Orson bringing him the guitar package down to the ranch when there was no need for such service, yet he and the whole village seemed to support him and his desire to perform. So, bringing the band to Sun Valley was a good idea. Perhaps he could do something special.

However, he did not know just how special that evening would become.

His mind started playing little tricks by keeping the Sun Valley concert in the back of his mind. It didn't affect his performance, but waiting to see and sing for his family now seemed like an eternity.

34

HOME AGAIN

On the plane ride home, reclining on one of the lounge chairs in her plane, Sarah decided the visit with Boris was a mistake. Bored and lonely, it seemed like a good plan a few days ago, but that damn Opry concert made her remember another lonely person she had met for just an instant. *Is he married yet? Does he have a lover? Would he even remember the lady on the train?* Well, she knew the answer to that last query. There was no question in her mind that when he originally wrote and sang *A Brief Encounter,* he was thinking of her. Ten years isn't such a significant age gap. Maybe there could be a relationship.

Oh, hell, Sarah, stop dreaming and get real. He's a singer with a great life, and I have a pretty damn good life of my own. Boris didn't work out, but now I know why our relationship wouldn't work. Charming, good-looking, intelligent, and a pleasant companion, he was just too dull.

She had met hundreds of men with money, looks, power, and prestige, but they all seemed like empty suits. Outside of pleasure-seeking, they didn't have anything to offer of significance. They weren't contributing anything of value to the planet. Playing, partying, and proving that they had the biggest organ in town seemed to be their whole lives. There were also plenty of extraordinary gentlemen like Boris, but their lives seemed so dull.

Of course, there were many adventurers in life, too, like archaeologists who traveled to distant remote sites digging into our past. Or explorers in other areas, such as our ocean's deepest places. Yes, those men were intriguing, but it wasn't her lifestyle to live in a tent somewhere in the desert where it's a hundred degrees in the shade, and there aren't any shade trees.

If there isn't anybody for me, I still have one hell of a nice life.

Looking out of the plane window, Sarah saw they were circling the Sawtooth mountains preparing to land at the Sun Valley Airport. Sarah was happy to be home, and she could stop her ruminating. Looking in the parking lot as the plane taxied to a stop, she spotted Arlene's yellow Chevrolet, with Arlene standing outside of the car by the front door. *Now, what is that all about? No one ever comes to meet my plane.*

Her friend was waiting for her at the foot of the stairs as Sarah exited the plane.

"Welcome home, traveler. Did you have a wonderful time back east?"

"Hi Arlene, it's great to be back, and what are you doing here? Not that it isn't pleasant seeing your beautiful self."

"We have a bit of a problem with the concert, Sarah. There aren't enough seats."

"What? My God, Arlene, we've got five thousand seats. What's the problem?"

"That isn't enough like I just said. The concert is sold out, and we have requests for hundreds of more seats. We could easily sell out another show, but we have to get The Weeds to agree to play an extra concert. There was such a fuss getting their manager to agree to play for one night; we didn't know how to proceed with a request for another show. We've been waiting for you since you were so persuasive last time. Would you see if you can get this man, Larry Perkins, to agree to play one more night?"

"I can try, but where are the requests for these tickets for the show coming from?"

"Oh, Sarah. It's mostly Cache Valley, the home of Roy Dalton. There are at least ten busloads of people coming from all over the valley. Apparently, when Roy started his band, they played all around the valley for dances, weddings, and special events. They love his music and are eager to see him perform live now that he's a big-time star. We have requests for seats from all over Idaho and Utah, plus Oregon and Washington, even Colorado."

"All we can do is ask. I believe these popular bands have their tours pretty well organized before they hit the road. The band may not have the luxury of extending their stay at any stop on the tour."

"Yes. I'm aware of that, Sarah, which is why I'm here. The committee believes that the sooner we ask, the better chance of getting an extra concert. The committee will give up their share of the gate if the band agrees to an extra show."

"Well, friend, let's find a telephone, and I'll place the call. Then you owe me a cocktail."

35
MIAMI

Following their successful concert in Nashville, The Weeds headed for Miami and the sun. After checking in at the Hilton, Larry asked Roy to meet him at the outside bar for a cocktail and a little chat. The open-air cocktail lounge was next to an Olympic-sized swimming pool with a large blue dolphin laid in colorful tile on the bottom. The pool was on the second level, overlooking the beach and the turbulent, dark blue Atlantic Ocean. When Roy finished unpacking and found the bar, Larry was already sitting in a padded wicker lounge chair, scoping out the view and sipping on a rum drink with a pineapple wedge on the glass rim. Lying by the pool and catching the sun were several ladies wearing the latest swimwear fashion, brief bikinis.

"Look at those swimming suits, Roy. They sure leave little for the imagination."

"Yeah, and the ocean looks pretty good as well. Are you planning on swimming or just gawking at the ladies?"

"Oh, I think I'll just surf the view from here with my eyes. The ocean is undoubtedly cold, and the pool is full of chemicals."

"Oh yeah. You wouldn't want to subject that swell body to kiddie piss and chlorine."

"I see our cocktail girl heading over here, Roy. What are you drinking?"

"Well, I don't want a fruit salad for my drink; how about a Johnny Walker scotch and water?"

"Sounds like a real country-boy drink. Happy to see you sticking to your roots."

"Oh yeah. My roots. I doubt my dad ever had a drink of alcohol in his life."

"Was it religion or just old-fashioned values?"

"It was probably poverty. We had little in the way of money, and dad could never afford to squander anything on liquor."

"So how come his son discovered the evil of booze?"

"Just lucky, I guess. So, what is it you wanted to chat about? Not my drinking habits, I'm sure."

"I had a message when we checked in to call the lady in Sun Valley who arranged for our concert there. She wanted to add a second concert the following day. I told her I needed to check it with you. We have an extra day we could spend in Sun Valley, but that doesn't leave you and the band any downtime before our appearance in San Francisco."

"What's going on there, Larry? You were initially worried they wouldn't even sell five thousand tickets to fill their auditorium."

"I guess everybody in Cache Valley wants to see you perform live with the band. Apparently, you developed a fan base when you and the Tumbleweeds played for dances. The lady said there were busloads of people coming from all over, and they inundated her with requests for tickets. She is positive they can sell out the second night. I know it's only five thousand seats, but what do you say since we're already there? It's your call."

"Well, they are my people. I received a letter from mom telling me the family was planning on attending the show. So, let us give the home folks a second show if there is that much interest. Besides, I'm looking forward to seeing Sun Valley.

Growing up in Clifton, we often heard stories about how great the place was, but it was never in the Dalton family budget to visit there."

"Okay, great. I'll call this Peroni gal and tell her to book the second night."

When Larry said the name Peroni, Roy felt goosebumps running up his arms. Despite the heat and humidity, he felt a sudden chill.

"What did you say her name was?"

"I believe she said her name was Peroni on the phone. Why? Do you know her?"

"No. I don't believe I've ever heard the name. However, it sounded familiar, like it was a name I should know. When you said her name, my body reacted weirdly. It gave me chills."

"Maybe it's your long-lost love, Roy. Probably one of the groupies from your past."

"Yeah. I don't know. Maybe I'll know when we meet. I suppose you'll see her when you check out the arrangements."

"Right. I'll fly in a day early as always. I'll check her out for you."

"Thanks, pal. I can always count on you to watch my back. It's strange, though. It feels like Sun Valley should mean something to me. I just haven't been able to figure out what. I know it's an iconic fixture in Idaho lore, but I cannot figure out why it's meaningful. Growing up in Clifton, we heard stories about the beautiful mountains and ice skating shows in the summer. In the middle of July, when the temperature reaches a hundred, stories about ice skating stir the imagination like no other. And pulling on a loose barbed wire to nail it to a post in that heat with sweat running down your face, thinking of someone ice skating seemed unbelievable. I would dream about what it must be like to feel all that cold. It was a fantasy to think about such things. I guess I'll find out in a few weeks."

36
THE LAKE

The concert was still a few weeks away, and Sarah was restless. She needed a new project to keep her mind off Roy and the damn Weeds. At times, she was sorry she ever saw that blooming album cover in that New York shop window. But now, living with the thought of meeting Roy after all these years, their meeting in the flesh seemed like fate. With reluctance, Sarah admitted she found Roy's version of country music pleasing and even beautiful. It even had a classical feel, something she experienced while listening to Beethoven or Mozart.

Highway 75 follows the Sawtooth Mountain range north out of Ketchum. Thirty miles from Sun Valley along the highway is Redfish Lake, one of the most scenic lakes in Idaho. Surrounded by mountains with pine trees lining its shores, the lake's remote location makes it an ideal getaway spot for someone seeking privacy, beauty, and solitude.

Sarah saw pictures of the lake hanging in the Pioneer Saloon, but she had never visited the lake, for it was an hour's drive along a narrow two-lane road against a steep mountain range. She had once heard a regular at the Pioneer Saloon say that Redfish Lake is the perfect place if you ever want to spend time in a beautiful spot to relax and commune with God. Deciding the time had come to get away, she invited Arlene to go with her and spend a few days painting by the lake. Arlene was thrilled with the prospect of spending time by a remote mountain lake. Patrons of the saloon who had visited the lake assured both ladies there were cabins by the lake they could rent. With that information, Sarah and Arlene packed up their easels and paint supplies, and with Arlene riding shotgun, they headed up the mountain road.

When she first glimpsed the lake, Sarah felt like she was coming home. The lake seemed to call to her in a voice she seldom heard anymore. As a young girl visiting the ocean near her home in Atherton, she felt like the sea was her friend, and standing by the shore she could hear sounds in the gently breaking waves that seemed to send her messages of comfort. Standing by the shore of Redfish Lake, Sarah listened to the same message as the lake's waves kissed the rocky shore. It would be a fantastic retreat, and she was sharing it with her best friend. Thoughts of Boris and Roy were swept away in the whispering breeze as it sifted through the needles of the tall Douglas fir and ponderosa pine trees.

Their bungalow, nestled in a beautiful aspen grove was a typical Idaho mountain cabin with a high-pitched roof for the heavy winter snow loads. Sheathed in redwood siding that had weathered into a dark brown the color of chocolate, their new lodging appeared inviting. Two square windows with fake green shutters flanked a door painted a coppery red.

Inside, a double bed with a homemade patchwork quilt bedspread with the double ring's motif rested against the rear knotty pine wall covered with pictures of the lake during all four seasons. On both sides of the bed stood a small nightstand with a knotty pine lamp base topped with a green cloth shade. Two wooden chairs, which looked homemade from pine branches stripped from their bark, stood against one wall with a lamp table between them and another green-shaded lamp. The homemade bone-white pinewood chairs gave the room an added homey touch.

A doorway in the opposite wall led to a small bathroom with a plastic shower stall and the other necessary bathroom fixtures. This room also featured knotty pine paneling. The cabin, while small, was homey and comfortable. Sarah and Arlene dumped their bags and took off for a walk along the lakeshore without bothering to lock the door. They appeared to have the lake to themselves, and besides, they were always within view of their cabin. Both ladies were eager to grab their easels and stools and begin painting. Spectacular views were prevalent in every direction.

Rushing back to their cabin, Sarah and Arlene grabbed their painting supplies and water bottles before heading back to the lake to set up their easels. The afternoon sun cast long shadows along the shoreline, and the lake's still surface reflected the snowcapped mountains. Arlene set up her station to paint the mountains reflected on the lake while Sarah went fifty yards away to look for a suitable subject. She enjoyed painting animals and looked for something to stimulate her imagination. Finding nothing of particular interest, she decided to set up her easel in a small, shaded cove and wait for something to happen. Her decision proved rewarding.

Taking a sip of water, Sarah sat relaxed, enjoying the clear mountain air and spectacular scenery when a small herd of elk visited the lake for their afternoon drink. A large bull stood guard while two cows and their calves went to the lake for their drink. Mesmerized by the beautiful animals, Sarah sat still while watching the cows and calves drink. The bull scrutinized Sarah, but he didn't appear alarmed by her presence. After the cows and calves drank their fill and moseyed along the lakeshore, nibbling at small tufts of grass growing between the rocks, the bull took one last, long, lingering look at Sarah before he went to the lake for his drink.

The bull was magnificent. With an antler rack spanning nearly four feet, the large animal held Sarah's attention while she registered every nuance of his presence at the lake's edge. When he dipped his head into the lake for a drink, the sun glistened from his antlers like shafts of white light while the lake reflected his full head in its waters. Sarah was afraid to move. She didn't want to startle the animal, but she ached to grab her sketch pad and record the scene. She knew there was no way she could paint the animal before it left the area, so she contented herself with memorizing every aspect of his being with sketches. After the elk family left the lake, Sarah grabbed her paints and started painting.

She worked until the fading sun left her no choice but to join Arlene, who was already back at their cabin, enjoying a glass of chilled Chardonnay. Arlene was proud of her lake scape until she saw Sarah's painting of the bull elk drinking from the lake.

"Oh my God, darling. What a truly magnificent painting. How on earth did you capture that beast drinking?"

"I had to wait for him to leave before starting the painting. I did this from memory."

"I know you do animals, Sarah, but this is one of your very best. Don't let Peter at the Pioneer Saloon get a gander at this picture, or you might not resist his offer to purchase it for his restaurant."

"Don't worry about that, Arlene. Old Peter and his money don't interest me in the least. However, this picture would go great in the Pioneer. Maybe I'll loan it to him for a year."

Later, as they dined on cold chicken and potato salad, Arlene asked, "Are you anxious about meeting Roy and the big concert?"

"Don't remind me. This little escape into the mountains is just my way of killing time. The waiting is nearly driving me crazy. I'm just afraid that he already has his true love and will hardly give me a second look."

"Don't be so sure, Sarah. Anybody who went to as much trouble as he did to attract your attention will not give up so easily."

"But it's been such a long time. I'm afraid Roy has moved on by now."

"Well, we'll find out pretty quick. It's not that far away now."

"Yes. I know. I'm just not very good at the waiting game."

"I'll bet he will be in for a big surprise when he meets you, girl."

Neither lady had any idea just how big of a surprise it would be for everyone.

37
WOHALI

The striking young Cherokee man went by Wohali, which meant eagle, the only name he had. Standing five foot six and a half inches, Wohali projected a much taller image, mostly because he had an attitude of six feet tall and a broad smile full of sparkling white enamels.

Driven from her home in Georgia by the United States Government's quest for land and gold, his great-great-grandmother, Ahyoka, survived the thousand-mile walk known as the Trail of Tears carrying Immokalee, Wohali's grandmother, on her back in a papoose carrier. Raised on a reservation in Oklahoma, Wohali received a rudimentary education from an unhappy drunkard named Mortimer Wilcox. Despite his impoverished background, Wohali grew up smiling and playing tall, even though it meant slashes across his back from a willow whip wielded by a mean-spirited man with no pleasure in life except to beat the starving brown-skinned school kids entrusted to his care.

An old Indian male known as Tsiyl made the young boy named Wohali a wooden flute from a willow branch. This gift may have accounted for the boy's beaming face as he carried and played the flute every chance he got. As he grew older, the boy learned to make flutes from different woods with more holes, each longer than his last one. Wohali became an accomplished flute maker by the age of eighteen and entertained the tribe with his original composed melodies.

From Miami, The Weeds flew to New York for three concerts. They arrived in the Big Apple in the afternoon, and after checking into their rooms at the Waldorf, Roy hit the streets for a brief excursion about town. Walking down Broadway towards Times Square, Roy heard a sweet soft sound floating in the humid summer air. Following the sound, he saw a small Indian man on the sidewalk sitting on a patterned Navajo blanket, playing a wooden flute. Roy loved the sound and waited for the melody to end before approaching the flute player. He dropped a hundred-dollar bill onto the flute player's blanket with the other bills and change sprinkled on the orange and black cloth.

"Hi," Roy began in his Idaho twang. "Do you have a minute to talk?"

"Man, your Benjamin buys you all the time you want."

"I'm Roy Dalton, and I'd like you to come with me back to my room and listen to some music."

"What? You don't like my playing?" Wohali asked with a grin.

"No, quite the contrary. I love your sound and want to hear you play the flute while listening to some whales sing."

"Well, Mr. Roy Dalton. I guess your Benji will buy you a few minutes. You aren't into any funny business, are you?"

"Not unless you consider playing music a funny business. I play a little too. Although not a flute, my thing is a guitar. By the way, what's your name?"

"My name is Wohali," answered the curious young man.

"Just Wohali? No other name?"

"Just Wohali. My mom couldn't afford two names for me." As he spoke, he had a sly smile on his face as he looked at Roy to see if the big white man liked his humor.

After picking up his money and blanket, they began walking with Wohali following Roy, who had not responded to the comment about not affording two names. As they passed an art gallery window, Roy paused to look at a picture featured by the gallery. Propped on an easel by the front window was a painting featuring a palomino racing across a moonlit meadow in full gallop. The horse's silvery-white mane flew in the breeze like fine silk threads in the wind. The eyes made the picture stand out from simply being a magnificent horse caught in full gallop. The artist had captured a look that made the horse appear to be enjoying the time of its life. The caption printed at the bottom said it all, *Doing Life*. Peroni signed the painting. Now, where had he heard that name before?

"Come inside with me, Wohali; I need to check this out."

"Sure, boss. Got nothing better to do than traipse around the streets with the likes of you."

"Don't get testy, Wohali. This stop will only take a minute, and I'm sure it will be worth your while."

Wohali frowned, but followed Roy inside the gallery.

The inside was a cool 70 degrees, with controlled humidity to keep the canvases supple. A high textured ceiling with recessed lights was surrounded by silvery gray walls. The floor appeared to be white marble. Elegant room dividers painted in bright colors and featuring Japanese flower blossoms were strategically placed around a large room with live potted plants adding an elegant touch. The walls were hung with large, expensive-looking paintings, each lit by its own special spotlight. A beautiful lady in a silvery sheath dress appeared as though summoned by a remote alarm when the door opened.

The tall, dark-skinned lady had gray hair twisted into a French bun with a string of pearls around her slender neck. Friendly brown eyes carried a beaming smile and flashing teeth to match the pearls. "Good afternoon, gentlemen. My name is Ember. Can I be of service?"

"Good afternoon, madam. I would like to inquire about that picture in your window. It's the Palomino mare running across the meadow in the moonlight. I believe it's named *Doing Life*. The picture, not the horse."

"That would be the Peroni. It's the only painting we have of hers at the moment. It isn't easy to acquire one of her paintings. They are in such a big demand."

"Did you say, Mrs. Peroni?"

"No, I said, Peroni. Her name is Sarah Peroni, and I don't know her marital status. Are you interested in the lady or her painting?"

"Oh, sorry. I recently heard the name Peroni for the first time, but I can't remember where I heard it. Anyway, I stopped in to inquire about the picture. I presume it's for sale?"

"Of course, the price is thirty thousand dollars."

"Whew. And here I thought it might be expensive. Does that price include the frame?" Then, seeing the look of disgust on the lady's face, Roy hastily added, "Just kidding, ma'am."

"If that price is a bit out of your budget," the lady added with a stiff smile, "I can suggest some works that are a little less expensive. It's just that the Peroni's are rare and are worth every penny."

"No doubt. Why are the Peroni's so rare?"

"Well, Sarah is primarily an interior designer. She has probably decorated more Manhattan mansions than any other decorator in the business. She also has a line of furniture and accessories. Although, like her paintings, they too are scarce. We only have two of her pieces in the gallery."

"My, she sounds like a very talented lady, Ember. Could I see her furniture?"

Frowning at what must be another wasted effort, the lady led them on a weaving trek through the gallery around the Japanese dividers and potted ferns to a room with several expensive-looking pieces of furniture.

Pointing to a polished sofa-back table that appeared to have been carved from a single rosewood tree trunk, Ember told the men that this was her only piece of Peroni furniture, plus the chandelier hanging above on a large silver chain. The table and chandelier were exquisite beyond anything Roy had ever seen.

"And how much are these two items?" he inquired politely. The woman's frosty attitude had not escaped his notice.

Sensing that she may have made a mistake, Ember tried to compensate by flashing her warmest smile. "The sofa table is $7,400.00, and the chandelier is $9,500.00."

"Great. I'll take all three pieces. The picture of the palomino, the table, and the chandelier. I need you to take care of shipping them for me. Can you take care of that?"

"Why certainly, sir. We'll cover the shipping because you are taking all three items."

"Thanks, I'm staying at the Waldorf. I'll have my manager come by with the payment and arrange the shipping. How late do you stay open?"

"We stay open until six."

"Oh, that doesn't give me much time. Would it be okay if he came by tomorrow? His name is Larry Perkins, and we have a show tonight, so he may not be available this afternoon. But definitely tomorrow."

Believing she might be the victim of a scam, Ember started backtracking. "And what did you say your name was?"

"I'm Roy Dalton, ma'am, and this delightful gentleman at my side is Wohali."

"Oh, my God. Are you that Roy Dalton? You're my daughter Caroline's favorite singer."

"Yep, the only one, as far as I know, and your daughter has excellent taste in music, I might add."

"Heavens, I cannot wait to go home and tell her who just came into my gallery," she gushed.

"I'll tell you what, Ember; I'll leave two tickets for you and your daughter at the box office. I can't guarantee how good they will be as it's getting late in the day, but I'll do my best. Now I have to get this gentleman back to my room for his tryout. But first, what can you tell me about Sarah Peroni?"

"She lives in Sun Valley, Idaho, and travels worldwide in her own airplane. I have never met the lady, but I have seen her picture, and she's a real beauty. I've heard she loves the opera and ballet, often coming to opening shows here in New York. Although, I don't think she is a fan of folk or country music. That's all I know, I'm afraid."

"No. That's okay. I remember now where I heard the name. Well, thanks for your time. Enjoy the show."

"Oh, Mr. Dalton. Thank you for the tickets. Caroline will be so delighted. I don't know how to thank you."

"Well, ma'am. Your smile is all the reward I need. Good afternoon." Turning to his new friend, Roy said, "Come on, Wohali, I need you to listen to some music."

38
THE PIONEER SALOON

It was an ordinary summer day in Sun Valley. The air was crisp and clear, with a slight northern breeze. Leaves on the big maple trees along the main street rustled, and everyone, residents and visitors alike, smiled for no reason except that being alive and in that place was pure pleasure. Strolling towards the Pioneer Saloon, Peter Drake, proprietor, couldn't help but feel like a man on top of the world. One of his favorite people in town had asked for a private meeting, and when Sarah Peroni asked for an appointment, it must be something special.

Coming towards Peter from the opposite direction walked Sarah, carrying a large object wrapped in brown paper. Peter stopped at the door to his saloon while waiting for Sarah to arrive with her package.

Dressed in a cream-colored pantsuit with gold band trim with her long black hair swishing as she walked, Sarah looked like a vision from heaven.

"Hi Sarah, you look more beautiful every time I see you. Are you in love, or is it just our fine mountain living?"

"Hello, Peter. Your flattery gets more outrageous with every meeting, but thanks, all the same. I see you are also in excellent shape for an old geezer."

"What's with this old geezer business? I thought we were friends?"

"Hey, some of my best friends are old geezers," Sarah answered with a broad smile.

Opening the door to the Pioneer, with a bow and broad arm sweep, Peter ushered Sarah inside.

"Why, thank you, dear sir. That's very thoughtful."

"Not at all, Sarah. And what's with that big package you're carrying?"

"Peter, with all these dead animals hanging on your walls, I thought your place could use a little life. You always wanted to buy *The Black Stallion,* my black stallion painting, so I brought you a present. Here," she said, handing him the package.

"Follow me, Sarah. Let's find a room in the back so I can see what you've given me."

Peter led Sarah on a meandering walk through the saloon and restaurant, dodging tables and chairs until arriving at a small room in the back with only two tables, neither of which was occupied by patrons.

"This is my favorite room," Peter said, while pulling out a chair for Sarah. "I reserve this room for exceptional customers. We seat no one back here unless I approve, which rarely happens. I always want a table available if someone like Lombard or Gable walks in, which happens occasionally."

"It is a lovely private room and quiet. I could get used to eating here," Sarah responded as she waited for Peter to sit down and open his package.

Recognizing it as a picture from its shape, Peter sat down and unwrapped the large, bulky package. The beautiful elk came into view as the wrappings fell to the floor. Peter sat open-mouthed, speechless, as he stared at the scene. A large bull elk standing by the edge of a spectacular mountain lake with his head hovering over the still water reflecting his image perfectly. The sun was glistening from his large antler rack, making the animal seem almost ethereal, the dream of a magnificent creature. The bull's eyes sparkled with reflected light from the lake, giving him an aura of perfection.

"Oh my God, Sarah. This picture is fantastic—what a stunning piece of art. I love how you captured his strength and power. However did you catch this guy in your sights?"

"I visited Redfish Lake with Arlene last week and saw this family of elks visiting the lake for a drink. I had my easel set up a few yards from the shore, and the animals never seemed to be afraid of me."

"Surely this big guy didn't just sit there posing for you to paint him."

"No, I quickly sketched him as he drank and then painted him from memory."

"You couldn't know this, but Redfish Lake is my favorite lake in the world."

"Well, I saw photographs of the lake in one of your other rooms, which prompted me to visit it. It is peaceful and beautiful. I'm happy that we went."

"But Sarah, I cannot pay you what this picture is worth. I know your work sells for big bucks, and this picture is spectacular. It would break my bank to pay you."

"Peter, what about the word present don't you get?" Sarah said with a grin. "You have always been gracious and supportive of my work, and I just wanted to say thanks. This is my thank you."

A lump formed in Peter's throat, making him speechless, and he ducked his head so Sarah would not see the glistening tears in his eyes. After composing himself for a few seconds, he stood up and motioned Sarah to remain seated, then set the picture against the wall before leaving the room. He returned a few minutes later with a white table reservation card. Then, taking a pen from his pocket, Peter wrote the words RESERVED

PERMANENTLY FOR SARAH PERONI on the card and placed it on the table in front of Sarah.

"From now on and forever, Sarah, this table is reserved only for you whenever you choose to visit the Pioneer. We will never sit another party at this table, and it will always wait for you. And you will never pay for another meal or drink at the Pioneer Saloon." Peter still had a glisten in his eyes from tears not quite shed, but the smile on his face was worth a million.

"But Peter, what if Marilyn or Gable come in and the place is packed?" Sarah had a wicked grin as she tormented the saloon keeper.

Not to be put off by the beautiful artist, Peter responded a little gruffly, as his throat still had a residual lump bobbing around his Adam's apple, "In that case, my dear, they'll just have to wait for another table like everyone else."

39
LESSONS IN MUSIC

The Weeds occupied a series of suites on the tenth floor, with Roy's suite 1006 in the middle. Entering the Waldorf and then Roy's room, Wohali's eyes were popping from his head, which looked like it was on a swivel. He made enough money as a street musician to rent a tiny one-room apartment on the Eastside and never in his life had he experienced such luxury firsthand.

In the center of the room were Roy's two guitars with the Gibson plugged into an amplifier. Seeing such expensive instruments told Wohali that he was in the presence of a serious musician. He had seen such guitars in the windows of some fancy music stores, but never up close and personal.

"Say, man, these are your guitars?" But, even to his ears, the question sounded stupid. Who else would they belong to except for the man who invited him into his room?

"Wohali, I'm a professional musician with a band named The Weeds, and tonight we have a concert at the Garden. Recently I spent time in Australia with the Aborigines and later in Hawaii listening to whales sing. I've composed some music for our concert featuring Aborigine chants and whale songs. I want to play them for you and see if your flute can help set the mood and add another dimension to the music."

An hour later, Wohali, a new member of the band, worked with Roy on a composition when there was a knock on Roy's door. It was Larry, checking in to make sure Roy was getting prepared for the evening's concert.

"Hi Larry, come on in and meet Wohali, the newest member of our band."

Larry looked at the small Indian man dressed in shabby street clothes and wondered if Roy had lost his mind. "What do you mean, he's a member of the band?"

"Yeah, just listen. Wohali, let's play the opening piece for Larry here. He needs to hear what we're doing. Oh, and Wohali, Larry is our manager."

Larry sat down in one of the oversized easy chairs decorating Roy's suite, chaffing how Roy had hired a new band member without consulting with the band manager while Roy keyed in the tape player to start the chanting. Wohali accompanied them with his flute when the chanting began, perfectly mimicking the rhythm and cadence. Then the whales started singing, and Roy played the harmonica while Wohali played the flute. The juxtaposition of chants, whale songs, Wohali's flute, and Roy's harmonica blended perfectly, making a unique composition that stirred the soul. As the piece progressed, Roy picked up his acoustic guitar and started the melody he had written to go with the chants and whale songs.

After the piece ended, Roy asked, "Well, what do you think?"

"That's beautiful, Roy, but it ain't country music. You can't play that; you'll lose your base."

"Larry, that's about as country as you can get. Sure, we call it folk music, but in my world, it's folks that make us a country, and folk music is **real** country music. Ancient people's chants- those were our ancestors' very first music. Then the wooden flute. Probably the first musical instrument ever made. It could mimic the wind and the sounds of birds. And come on Larry, whale songs are as real as music can get."

"That's all true, Roy, but you have made a great reputation singing what for forty years or more Nashville has dubbed country music. It's a sound of heartbreak stories with fiddles and harmonicas and guitars. It isn't flutes and chanting. Your fans don't come to hear someone play the flute."

The tension in Roy's room was getting stronger by the minute, and poor Wohali could do nothing but sit there on his blanket, looking back and forth between Roy and Larry like he was watching a tight tennis match.

"Okay, it isn't yodeling and heartbreaking love songs, but it's damned good music and as country as you can get. I'm not devoting a whole concert to flutes, chants, and whales, but adding in a bit of variety will not hurt the Weed's reputation. I believe Wohali adds a dimension to our band that distinguishes us from other country western music bands. You know damn well that the flute is mesmerizing. And tell me you don't find those ancient chants claiming a piece of your soul, along with the singing of whales."

"All right, Roy, I can tell that you will not be persuaded to forget about changing your mind. Let's see how it plays tonight."

The tension in the room dropped dramatically when Larry capitulated, and Wohali breathed fully for the first time in minutes.

"What were you thinking about for tonight's show? I mean, how do you want to introduce Wohali to the audience?" Now that he was resigned to Roy's new program, Larry smiled and said, "Welcome to the Weed's Wohali. We aren't always this confrontational."

Wohali was overwhelmed by the entire afternoon. A few hours ago, he was a street musician struggling to survive. Then, he saw this handsome man stop and drop a hundred-dollar bill onto his blanket, followed by the man spending a God-awful lot of money on a picture and things, and then this hotel scene and talk of being in a band. It was all a bit much. "What does this mean, being part of The Weeds?" he asked the room at large, not knowing who was who or to whom he should address his questions.

"Wohali," Roy answered, "The Weeds are a professional band making records and performing in concerts worldwide. You will travel with the band, stay in luxury hotels and eat in fancy restaurants. You'll have ladies throwing themselves at you every night after your performance on stage. I guess I should ask you if that is a lifestyle you could get used to for a year or so?"

"Can I bring my cat?" Wohali was serious, but he had a broad smile on his face and a look of disbelief in his eyes.

Larry picked up the answer. "Wohali, you can bring along anybody or anything you want. We only ask that you are sober and ready with your flute when it comes time to rehearse or perform."

"You," Wohali said, pointing to Larry, "mentioned a concert tonight. Am I expected to play?"

"Well, hell yes, we just had our rehearsal," Roy answered instead of Larry. "There is just one more little song I want you to listen to and play something proper as an introduction. We'll do that after our fearless leader goes and informs the band about its newest member."

40
SARAH SEEKS ROMANCE

As Peter and Sarah left the back room of the Pioneer Saloon, the elk picture was leaning against the wall. Peter summoned a staff member with instructions to hang it out front where everyone entering the establishment would see a Peroni hanging on the wall. He grinned and said, "It gives the place some class."

"Sarah, I would like you to have dinner with me at my home. I have an excellent chef who makes elk taste like the finest Black Angus beef in the world. But, until you've tasted his veal parmesan, you haven't lived. And I haven't even mentioned his Wiener Schnitzel. Oh my God, Sarah, you must let Andre make you Wiener Schnitzel. He has the makings in the refrigerator already for the stove. Please say yes."

"But Peter, you have this fabulous restaurant; why not eat here?"

"Yes, we try to serve the best possible meals, and our cooks do the best with whatever quality produce is available. However, cooking for crowds is not the same as cooking an individual meal where the chef can devote full attention to the preparation and food quality. It takes time to prepare extremely high-quality food, which is impossible to do in a restaurant where suppliers must be paid. Trust me, my chef at home will prepare a dinner like none you have ever tasted."

"Well, Peter, how can I refuse such an enticing invitation? You're on. Let's see how good this chef of yours is compared to, say, fine French cuisine. I've eaten some pretty fantastic meals in France."

"Thanks Sarah. You won't regret it, I promise."

Peter didn't live in Ketchum or even Sun Valley, but up the canyon away from the ski lifts, tourists, and commotion of communal living. From the outside, his house looked like a miniature version of the Sun Valley Lodge; large pine tree logs fitted together like an elegant European building you might see in the Swiss Alps. Big flat red flagstone rocks served as the walkway from the driveway to the broad railed steps leading to a covered, wide plank porch. Although missing the city gutters and sidewalk, his house had what realtors would call curb appeal by the bucket load.

If the outside looked like the smaller version of a ski lodge, the inside looked like something you would see in Architectural Digest. The outside looked like your typical rustic, high-priced mountain dwelling, but inside, you felt like you were entering a magnificent mansion on New York's Park Avenue. Starting with a parquet floor in a dazzling phi spiral interspersed with handwoven rugs and overhead sparkled some of Peroni's most spectacular chandeliers. You knew you were in the home of someone who wanted beauty. As seen in the White House in Washington, DC, the walls were covered with elegant fabric, and hanging on almost every wall was a Peroni painting. Beautifully sculptured Peroni furniture was arranged in pleasing formations, and at the far end rose a majestic two-story fireplace made of river rock with an opening large enough to accommodate a Shetland pony.

"Peter, this place is magnificent. And how on earth did you acquire so much of my work?"

"From the time I first saw you, Sarah, I felt like I was standing in the presence of someone special. It isn't just that you are one of the most beautiful people on the planet with the presence of an extraordinary person. Yet, you behave towards everyone with a common touch and pleasant demeanor. I wanted to own you, have you for myself, but of course, that was impossible, so I did the best next thing: I bought everything of yours I could find that would fit into my home. Since I am at least twenty years your senior, I didn't think it possible for a personal relationship, so I purchased the Peroni's I could own."

"Wow. Such a fantastic compliment. I did not know you felt that way."

"I hope I haven't frightened you off, but until you gave me that painting of an elk, I would have never presumed to ask you to have a private dinner in my home."

"Well, I'm glad you did, but I still want to experience that fantastic chef you talked about."

"I rarely entertain here. As you might have guessed, I enjoy privacy and seclusion, but I built the place to host private parties from time to time. The dining room feels too large for just the two of us, so I suggest we dine in the study. It's over here," he said, pointing towards a white, multifoil arch.

The study was another architectural dream with custom teak bookshelves and light brown sand-colored suede leather couches. A hand-carved wooden stand held an unabridged Webster dictionary standing next to an illuminated world globe, two feet in diameter, resting on a bronze tripod. A fine Berber carpet with a stunning fleur de lis design covered the floor, and at the wall opposite the door was another small, intimate fireplace. A small ornate Peroni table with two matching chairs was placed before the fireplace. The table was covered with a bright white tablecloth and two place settings. A wood fire crackled, sending sparks flying up the chimney.

Seeing the table and place settings, Sarah commented, "It looks like you were expecting company, Peter."

"After you consented to have dinner with me, I had my hostess call home and inform the maid so she could make the preparations. Dinner will be along in a few minutes. Can I fix you a drink to enjoy with the fire before then?"

"It would be a pleasure. This room is so comforting. I expect you spend a great deal of time in here reading."

"Yes, I find the room very restful. This place is my sanctuary away from the world. I'm glad you like it. What would you like to drink?"

"I would love a glass of red wine if that were available."

"Sarah, let me show you my wine cellar. I have a modest collection, but I try to select only the best."

Peter led the way through another multifoil arch; only this one was a dark brown arch with touches of red accents. He led the way down a wide rock circular stairway into a room that looked like it belonged in a Hollywood movie. The room was paneled in dark wood with massive overhead beams that reminded Sarah of similar beams at the bottom of a third-century courthouse in Germany. The beams were nearly black and two feet square. A small rosewood bar stood in front of several rows of wine bottles on wooden racks. In front of the bar sat two black leather overstuffed armchairs with end tables on either side.

"It looks like you spend some time down here, Peter. Is this your other refuge?"

"Well, it's quiet and a good place to dream, if you get my meaning."

Sarah gasped as she stared at a life-sized portrait of herself on the wall next to the stairway. In the photograph, Sarah was wearing a form-fitting white pantsuit, and it looked like she was about to enter a building. A breeze had teased her hair, almost covering one eye, appearing like a provocative pose. "Peter, what is this?"

"Well, Sarah, as I never dreamed that you would visit my humble home, I did the next best thing. I had a photographer friend of mine snap a picture of you one time. This cellar is where I come to dream."

Peter had always been courteous towards Sarah, yet she never dreamed he had this obsession with her.

"Oh my God, Peter, I'm afraid I may never live up to your expectations."

Hidden behind the wine racks, Peter searched for a particular red wine bottle so Sarah could not see his face, but his words were plain enough. "Don't worry about that, dear Sarah. You have already exceeded my greatest joy. Ah, here's the bottle I wanted. Let's go back upstairs and enjoy the fire while exploring this wine together. As I remember, it's extraordinary for a special person."

41
MADISON SQUARE GARDEN

The band was already backstage at the Garden when Roy walked in with Wohali. When they entered the room, everyone stopped what they were doing and stared at the short Indian. He wore a colorful serape with an Apache design woven into the threads. Wohali was nervous, but he still flashed a million-watt smile, showcasing his brilliant enamels.

"Greetings, everyone. I want you all to meet Wohali. As of tonight, he is the newest member of our band. He plays the flute. I'm sorry to spring this on you at the last second, but wait until you hear him play. Walking down Broadway today, I heard this sound that stopped me in my tracks. I found the musician and took him back to our hotel and worked on a couple of arrangements to open our show tonight. After that, Wohali, you get to sit and listen. If you find a song where you think you can contribute, by all means, join in the fun. We'll work out with the full band tomorrow and find places where you can contribute. So that everyone knows, I already discussed this new addition to our music with Larry. He thinks the band is moving too far away from country music with the whales and chanting, and now the flute. I agree it's more folk music, but dammit, folk music is country as far as I'm concerned. So, I agreed to see how the audience reacts and read the reviews before jamming this music down everyone's throats."

To everyone's surprise, Kathryn walked over to Wohali, and, at six feet tall, she made a striking picture with the short, smiling Indian. Then, grabbing him in her long arms, she gave him a gigantic hug and a welcoming kiss on the cheek. This scene broke the ice, and everyone made it a point to shake the man's hand and give him a warm welcome.

Showtime arrived, and the house lights dimmed, leaving only the exit and step lights glowing. Then, with the crowd quiet, a spotlight lit up the stage showing a small Indian man in a bright serape holding a flute sitting on a colorful blanket. Then, taking a deep breath, Wohali played, and the crowd was mesmerized by the soft, sweet melody. Backstage, the band members stood transfixed by the sounds while Larry stood off to the side with a broad grin as he saw the band's reaction to Wohali's flute.

After about a minute, a soft harmonica joined the flute, although the harmonica player was out of sight. Then a new spotlight illuminated another figure sitting on a stool. The two sounds played with the senses. The listeners felt like they were floating on a celestial cloud listening to angels sing, and then the aboriginal chanting started. The cadence perfectly matched the flute and harmonica, almost as though the chants were accompanying the music and not the other way around. In another minute, the chanting became muted, and the whales began singing. The whales sang and then paused. Then, the flute seemed to answer their call with a soft rift that talked back to the whales. The whales grew silent while the chanting seemed to float in the air on the flute's notes.

Kathryn sensed the mood and, feeling the rhythm, started strumming the big bass, which added a soft beat that prompted Jackson Wood, the drummer, to join in with his own smooth, pulsating brush strokes on the snares. Roy exchanged the harmonica for his acoustic guitar, and the music morphed into a new version of *A Brief Encounter*. As the opening song ended and *A Brief Encounter* began, the lights came on to show the entire band. Les Aranson began playing his baritone saxophone in a haunting counterpoint to the flute and guitar, and then the whole band joined in as the song reached its zenith, with Roy singing his heart out.

Roy switched guitars before the song ended and launched into a ringing version of *Chime Bells* while playing the Gibson. While the last high notes on the Gibson sounded, and with Roy's spine-tingling, rafter-raising voice signaling the end of their opening series, the entire Madison Square Garden erupted in a standing ovation lasting nearly five minutes. Backstage, Larry Perkins could only smile at his friend's success. Roy had nailed it. The flute was here to stay.

The concert went ahead with songs from various albums mixed in occasionally with some of Roy's music from Somewhere in Time, which Horace Walpole had rearranged for the entire band. Sometimes Wohali would add a haunting rift from his flute that seemed to have been planned from the beginning. As a whole, the concert may have been the best one ever performed by The Weeds.

Music critics couldn't find enough positive adverbs and adjectives to describe the performance the next day. Roy and The Weeds were used to excellent reviews, but the Garden concert seemed their zenith.

Back at their hotel, no one was surprised when Kathryn and Wohali seemed to find themselves wrapped in romance. Who would ever have guessed that the tall, gorgeous bass player would fall for a short little Indian who played the flute? No one was happier for the couple than Roy, who gazed wistfully at the pair while sipping on his Johnny Walker Red. Maybe one day, he would find his own true love.

Roy dreamed about romance and loving some woman. There was no shortage of ladies throwing themselves at him whenever he appeared in public, yet he rarely invited anyone to share his bed. Anita taught him to enjoy sex, and Roy had fond memories of his therapist, yet he couldn't just hop into bed with anyone. Roy had to have some deeper feelings for his companion before committing to spending a night together. There were moments when he wished otherwise, but something held him back. Perhaps it was his mother's warning to remain pure for his life's companion. Roy remembered how guilty he felt the first few times he made love with Anita, but he also remembered how quickly the guilt faded and how lustful he became. Perhaps he should relax and enjoy having sex more often.

With these thoughts, Roy excused himself and went to his room alone. Perhaps, next time some voluptuous woman threw herself at him, he would let himself succumb to her charms—next time.

42
PETER DRAKE

Sarah enjoyed Peter's company and attention and was flattered that he had such a crush on her. Maybe twenty years wasn't so much after all. Hell, she was half in love with a man she had never met ten years younger than herself. Romance with Roy was a fantasy. A dream. Who knew if there could ever be a relationship with a phantom? Hell, she wasn't married, had no genuine love interest, and was as horny as a beautiful young lady could ever get. Peter was here now, a real man who adored her beyond measure. Perhaps she should reconsider her actions and behavior. For the first time in a long time, she fantasized about making love again. Maybe the time had come.

Peter was handsome, wealthy, intelligent, and already in love with her. What more does a woman want or need? Sitting in front of the fireplace upstairs with Peter and sipping on a beautiful red wine, Sarah decided she would consent if Peter suggested going to bed. It was time to treat herself to sexual pleasure once again. Her romantic interludes were far too infrequent. Roy Dalton was a dream. Perhaps that was all he would ever be. Peter was a real, warm body, here and now. Maybe it was time to get real and stop dreaming.

Relaxed and comfortable in the study, Sarah enjoyed herself and felt almost disappointed when Peter's maid came in to announce that dinner was ready to be served. As Peter and Sarah moved from in front of the fire over to the intimate dining table, the maid held their chairs and unfolded their napkins. They were barely seated when she returned with two Royal Daulton salad plates heaped with Casseroles Et Claviers or exotic lobster salad. The salad hinted at a memorable dinner, just as Peter had promised.

The salad was followed by pea and mint soup served in a small bowl with cup handles on each side, allowing the soup to be drunk from the bowl rather than eaten with a spoon. Homemade crab cakes accompanied the soup.

"I know we should drink white wine with this seafood, but this red does the salad and soup justice. It seems to blend harmoniously. Don't you agree?" Peter seemed eager to please his guest and hoped to hear her approval.

Sarah had not thought about the wine, but it seemed perfectly matched to both the salad and soup. "You know, Peter, I think we pay too much attention to what the so-called experts say we should drink with our food. I believe this excellent red would go with almost any serving."

"I don't mean to brag, Sarah, but this wine is a unique selection of Cabernet from Chateau Lafite Rothschild. When I visited there five years ago, the current Rothschild manager told me the average age of their wines was 40 years. He offered to let me buy ten bottles of this Cabernet from one of their premier vintages. It was an emotional purchase, but one I have never regretted. This bottle is only the third one I've opened in the past five years."

"Oh, my God. I feel so honored. I knew it was exceptional from my very first sip. No wonder it pairs with almost any food." Sarah had a sparkle in her eyes, and it wasn't only the wine causing the warmth in her chest.

The maid cleared their soup and salad dishes and then brought a silver tray with two heated moist towels scented with lilac water. Peter felt it was necessary to explain. "I always like to freshen my lips and hands before beginning the main meal. It's become a sort of tradition. I hope you don't find it too strange."

"Why no," she responded. "It's a charming custom. Before I got my plane, I often traveled by foreign airline carriers, most of whom provide this service. I always looked forward to the towels."

Dinner was Cornish game hens cooked in a plum sauce served with buttered asparagus laced with melted Gouda cheese and a light, tasty balsamic vinaigrette. It was one of the most delicious meals Sarah had ever eaten.

"Well, Peter, your chef certainly knows how to cook. I loved my Cornish game hen, but I thought we were eating your fabulous Wiener Schnitzel?"

"Yes, I mentioned that back at the restaurant; however, when we arrived here, I discovered Andre had already begun prepping the hens, so I let it continue. I hope you aren't too disappointed. And this way, I get to bring you back for another dinner."

"No, I'm not disappointed in the least. You already know the meal was fabulous, and I look forward to trying the schnitzel some other time."

Andre had prepared Tiramisu for dessert, which the maid served with an aromatic coffee liqueur in Peroni crystal glasses.

"Oh, my Peter, this dessert is so rich and flavorful. And you keep surprising me with all the Peroni acquisitions you have made. These glasses are some of my favorite pieces."

Engaged in small talk, the couple sipped on the coffee liqueur for a few minutes, as each one felt the mounting tension building towards an even more eventful evening. After a few minutes, Peter suggested, "Let's move over to the couch in front of the fire and get comfortable. I have an excellent Grand Marnier for you to try. Then, I want to play one of my favorite romantic songs. I know you prefer classical music, as you're always jetting all over the world to operas, ballets, and concerts, but I have something very romantic I want you to hear."

Peter served the liqueur himself before selecting a long-playing LP that he placed on a Rega turntable. He carefully set the needle onto the beginning of a chosen track and then hurried to the couch, where he settled close to Sarah.

The room seemed to swell with the opening chords played on an acoustic guitar, and then Roy Dalton's famous voice began singing *A Brief Encounter*. When the song ended, Sarah was in tears.

Peter hurried over to the turntable with a worried look and stopped the music when the song ended. "Sarah, it's a love song; you shouldn't be crying. Did I do something wrong?"

"Oh, Peter. There is no way you could have known. Let me tell you a story." Sarah took a moment to compose herself before beginning.

"I fell in love with a young boy; we were both twelve years old. When he turned eighteen, he was drafted into the Army, and before he went to special training in Fort Belvoir, we got married. We were happy, in love, and ecstatic with each other. I went to work at Walter Reed Hospital to be near him during another part of his training before they shipped him over to Europe and the war."

"A few months later, I got the knock on my door by two uniformed men telling me my husband had been killed in the war. I was devastated."

Sitting by her side, Peter listened and wondered what this marriage had to do with the love song he had just played.

"I decided to return to my home in California to visit my parents. The train I was on stopped at a small mountain town in Idaho to take on water. I didn't know where we were, nor did I care. My face rested against the train window, my eyes were red, and my cheeks were blotchy red and swollen. Just as we were stopping, I saw a ragged farm boy standing by the side of the train tracks and leaning against a beautiful bay horse. The boy's pants were torn, he wore an old tattered straw hat with a bandana around his neck, his hands were bleeding, yet he had this great look of happiness on his face."

Sarah almost lost it as she took a few deep breaths to control her emotions. Peter sat in rapt attention, wondering where this story was heading. He wanted to reach over and comfort the lady, but felt compelled to sit still and listen.

"I barely had time to notice that his eyes were not smiling before something extraordinary happened. I suddenly felt myself inside of this boy, feeling his loneliness and sort of trapped desperation. I later learned his brothers were away in the Army, and his father was laid up with a broken hip. This eleven-year-old boy was running this ranch all alone. He had no chance to play with friends or enjoy any social life; all he knew was work from before sunrise until late after sundown every day of the week. He was trapped in a life of labor and despair. His only joy, the only happiness in his life, was watching the trains go by the ranch, dreaming about the beautiful life of those people riding along in comfort, drinking, eating, and laughing."

Sarah took a moment to take a few more breaths and grab some tissues from a handy box set on an end table. Of course, Peter still had no clue where this recitation was heading.

"While I was inside of this boy, he was inside of me at the same time. It was like, for just a moment, we traded souls. He knew my sorrow and unhappiness, and Peter, my God, this poor ragged boy, actually felt sorry for me. I could feel his deep empathy. I know it makes little sense, but we had a very brief soul encounter."

When she said those words, Peter started feeling like he had lost her for the evening, perhaps forever. However, something powerful in her voice and demeanor suggested there was still a lot more to come.

"I was very touched that a lonely, ragged boy could feel sorry for me, and when I had a chance, I hired a detective to find this little Idaho town and see if he could find out who the boy was. It was important to me that no one would know who I was, so the detective never let on that I existed. I sent the boy a small gift of money which he used to buy a cheap Gene Autry guitar, with which he taught himself to play and sing Gene Autry's songs. After learning about this guitar, I had my detective buy him a good guitar, and it turns out the electric Gibson Roy plays today is that guitar."

Sarah stopped for another breath, and by now, Peter knew Sarah was the lady on the train, the name of the album from which he had played the song earlier.

"For my next gift, I bought a silver pocket watch on which I had engraved his initials on the back, **R. D.** I figured he could not afford a watch of his own. I continued with gifts until he turned eighteen, and then I left him alone and went about my own life, which was taking off like a rocket. Designing, traveling, sketching, and then painting. Years went by and I forgot about the boy who was now a young man until I was in New York on an assignment when I spotted an album cover featured in the window of a music store on 5th Avenue. On the cover was the picture of a silver watch which showed the time, and also on the image was the back of the watch with the initials **R. D.** I knew that watch because I had bought it myself."

Even though his heart was aching, Peter found himself fascinated by the story. Here he was, sitting by the famous *Lady on the Train*. Her name and image were a mystery to millions of Roy Dalton fans worldwide, and here she sat next to him in his house.

"It was not until I entered that store that I found out what happened to young Roy Dalton. But, of course, that song you played was the song Roy wrote for me, hoping to discover who I was. Dear Peter, I was prepared to spend the night with you;

however, I'm afraid that won't be possible right now. Perhaps another time. I am thankful for your magnificent meal and kind attention. And now, if you would please see me home."

Peter was gracious and understanding. He marveled at his poor luck as he drove Sarah back to Ketchum. Damn. He almost had the women of his dreams in bed.

Sitting quietly by his side, Sarah wondered if she had made a big mistake. Oh well, she would know in a few extremely long days.

43
LOVE IN THE AIR

The Weeds were all in Roy's room, where they rehashed the evening's performance. The mood was euphoric; their laughter and joy were contagious, infecting everyone. No one was amazed when Kathryn seemed to monopolize Wohali. The tall bass player seemed to have found her soul mate as she continually hugged and kissed the shy Indian.

Everyone was happy to welcome Wohali into The Weeds, and when Roy looked deeply into the man's eyes, he could see that the relief at having found a home was almost more than Wohali could bear. While enjoying the administration from Kathryn, the tears were close to forming. Working and living as a street musician didn't allow for a healthy lifestyle.

The Weeds were celebrating, but their only drug was alcohol. Roy and Larry, their manager, made it clear from the beginning that no street drugs were allowed, ever. No exceptions. The band made up for the lack of coke or heroin by drinking copious quantities of wine, vodka, bourbon, and Roy's scotch. The participants got loaded and staggered off to their rooms (Kathryn took Wohali to her room) until only Larry and Roy remained.

After the room had cleared out, Roy addressed their manager. "Larry, I would appreciate it if you would do me a big favor?"

"Sure, Roy. I will admit that you were right about the flute. We'll rehearse tomorrow and put him in some other arrangements."

"No, that's not it. I want you to see that my parents get some of the best seats for our concert at Sun Valley."

"Hell Roy, that's a given. I've already talked with their coordinator and told her about your parents. I'll follow up and make damn sure she gives your parents the best seats in the house."

"Okay, thanks, Larry, but I have another huge favor to ask. I would like to see my horse, Jupiter, again, and I won't have time to visit Clifton. That would take a whole day. I want to hire a carrier to bring Jupiter to Sun Valley, but I want him treated with kid gloves. The old boy shows his age, and I want him happy."

"Hey, I know what that horse means to you, and I'll make sure we hire some professionals who know how to pamper thoroughbred racehorses. I'll take care to ensure they give Jupiter the same attention. What do you want to do with him in Sun Valley?"

"Have that coordinator lady you're talking to ask around for a good boarding place? From what I remember reading about Sun Valley, horses are a big part of the local lifestyle. The area has horse trails all over the valley, so the rich and famous can show off their horses and riding skills. I would like to have him as close to the venue as possible to spend more time with the old boy."

"Sure, Roy. First thing in the morning. I'll take care of it. Don't worry; we'll take good care of Jupiter."

Roy took another swallow of his scotch before asking his next question. "Do you think we will have a problem with Kathryn and Wohali?"

"I don't see why that should be a problem. As you know, Kathryn has been a big flirt, but as far as I know, she hasn't been serious with any of the other band members. So, there should be no jealously issues."

"That's good to hear. I haven't kept up with the personal lives of our band members since I came back from Australia and Hawaii. I've seen jealousy wreck more than one group of musicians."

"We have a pretty solid troupe, Roy. They all take their music seriously. I learned from Wohali that he makes his own flutes. His father started teaching him how to make flutes when he was just a young boy. This dedication is what I mean by serious musicians. They take their music seriously, and they all love the band."

"Okay, thanks Larry. I'm not sure how long I want to tour and live on the road. It's been fun and exciting, but those Aboriginals in Australia taught me a few things about living, and while entertaining people gives me a lot of pleasure, I feel like I'm missing out on other aspects of life."

"Well, hell, son, and don't take offense by the word son. We've had a great run. We've all made some serious money, and if you want to hang it up, you've earned the right to do what you want to do with your life. You don't owe the band anything. In fact, it's the other way around. We all owe you for giving us one hell of a great ride."

"Ah, you're just saying that cause it's true." Roy couldn't help but jibe at his business partner. "Let's pack it in, Larry. I'm bushed and ready to hit the sack. We'll pick it up tomorrow and work Wohali into some more pieces."

"Oh, Larry. One more favor. I bought some art objects I need you to take care of for me." Then Roy explained his purchases and the need to make the payment and supply shipping instructions.

"Sure, no problem. Goodnight Roy. See you tomorrow."

After Larry let himself out, Roy went into the bedroom and flopped down on the bed, fully clothed. Seeing Kathryn making out with Wohali reminded him of Anita and how much he enjoyed having sex with the energetic Aussie. For perhaps the first time in a long time, Roy felt lonely. He hadn't felt this way for years, and now his loneliness seemed to have returned. Strange seeing two other people enjoy each other should evoke feelings of loneliness, but a lonely life was his chosen life. Maybe realizing this was behind his remarks to Larry about getting on in life. Perhaps he was seeking his own mate. Well, hell, it was about time he found a woman to share his bed. There was certainly no lack of opportunity. Maybe tomorrow.

44
GIRL'S NIGHT OUT

The day after her dinner with Peter, Sarah called Arlene.

"Hi, this is Arlene."

"Arlene, this is Sarah. How about meeting me at the Pioneer for lunch?"

"You sound serious. Is there a problem?"

"No. I don't think so. Maybe. I could have made a mistake. I don't know. I just want to talk with somebody I can trust, and you're the one."

"Sure. I'll be happy to meet you. What time?"

"It's Saturday, and the place will be jammed. So, let's try for twelve-thirty." Sarah had forgotten her reserved table promised always to be free.

"Okay, darling Sarah. See you at twelve-thirty. Do I need to bring anything?" It wasn't clear what Arlene had in mind with the question. The inquiry made little sense to Sarah.

"Just your lovely, beautiful self." Then Sarah immediately forgot about the question; her mind was racing, figuring out how much to tell her friend.

When Sarah arrived at the Pioneer Saloon, Arlene sat on a bench outside on the sidewalk. It was a beautiful sunny day, and the air was clear and sparkling. You could see forever, as the song proclaimed.

The two ladies hugged each other in greeting before venturing inside. Neither one felt the need to say anything.

A blond twenty-something hostess with hair that hung down to her waist (one of the ski bums who moonlighted during the summer months) greeted the two ladies by the check-in stand. An expert seamstress had tailored the silky red hostess dress she wore to display her taut, firm body. "Are you ladies joining us for lunch or just cocktails?"

"We're here for lunch when a table opens up. The name is Peroni, Sarah Peroni."

"Oh, Ms. Peroni, your table is waiting. Just follow me, please."

Arlene gave Sarah a look that said, *"What's this?"*

Sarah shrugged her shoulders in a *"how the hell do I know"* sort of move, and then she remembered. Is there really a table reserved for her whenever she arrives? Last night, she thought Peter was making a joke. It never occurred to her that such an extravagant gesture was made in earnest. Slightly embarrassed and self-conscious, Sarah followed the hostess, with Arlene close behind.

Sure enough, the hostess led them back to the private room, and there in the corner was a table set for two with a wooden placard announcing, THIS TABLE IS RESERVED FOR SARAH PERONI. Then, the hostess pulled out a chair for Sarah while remarking, "Everything is on the house, Ms. Peroni. I'll send your server in right away."

Seeing the placard, Arlene had to comment. "My God, Sarah, I guess we should talk. What did you do last night to deserve this treatment?"

After the hostess left, Sarah said, "Well, I didn't get laid, if that's what you mean."

With a wry grin, Arlene said, "Yeah, that's what I meant."

"Well, it's like this," Sarah started, but the server appeared, and she had to stop. "I'd like a bottle of your best Cabernet," Sarah ordered, and then with a sly grin of her own, she looked at Arlene and said, "And what do you want, Arlene?"

Having been taken in by the question and grin, Arlene sputtered, "I'll have the same," she managed, and then they both burst out laughing.

The poor server girl stood there trying to decide what to do, listening to these two minor celebrities laughing. Finally, Sarah composed herself enough to tell the server, "One bottle will do, for starters. Just bring two glasses, please."

"As you were saying, dear heart, before we were so rudely interrupted," Arlene started the conversation again, having regained her composure.

"So," Sarah began, and told Arlene all about her evening with Peter Drake and her insistence on being taken home after listening to Roy Dalton. "I was going to go to bed with him Arlene, and then he played that damn song. How could I be such an idiot? I have never even met the damn singer. Well, not in person," she added, thinking that perhaps that brief encounter by the railroad tracks counted as a meeting.

Arlene looked at her friend and said, "I know how emotional you are about that song and your long-ago encounter with that strange little boy on the side of the railroad tracks. Still, if old Peter wanted to ride my skinny bones, I sure as hell wouldn't turn him down."

"Come on, Arlene. Your bones aren't all that skinny, and I don't believe for one second you haven't spent at least one night camped out at the Drake mansion."

"Well, it was twice and a long time ago. I sure as hell didn't get a table always reserved for me, plus everything on the house. What did you do for such a splendid reward?"

"Honestly, Arlene, all I did was give him that painting of the elk I did with you up at the lake. He claimed the lake is one of his favorite places in the world. He has his own cabin someplace up there. I told him that with all the dead animals he has hanging on the walls of this dump, he needed something alive."

"Take you home and seduce you. It sounds like an excuse to do what he has always wanted to do, anyway. God, I wish it had been me."

"Well, he almost succeeded. Part of me wishes he hadn't played that music. I haven't made love with a man for such a long time. I'm almost afraid to try it again."

"Oh, I don't think you fear making love, Sarah. I say give ole Peter another chance. I can tell you, darling, he ain't all that bad in bed. However, don't fall in love with the man. He loves himself too much to accept a rival."

"Arlene, such a cruel thing to say. He acted like a perfect gentleman."

"I never said he couldn't be charming, pleasant, and entertaining. He loves to hold court. But, and I'm only guessing, he wouldn't take too kindly to a rival for his affections. Bowing down to the altar of Peter Drake every day could get wearying. Why do you think I stopped seeing him?"

"Hell, Arlene, I didn't know you ever dated the man. You never told me."

"Yeah, it was a long time ago, probably before you moved to Ketchum. Anyway, if you get the chance, go screw his brains out, but don't take him seriously."

"Okay, thanks, I guess. Although I will say, Arlene, he served me the best damn wine I've ever tasted. So, let's order something decadent and expensive. Maybe I'll invite him up to my place next time."

The girls both ordered prime rib, baked potato, and Caesar salad. Between bites, Sarah told Arlene about the forthcoming concert.

"I've been in touch with a man named Larry Perkins. He's the business manager for The Weeds. Larry asked me to make sure I get front row seats for Roy's parents for both nights. Also, he wants me to help him get Roy's horse, Jupiter, up here to Ketchum. Roy wants to see his horse and doesn't have the time to go to Clifton. Got any ideas?"

"Your good buddy Peter Drake has a heated, air-conditioned horse van he uses to transport his horses. I'll bet for a front-row seat he might even let you borrow his van." Arlene couldn't keep the wicked smile off her face as her eyes lit up just thinking about the scene with Sarah begging Peter for his van.

"Well, Peter already has front row seats, right beside you and me, although I think I'll seat him next to you just because you're so mean."

"We've already played grab-ass; it's your turn. Besides, putting me between you two lovers would be just plain cruel."

"Our venue seats 5244 people," Sarah explained, "and we can squeeze in another fifty as ushers and bouncers. Our contract with The Weeds gives the band 50 comp seats, and we get 50 seats. These seats do not count against the house receipts. I've got five seats with two left after you, Peter, and myself. I don't have anyone in particular to invite for a free concert. You are welcome to the tickets if you can use them."

"What about those ushers and bouncers? Don't they need tickets?" Arlene seemed confused.

"No. Those tickets come under the same category as the lighting technicians, sound technicians, and stagehands. They don't need tickets. Instead, they'll be wearing badges."

"Oh, well then. Since you're treating me to this swell lunch, the least I can do is take those two extra tickets off your hands. One less thing to distract you from paying attention to Peter." Arlene was having fun and couldn't keep the grin from her face.

"Just you wait, dear friend. I'll think of something to make you pay for your snide remarks."

45
CAROLE

The Weeds had two more stops before appearing in Sun Valley. After playing at the Garden, they headed to Dallas for one night and two nights in Seattle. On the plane to Dallas, Kathryn and Wohali sat together, nuzzling each other like they had not known love in a long time. As always, Roy sat in the back alone, trying to work on a new song. The loving couple made little noise, but Roy had difficulty concentrating on his music. Occasionally glancing at the pair, he thought about what he was missing. Over their years of traveling the world, he had every opportunity to score one or several band groupies at each stop, yet he almost always skipped out, leaving the girls shouting his name. Well, by damn, it was time to get laid again as visions of the naked Anita flooded his brain. *Now that was some fantastic sex.* Why not have some more fun while he could? Maybe he would find his own true love.

For the moment, Sun Valley was not even in his mind, and he did not know if the lady in his brief encounter still existed or if she had remarried and had a passel of kids. There had been no communication since he turned eighteen, and there had been no response to either of the albums that featured her. Indeed, if she still existed and was aware of him, she would have made contact by now if she wanted to. He figured she was ten or twelve years his senior, but hell, age was just a number. In the end, he decided their encounter meant much more to him than it did to her. Perhaps in her sorrow, she forgot about the ragged boy by the railroad tracks before the steam engine had even been filled with water. Yes, it was time to let go of the dream and find some girl willing to share his bed and perhaps his life.

The Dallas concert took off with the same opening used at the Garden, Wohali playing his flute on a rug in a spotlight and Kathryn coming in a few bars later with her bass. Dallas country music fans were boisterous, loud, and appreciative of the music offered by The Weeds, and Kathryn seemed to glow on stage. She looked incredibly alluring in a hip-hugging white pantsuit with her pony-tailed black hair swishing around and hiding her face from time to time.

The concert built up in momentum, with Roy's yodeling, Arlo's fiddle playing, Ted Balls' trumpet, and a blistering solo by Jackson Wood with his drums. They slowed it down just a notch with a romantic song featuring Les Aranson on the sax before climaxing with a musical number from their first album that built into a crescendo with everybody playing and singing. The band did three encore numbers because the audience refused to let them leave the stage. Although they had not planned on performing *Chime Bells* for this concert, Roy relented and finished the night with one of his trademark songs that left the audience in a complete uproar.

As the band escaped the concert auditorium, a statuesque blond caught Roy's eye. The lady was almost six feet tall, with an eye-catching figure and a full-on number ten face. Their eyes met briefly, and the woman favored Roy with a dazzling smile while he and the band were hustled out of the building and into waiting limousines.

Back at their hotel, the band met in Roy's suite for a nightcap and to revel in the success of another concert. Traditionally, the double doors to the suite were left open, allowing groupies to come in and mingle with the band members. As the party progressed, the beautiful blond lady walked in and up to Roy and, to Roy's surprise, planted an enthusiastic kiss on his lips.

After his first shock, Roy kissed her back with equal passion. Something about the lady excited Roy, a feeling he had rarely experienced since the days in southern Utah with Anita. After exchanging kisses, Roy asked her name.

"I'm Carole, with and e," she said in a husky, adrenaline-driven voice.

"Well, Carole with and e, let's go find someplace to sit down and get acquainted."

The band members did not do drugs other than cigarettes and alcohol, so Roy asked Carole what she would like to drink.

"Could I have a gin and tonic with some lime juice?" she asked.

"Most certainly," Roy answered. "Let me find a bartender."

One of the hotel's off-duty bartenders usually offered to tend bar for the visiting bands to associate with the band members and load up on free drinks and food, not to mention that the groupies who were unsuccessful in snagging a band member could be persuaded to favor the local help.

Roy and Carole found a quiet corner with a love seat and were promptly served their drinks. Scotch on the rocks for Roy and a gin and tonic for the lady.

After a couple of minutes of friendly conversation about items that didn't interest either person, Carole took the lead and turned side-wise to lie in Roy's arms. Her loose-fitting top exposed most of her right breast, causing Roy to get an erection. As their kissing and making out became more adventuresome, Roy stood, pulled Carole to her feet, and searched for an unoccupied bedroom. It wasn't unusual for two or more band members to share a bed and companions, but Roy wanted Carole all for himself.

Finding an unoccupied bedroom in his suite proved to be difficult, so Roy went down the hotel hall with Carole and looked for an unoccupied room of another band member.

Every room in this hotel wing belonged to the band, and every door was open. The third room they checked proved to be empty of guests. With Carole locked in his arms, Roy found a room, and the couple stumbled into it. Roy quickly shut the door. The pair at once began shedding each other's clothes, and in seconds, both were naked. Roy couldn't believe his luck. Carole had a magnificent body, and poor Roy couldn't wait to begin serious foreplay as he admired the statuesque blond.

Just as Roy was about to throw Carole on the bed, she held up a hand against Roy's chest and said, "Gimme just a minute, okay?" She slipped into the bathroom, clutching a tiny purse Roy had not noticed before.

Roy assumed the lady needed to respond to a call of nature, so he flopped down on the bed and tried to ignore his throbbing penis as he waited for her to return. She was gone only a couple of minutes before returning with glazed eyes.

"Here," she said, handing Roy a small red pill. "This makes sex so much better."

"What is it?" Roy asked.

"I don't know. All I know is that with one of these, I can go all night."

"I'm sorry," Roy said. "I put nothing in my body unless I know what it is and what it does to my health."

"Oh, don't be silly," she said, rubbing herself against his swollen penis. "It's harmless. All it does is make the sex last forever."

"It's no good, Carole. You have a fantastic body and are undoubtedly a very accomplished sex partner. I would love to have you all night, but I will not take your pill. Perhaps you had better leave."

"What? You're throwing me out just because I want to share an experience with you?"

"No, I'm leaving. You can stay here. I'm sorry. You will never know how sad I am. Damn, but I was so looking forward to tonight."

Roy got up and pulled on his pants. Then, grabbing his other clothes, he left the room to look for someplace to crash where he could be alone.

46
FRUSTRATION

Sarah did not know what Roy was doing down in Dallas. She barely knew that The Weeds were playing in Texas. So, while Roy, down in Dallas, was tossing and churning in frustration in an unoccupied bed he found, Sarah was thrashing around in her bed, frustrated that she had not slept with Peter. For weeks, or perhaps months, sex had rarely been on her mind, and now she felt like a horny teenager. Oh well, thank God for vibrators. Self-gratification was a hell of a lot better than no gratification at all. *Peter, where are you when I want you?*

The trouble with being rich and famous is that when you hit a dry spell and the opportunities for relaxation and pleasure are limited, how can you possibly complain to someone about your boring, empty life when you can have almost anything in the world? Sarah had offers for her services as a decorator from around the world, but the thought of spending her time trying to make some other wealthy people happy with their houses or belongings no longer pushed any of her buttons. Instead, she wandered around her studio and admired her paintings, but couldn't find the motivation to splash paint on a new canvas. Instead, she thought of calling Arlene, but she felt rather stupid after the last exchange with her only real friend. Hell, she should have known that Arlene, who had the morals of an alley cat always in heat, would have slept with Peter and probably every other available man in town, married or not.

Down in Texas, Roy didn't have it any better. His sleep was interrupted by images of a naked Anita and Carole teasing him into bed, only to wake up every time their advances reached a certain point. Unable to get either woman in his dreams to complete a succubus sexual transaction, Roy constantly woke up just as they were about to make love. He finally gave up and went back to his room, where he had a desk and some paper. Maybe he could write a song about unrequited love. No, that was love not returned, wasn't it? What do you call it when your sleep doesn't let you make love to another woman? Whatever happened to the damned succubus? Weren't they supposed to make love with you in your sleep? Hell, he could never count all the wet dreams he had as a boy growing up in Clifton. Every time he saw a sexy woman around town, his thoughts went wild, along with his wet dreams. Funny, though, his succubus never looked like any of the women in town that provoked his fantasy.

Sarah decided to take off for Paris. She had not been in France for almost a year, and the Parisian men were easy to get into bed. She wouldn't have to worry about her reputation or sleeping with one of her friend's former lovers. Her pilot would not be happy to be aroused by an early morning telephone call, but Sarah knew he loved flying into Paris and would not have any trouble entertaining himself.

Two couples were sleeping in Roy's bed, but they were too exhausted to be bothered by his desk lamp as he started working on a new song about unrequited love. Damn, if only Carole had not had those freaking pills, he could have screwed his brains out. Oh well, maybe this song would offer some solace. Everything else faded into the background when he got into a rhythm of writing new material. If the song worked out, he might have to give Carole a pass for disappointing him. Musicians took inspiration from what they had to work with, even if it was only frustration.

As she was winging her way across the Atlantic, Sarah remembered a request for decorating services from a Russian mobster living in Paris. He had a villa outside of Paris and wanted Sarah to redecorate the entire estate. She didn't know he was a mobster, but he was not a diplomat, and honest Russians didn't gain the fortune needed to purchase French villas. But, anyway, it didn't matter. She could take a quick look at the project and perhaps pay for her Parisian trip. If Paris proved to be disappointing otherwise, she still had her vibrator.

When the sleeping couples woke up and left Roy's room, he finished his song about unrequited love. Maybe he would play it later and see how it sounded, but now he had to shower and get ready for their flight to Seattle. They were going to play two concerts there before heading to Sun Valley. As he was packing his suitcases for the plane, Roy couldn't help but think about seeing his horse and parents. It had been a long time since he had visited his hometown, and a feeling of nostalgia hit him hard. Old Jupiter had been such a faithful companion throughout his youth. And his parents had given their children everything the poor struggling couple could afford. His mom had nursed him through childhood diseases and the minor injuries suffered on the ranch. His father had slaved to support his family, and both parents had sacrificed their own pleasures for their children. He owed them for his life and the opportunities they had provided. Maybe he could do more than he already had to help make their lives more manageable. Although knowing his parent's pride, it might be a challenge to get them to accept more of his help.

When Sarah got to Paris, she discovered that her Russian mobster, if that was his background, had left France for a few weeks and would not be available to show her his wishes for a new look in his villa. Instead, she found her room at the Ritz lonely and disappointed. It was luxurious enough, with plenty of amenities to make anyone happy, but it seemed too empty. When she visited the bar, hoping to be picked up by some handsome playboy out for an evening of sport, the whole scene seemed too shabby. Too seedy. The hotel bar and lobby were lavishly decorated, but Sarah couldn't help herself. Everywhere she looked, there were noticeable changes to be made that could make the place seem more friendly.

My God, she flew 5000 miles to get laid and couldn't find anyone she wanted to sleep with, and all she could do was sit in her seat redecorating the bar. There were plenty of men giving her the eye. All she had to do was nod her head, and they would be at her table in a heartbeat. It just seemed so artificial. Yet, isn't that why she flew five thousand miles? She was here, and now she couldn't pull the trigger. Maybe she was doomed to be an old maid. If being rich and beautiful weren't enough to find someone to screw, perhaps she should find a nunnery. Maybe Jesus would have her for a bride?

Sarah almost went to bed with Peter. Still, in thinking about going to bed with Peter while drinking a Tanqueray and tonic, the gift of a reserved table and complimentary meals almost seemed like a bribe. Although she had not gone to bed with him and had given him a valuable gift, she still felt like a whore. Even Arlene suspected she had slept with him, and indeed, everyone who worked at the Pioneer Saloon thought the same thing. And by now, practically everybody in Ketchum thought the same thing.

Sitting here in a Paris bar hoping to get lucky was the last straw. So, what was the matter with her? My God, getting laid by some stranger was no big deal, was it? Sarah, sitting alone at a table and drinking a cocktail, caught a glance of herself in one of the mirrors strategically placed around the room. It was such a lonely sight. Part of her wanted to sit and weep, but another part caught the image and thought it would make a great painting, a scene called loneliness.

It was time to forget Paris and head back home. Since practically everybody who knew her in Sun Valley assumed she was sleeping with Peter, maybe she should just screw the guy. It wasn't like anyone would think less of her, and she would at least not be so damn horny.

As the band members boarded the plane for Washington, Roy couldn't help but see the satisfied looks on their faces. He could see the inquiring eyes they gave him, wondering if their leader had a great evening as well? Several had seen him with the delectable Carole and suspected that he had enjoyed himself as they had. Oh well, *let them wonder*. Seattle might be different. Maybe he could find a Carole without the pills to make sex last forever. It never hurt to dream.

47
SEATTLE

Besides being home to some of the finest coffee globally, Seattle has a reputation for enjoying good, lively music. Ray Charles moved there from Florida, and Kenny G was born there. Jimi Hendrix was from Seattle, along with a host of several reputable bands and lead singers. Playing Seattle was not like most other cities, even though Roy always found the audiences well behaved and respectful. Still, he worried a little about how they would take to whale songs and a flute. While Roy did not plan on another concert in Seattle after this run, aggravating the local audience would still not be wise.

Larry may have been thinking the same thoughts as he made his way back to Roy's luxurious lounge in the plane's rear.

"What are your thoughts about the musical selection for Seattle? Do you think they are ready for whale songs?" Larry asked as he sat down next to Roy.

"Well, they have the Seattle Aquarium, home to several fish species, although I don't believe they have a whale or a shark tank. At least, they didn't on my last visit. The aquarium is popular, but I'm not sure about the chanting and whale songs. Maybe just one number. What do you think?"

"I don't know, Roy. Maybe just Wohali's flute and a little chanting. They love wild music, but I'm not sure they're ready for whale songs."

Roy continued, "It isn't like we don't have enough material for both concerts, including the encores. We don't need the whales, although I love to hear them sing. So let's play it by ear. I want to have the tracks available, but we may not use them for this concert."

"Okay, but you should know that our lighting guys have done some magnificent scenes with pictures of whales swimming and breaching. Projected on the scrims, it gives the whale songs an ethereal quality. I'm not crazy about it, but maybe we do one piece the first night to see how it plays. If the audience likes it, we may do two the following night. What do you say?"

"Sure, Larry. That sounds good. Have the lighting guys show me their clips tonight so I can get a feel for the effect."

Roy leaned back and put his feet up, signaling the conference was over. Larry headed back towards the front to talk with the lighting guys and left Roy alone.

Not that he didn't enjoy performing or making music. It just felt like something was missing in his life. He had pretty much decided to leave the band after San Francisco. These two concerts were in Seattle, two in Sun Valley, and one in San Francisco. After that, the band would probably dissolve, which wouldn't be all bad. They had been making music for over ten years, including the gigs in high school, and Roy was just tired.

It was partly all the travel and living in hotels. Roy wanted a place of his own to relax for a few months and then maybe hit it again. He wanted someplace. He wanted someone. He wanted something. God, he didn't know what he wanted, but he wanted out. At least, for now. What to tell the band, and when? They probably sensed that he needed some time off, and it may not be that big a deal. Hell, they all had more money than they needed, except for perhaps Wohali. Well, he would make sure Wohali was taken care of, although Kathryn may already have solved that problem.

Seattle's outdoor venue was huge, seating over eighty thousand. The front crew had done a marvelous job setting up the speakers and lighting. It took almost two weeks to get the sound right so everyone in the audience could experience quality sound. Lighting technology has come a long way with laser lights, and each concert got a little more sophisticated.

Roy went with the lighting guys to check out the new light show and preview the whale scene. The stadium was still crawling, with men making last-minute adjustments to the sound. Getting the sound right was always the most significant challenge and running power cables around so they didn't pose a tripping hazard was almost as tricky.

While Roy was on stage waiting for the light show to check out the whale scene, an angry lady who assumed he was a member of the setup crew accosted him.

The large, heavyset woman wore a big mad on her ruddy face as she yelled at Roy, "You men need to be more careful! I almost got electrocuted by these damn cables running all over the place."

"What's the problem, madam?" Roy asked as politely as possible.

"Why just now, I walked by that panel," she said, pointing to the main power cable interface panel, "and sparks flew out, nearly singeing my hair."

Roy walked over to the panel in question. "You mean this panel?" he asked and pointed to the main power junction box.

"Yes, that's the one. With all these cables, it's a wonder no one has been killed with all the power you're using." The lady was overwrought about something, and Roy couldn't figure out the problem.

Confused because he could see nothing wrong, Roy said, "Madam, please come over here and show me the problem you have experienced."

"I will not come over there and get electrocuted," she scolded as though addressing some juvenile boy.

"May I ask what you are doing here, then?" Roy asked, still trying to be polite.

"I am the special events coordinator for Seattle, and this concert is my responsibility to see that it is safe for our citizens."

At that moment, one of the lighting technicians walked over and said, "Okay, Roy. We're ready to preview the whale scene. Just watch."

As he spoke, a scrim dropped to the middle of the stage, and whales could be seen swimming in the ocean and jumping out of the water. But, since the scrim was not fastened at the bottom, it undulated in the air, giving the scene an unearthly feeling.

Roy thought it was beautiful and thought he might use it after all. The large abusive woman charged over, "If you are the man responsible for this mess, I want to report you to the fire marshal. What is your name? We can't have people electrocuted who attend our concerts."

The electrician who had contacted Roy saw what was happening and intervened. "Lady, the light you saw a minute ago was laser light we are using for our production. No sparks were flying. That power junction box does not yet have any power."

"Well, you should be more careful. I'm still going to report this incident to the fire marshal."

"Please do, madam," the technician responded. "I'd love to meet the man. I've been trying to get in touch with him all week, but he seems to be preoccupied. So far, he hasn't seemed too worried about what we're doing here. And if I might be so bold, you don't have any business being here. This venue is a work area, and no unauthorized people are allowed on the set while undergoing prep work. Please leave."

"Listen, young man, I am responsible for this venue and have every right to be here," she screamed.

"Ma'am, if you would check our contract, you will find that until we are ready for an inspection, which should be in about two hours, and we invite the city representative to inspect our work, no one not authorized by me is allowed on the set. Please leave. You are not invited, you are intruding on our work, and you are a rude, abusive person who is unwelcome here."

The lady swished her mumu and left in a huff.

Roy watched her leave and then thanked the technician, but he didn't fail to let the man know he appreciated the light show and his handling of the situation with the woman from Seattle.

They included a whale song as part of the program that night, and the Seattle audience lapped it up. The following night, Roy included two whale songs with a lot of Wohali's flute accompaniment. The local reviews could not have been better. With every performance, the band seemed to get a little more respect. They had a versatile show, including a sexy lady on the bass with a songbird voice, a world-class pianist, and an alto saxophone that melted your heart. With the drums and guitars and Roy's singing, The Weeds played a three-hour concert that flew by in minutes. People couldn't stop talking about what a great experience it was to attend one of their concerts. The band was on top of the world and headed for Sun Valley, Idaho.

48
JUPITER

When the band landed at the Sun Valley airport, Roy immediately inquired about his horse. A representative of the concert committee met the band's plane and ushered everyone into waiting limousines for the ride to the Sun Valley Lodge. Marlene, their hostess, knew nothing about a horse but assured Roy that someone at the Lodge could answer his question.

A beautiful brunette with a dazzling smile met the limousines and ushered everyone into the lodge, where they were provided with their room assignments. Larry wasted no time getting on the telephone to inquire about Roy's horse, Jupiter. He found the horse was stabled only about a half-mile away in a private stable with access to a large pasture. Roy was given directions and went to see his horse without visiting his room.

Being members of the arts committee, Sarah and Arlene were informed about the plane landing, and Sarah suspected that Roy's first visit would be to his horse. With Arlene along to keep her company, Sarah parked across the street from Peter's stable, where Jupiter was housed and waited for Roy to show up. Jupiter was enjoying the pasture after being cooped up in the horse trailer yesterday and watching the beautiful horse brought back to Sarah all the memories of that long-ago experience. Arlene watched her friend tear up as she watched the horse and knew the reason. She kept quiet and let her friend relive the experience alone.

Roy's limousine stopped by the stable, and Roy saw Jupiter eating grass in the pasture. The ladies watched a tall, handsome man exit the limo and head over to the field. Arlene nudged Sarah with her elbow. "Oh my God, the man is a solid 10. You've got to do him, Sarah, so I can have the experience vicariously."

Roy whistled, and Jupiter raised his head. Spotting Roy, the horse took off in a gallop as Roy entered the field. Sarah watched the reunion between horse and man with a lump in her throat. Jupiter nearly knocked Roy off his feet as he charged toward his owner and best friend. Jupiter nuzzled Roy with his head and stamped his feet in happiness until Roy buried his head in Jupiter's mane and whispered into the horse's ear. Even across the street, Sarah and Arlene could see the tears in Roy's eyes as he threw his arms around the big fellow's neck and kissed his forehead.

"Go over and introduce yourself, Sarah," Arlene suggested. She could no longer see the tears in Sarah's eyes for the tears in her own.

"No. I can't. Not like this. It wouldn't be fair to spoil their reunion. I'll wait until later. Maybe tonight. I'll invite him to dinner, or perhaps for drinks, or something. Hell, Arlene, he doesn't even know who I am. To Roy, I'm just another woman hitting on him. Although it is special, watching Roy and Jupiter. God, but I'm bawling like a baby. I did not know it would be so emotional. I can still see his eyes as they touched mine."

"You can't imagine, Arlene, what it felt like to have a boy in ragged pants and bloody hands with a big smile of happiness on his face reach in and grab my soul, feel my pain, understand my loneliness while I felt his loneliness, his feeling of being trapped in a life of poverty. That big smile of happiness on his face never reached his eyes. Only the lonely, desperate part lived there. I think that prompted the gifts, as I hoped to end his misery. It looks like I succeeded. On second thought, dear friend, I may not want to meet him. He might be embarrassed to be confronted with the lady who bought him a guitar."

"Oh God, Sarah. Get a grip. Of course, it's an emotional experience for all three of you. Look how that horse loves the man and vice versa. It's bound to bring back memories, but remember all the songs and albums he made searching for you. Meet with him. You just have to."

Roy spent a good hour with Jupiter playing chase. He chased Jupiter, then turned around and started running so Jupiter would chase him. It's a game you often see dogs play and one Roy and Jupiter used to play whenever their chores permitted. Seeing the two old friends playing with each other, Sarah and Arlene watched in awe and pleasure. Although the scene was rural and peaceful, both gals often had tears in their eyes mixed with smiles of joy at seeing the man and horse enjoying themselves.

Sarah started the car and drove away to leave the man and horse alone. Roy saw the ladies parked in the car across the street but thought nothing of their presence. There was no reason for them to know who he was or what he was doing. As far as he was concerned, they were just two ladies watching a beautiful horse.

"I don't know, Arlene," Sarah said as they drove away. "I'm a coward when it comes to this kind of thing. That's one of the reasons I never wanted him to know my name. I didn't want him to feel obligated to anyone."

"Well, dear friend, we will have to get you two together."

49
TOGETHER AGAIN

After spending time with Jupiter, Roy had the limousine take him back to the Sun Valley Lodge, where his parents were staying. His parents had left to visit The Lamp Lighter, where their friends from Clifton were staying. It was an upscale motel built in the late 40s and featured a glass-enclosed swimming pool. The Daltons were enjoying the pool with their friends and were visible from the parking area when Roy's limousine drove into the large courtyard. The motel residents were used to seeing limousines around town, but one never stopped at The Lamp Lighter. This motel was not on the distinguished VIP guest list of places to stay in Ketchum.

It was a pleasant summer afternoon, and the pool was being enjoyed by several people who gawked at the limousine as it drove into the motel yard. Many motel guests were there for the Weed's concert, so Roy was recognized as soon as he stepped out of the car. Teenage girls started screaming and jumping for joy just spotting their fantasy man in real life. Roy waved at the girls and then spotted his parents and went into the motel's lobby which accessed the pool.

Mom and Dad, dripping wet, met their son in the lobby and, after everyone around, including the screaming girls, met the star, his parents left to change out of wet suits so they could have a proper reunion back at the Lodge.

Back in their room at the Lodge, Mother Dalton had tears as she hugged her handsome, celebrated son, and Roy's father ducked his head to hide his teary eyes. Mrs. Dalton brought her son up to date on all the happenings in Clifton, including a description of Frann's pregnancy and an expected delivery date, which was imminent. Marlow sent his best wishes, and Roy's mom had a letter for Roy from Arnold, who had a job in Utah working for the State. Christine, Roy's big sister who was also married and living in Colorado, had sent a letter to her parents for Roy.

It had been years since Roy last visited Clifton, and it took a long time for him to bring his parents up to date on his accident and subsequent recovery. His parents sat in awe as he described the Aborigines and their lifestyle. For simple country folk, it was inconceivable that a society of human beings could exist for ten thousand years without toilet paper. They were thrilled with his stories about the whales, and of course, they were familiar with all of his music, including the whale songs.

By the time they were through catching up with the news, it was getting dark and dinner time. People at the Sun Valley Lodge told Roy that Mr. Peter Drake, who owned the Pioneer Saloon, was the one who let Jupiter share his stable and pasture with his own two horses. Roy wanted to stop by and offer his thanks and inquire about payment and perhaps eat dinner there if his parents approved. While his parents were getting ready for dinner, Roy looked at the Sun Valley brochures and relived his childhood fantasy about this magical place.

Roy led his parents out to the limousine to ride downtown to the Pioneer Saloon. Ketchum's Main Street looked like the setting for an old western movie. Roy had the limousine drop them off in front of the Pioneer with instructions to check back in two hours. With business taken care of, the Daltons entered the Saloon, where Roy asked if Peter Drake was present.

Roy was recognized and immediately pummeled for autographs and handshaking. The front of the saloon was turning into a circus when the imposing figure of Peter Drake entered the area. He chased away the autograph hounds and led the Daltons into a private back room. This room had only two tables, and Roy noted that one table had a discrete wooden placard announcing that the table was reserved permanently for Sarah Peroni.

The magnificent painting of a giant bull elk in the front lobby did not go unnoticed by Roy, and having recently bought some of her work, the artist's name was familiar. Seeing a table reserved for the lady brought several questions to mind, but it was none of his business, so the questions remained unasked.

Roy asked Mr. Drake to join him and his parents at their table for a drink, an offer which the proprietor accepted at once. Even though the man's music cost him an evening of bliss with the beautiful widow, he was a big Roy Dalton fan.

Roy thanked Peter for allowing Jupiter to stay in his stable, which Peter graciously acknowledged and told Roy it was a pleasure and honor to see the famous Jupiter and let him share the stable with his two horses. Roy inquired about riding one of Peter's horses on the trails around town. Jupiter was too old to ride the trails Roy wanted to take him on. Peter agreed to let Roy ride his horses and offered to go along and show Roy some of the best riding spots in the valley. Roy and Peter made plans to meet tomorrow at noon for a ride, after which Peter left the table so the Daltons could enjoy a private meal together.

Sarah was home drinking wine with Arlene and discussing her fear of meeting the famous Roy Dalton. Arlene kept reminding her friend that Sarah was notable in her own right and should not be intimidated by meeting another famous person. What Arlene could not understand was that Sarah, who was not intimidated by reputation or stature- hell, Sarah associated with Presidents, Prime Ministers, and ambassadors- should be in such an agitated state. Meeting another famous person was no big deal. But Roy was different because he had seen into her soul one time, and Sarah was afraid of what Roy might see when they met in person.

Not that Sarah was ashamed of her life, who she was, or what she had become. She didn't have any big secrets or regrets, only she felt lost and was afraid that someone like Roy might see that she was a lost soul. What if he found her to be an empty shell, pretty to look at, possibly fun to be around, but devoid of substance? She could not even discuss this fear with Arlene because she didn't understand it herself.

Throughout the evening with his parents, Roy glanced at the empty table nearby with the reserved placard. Who was this lady to deserve such treatment? In the brochures Roy read back in his parent's motel room, he learned that Ketchum and Sun Valley were home to many celebrities and famous people who regularly visited the area. Surely big stars like Clark Gable and Marlene Dietrich, who had visited the place, would eat at the premiere restaurant in Ketchum, yet the table was reserved for a lady he knew only as an artist. There had to be a story here, but no way of learning what it was. Perhaps he would meet this mysterious lady. After all, he remembered Larry telling him that some Peroni lady was part of the arts committee responsible for sponsoring the concerts. He would have to remember to ask Larry to point her out to him.

Roy and his parents had a wonderful time together as they talked about old times and recalled their family history. Dinner was spectacular, with Roy and his dad opting for the prime rib while his mom had scampi. They had an after-dinner apéritif when Roy asked their server for his check. He was informed that their meal was on the house, for Mr. Drake considered it an honor to have such a famous person visit his restaurant.

Surprised because he was surely not the only famous person to visit the Pioneer Saloon, he compensated by leaving a great tip for their server.

On the ride back to the lodge after their excellent dinner, they made plans to get together again the next day. Roy finally went to check out his room. Band rehearsal in the morning to see the venue and do a soundcheck, after which there was the trail ride with Peter Drake. Another visit with his parents and then the Sun Valley Weed concert tomorrow night. Another busy day, just like he wanted.

There was no way he could know just how special tomorrow's concert would be or that it would become a classic.

50
RIDING TRAILS

The band checked out the concert hall the following day. After making a few adjustments to the sound systems and practicing a new introduction, they took the rest of the day off to see sights and enjoy one of the most spectacularly beautiful locales in the world. Roy left to get Jupiter and meet Peter to go riding on the trails. Peter had two bay geldings; both show horses and easy riding. Jupiter did not need a lead rope because he followed along like a little puppy.

Peter took them on a trail that led down to the Wood River. He warned Roy that there were bears around, and while they wouldn't charge a man on a horse, they could frighten the horses into running wild, especially Jupiter, who was not tethered. Not taking a chance, Roy dropped a rope with a lot of slack around his horse's neck, just in case.

About ten blocks east of Ketchum's Main Street, the Wood River is a major attraction to the area featuring some of the world's best trout fishing. Million-dollar mansions were scattered around, but with enough space to be completely private. The trail wound around and among pine trees, oak trees, aspens, and maple. The scenery was glorious, the setting peaceful and quiet except for dancing riffles in the water as the river swirled around rocks.

Peter knew Sarah was The Lady on The Train, but he didn't know that Roy didn't know this. As they rode along, Peter talked about his beautiful friend, who had painted the picture of the elk Roy saw in the Pioneer's lobby. Peter never mentioned Peroni's name, but Roy had noticed the painting and bottom signature and knew who Peter was describing. Without saying as much, Peter tried to give the impression that the lady in question was his very close friend, perhaps much more than a friend. This innuendo meant nothing to Roy, who barely listened. He was too enthralled with the experience, enjoying the ride and the beautiful scenery. Jupiter seemed to be happy trotting along and stealing a crop of grass along the trail now and then. The only phrase Roy remembered was when Peter mentioned that he and the mysterious friend were both huge Roy Dalton fans.

Peter seemed to take them quite far from the stable, so Roy reminded him he needed to be back before long to prepare for the evening. He also had to stop in and spend a few minutes with his parents. Larry had given Roy's parents tickets to their band's second show last night, and Roy wanted to make sure they were comfortable. He had arranged for a limousine to pick them up at the lodge and drive them to the stage door, where an usher would see that they were seated without going through the front doors with the mob.

Chores done, Roy had one last request. He wanted to bring Jupiter on stage for his signature song, *A Brief Encounter*. Since the horse was part of the original scene, Roy thought the audience would get a kick out of seeing the real McCoy. It was a frivolous request, yet Larry liked the idea, and the band seemed to think it would be great fun to share the stage with such a famous horse. Besides, Roy had a couple of other songs about horses he planned on performing, and if Jupiter were behaving, he would leave the horse on stage for these later numbers.

With a few minutes to spare before leaving for the concert venue, Roy wandered the Lodge halls and looked at pictures of the many famous guests who had visited there in the past. He visited the outdoor ice skating rink, vowing to come back for an ice skating show one day. Several kids and parents were out ice skating, and it was easy to spot the natives versus those who were visiting for perhaps the first time and just had to ice skate in the sun.

A shuttle ran around Sun Valley Village every twenty minutes, and Roy had time for one circuit. He wanted to take in the whole Sun Valley scene, for he was not sure he would ever make it back here to see an ice skating show. The shuttle passed the concert hall with giant banners advertising the Weed's concert and a gigantic picture of Roy Dalton. Roy had tried to remain incognito because he just wanted a peaceful, quiet ride to view the sights. His minimal disguise worked well until the shuttle bus passed the big poster featuring a picture of Roy, and an observant passenger recognized her famous bus mate, and the ride was spoiled. At least for Roy.

He was gracious, signing autographs until the shuttle deposited him back at the main entrance. The concert hall was filling up with entertainment provided by a local band. If Roy, Larry, and some of the old Tumbleweeds band members had been present, they might have recognized themselves years ago. A good group, but without the old band's talent.

Roy left early to check on Jupiter and see what arrangements were made to bring him to the concert and how the horse would enter the stage with all the wires and instruments. Where would they put the horse? Roy wanted him down front for the main song but to be visible throughout the remaining show. He needn't have worried. Larry had a very professional crew. They had made special arrangements to bring the horse over during the first half-hour and keep him outside until Roy called for his presence on stage. They already had a path marked out for the horse, and one of the stagehands familiar with horses was assigned the chore of minding the horse and taking him onstage.

Satisfied that all was as it should be, Roy relaxed backstage and enjoyed the reprieve before performance time. Just before taking the stage was his favorite evening time. Adrenalin was pumping through his body, heightening his awareness. His nerves were rattling teeth, but the remembered thrill of past performances built his confidence. Contrary to popular opinion, professional speakers, singers, and theatrical stage performers also suffer stage fright. The professionals know how to channel this fear into strength and power to enliven their performance. But even the best and most accomplished will admit to feeling fear just before going on stage. What you do with that fear makes the difference between the absolute professional and everyone else. Roy was the former, and he used this time backstage to put on his game face, a name used by actors and singers long before being popularized by the professional ballplayers.

51
NERVES

Sarah was a mess. My God, she was not this nervous when she met the Queen of England. She couldn't decide what to wear. Her hair was all frizzy. She had already drunk half a bottle of Cabernet, and the concert didn't start for another two hours. After trying on and discarding her fifth change of clothes, she sat at her dressing table, almost in tears. It wasn't like she knew anything about Roy. She had learned that he wasn't married but no word about another romantic interest. What was he like as a person? Could he still jump into her mind if they met? It was probably this last thought that worried her the most.

But, and this was a big BUT. But what if Roy didn't recognize her or want her in his life? Sitting on her bed and practically in tears, Sarah realized she had been waiting for Roy Dalton for the past fifteen years. That realization struck like a knife in her ribs. What in the hell had she been thinking? He was just a boy when their eyes held each other for mere seconds. Maybe these romantic fantasies weren't the same for him?

Fifteen years is a long time, especially for an eleven-year-old boy. Hell, he didn't even know what dating was or probably didn't know what it was to have a girlfriend. For sure, marrying some old lady ten years his senior was not part of his program.

How silly to think that the boy would remember all these years later or want some old lady for his mate.

Yet, there were those love songs and the name on his first album. That had to mean something, didn't it? Still, doubts persisted until, at last, Arlene knocked on her door before letting herself in.

Calling her friend from the bedroom, Sarah told her to bring her own glass. When Arlene saw her friend, the eyes gave Sarah away. Arlene never experienced the fear she saw in Sarah's eyes, and she was unsure what to do or say. Such fear must be experienced to understand how paralyzing it can be. Arlene's only experience with fear that extreme was in the eyes of a dog tied to a post whose master was beating it with a shovel. She remembered being sick afterward. Shit, she couldn't get sick now.

Sarah had tried to make her friend understand her fears earlier, but even Sarah was unprepared for the attack of nerves she was currently experiencing.

As Arlene poured herself a glass of wine, she noticed the level of wine left in the bottle. Sarah was not acting drunk, but the wine didn't seem to be helping her cope.

"Sarah, we have got to get you dressed. Let's look in your wardrobe for something appropriate."

Without waiting for a response that did not come in any event, Arlene helped herself to the wardrobe, searching for something fetching but not suggestive. There was a gray silk dress with many beautiful folds and swirls to suggest the body beneath without being too revealing. Perhaps subconsciously, she noticed the dress was the same shade as Roy's eyes. She pulled it off the hanger and handed it to Sarah with instructions to get dressed. Sarah took one look at the dress and held out her hand. She recognized that fighting with Arlene over her wardrobe would not be a good start to their evening.

After Sarah was dressed, Arlene sat her at the dressing table while fussing with Sarah's hair. A little curling iron, a bit of hair spray here and there, a couple of discrete pins to show off a pair of stunning earrings, and a plain gold necklace. As Arlene worked on Sarah, Sarah relaxed, partly from not having to decide anything and partly from her friend's calming presence. A third and last glass of wine from the bottle also helped. But when Arlene's glass came up empty, and she complained, Sarah, now dressed for the evening, took her friend out into the living room for another bottle.

Because they were both members of the arts committee, they had to leave early to help organize the ushers, the gatekeepers/ticket takers and check on the warm-up band. Sarah and Arlene pushed for a more accomplished prelude act, but budget constraints forced the issue, even though the committee would have plenty of cash after the concert.

They saw Peter Drake, who gave them a very sly smile, like he had some big secret he was keeping. But, of course, there are always minor snafus in any production. The warm-up band's amplifiers shorted out, but one of the Weed's technicians wired them up to some amplifiers used by The Weeds. There are always gate crashers, and the situation could turn ugly unless handled with care. Fortunately, the local police and the extra bouncers hired for the occasion maintained order. The vendor's ice machine broke, which sent someone scurrying down to Ketchum for more ice.

Thankfully, nothing major, and the concert was about ready to begin. Sarah and Arlene found their seats between Roy's parents and Peter Drake. Sarah and Arlene were introduced to Mr. and Mrs. Dalton, and for the first time, Sarah met Roy's parents. She was impressed by the Daltons. They seemed down-to-earth and pleasant people to be around. A comely couple, it was easy to see where Roy got his good looks and size. Mr. Dalton was almost six foot four inches, and Mrs. Dalton had the gray eyes that helped make Roy famous. Afraid of her reaction to Roy's presence on stage, Sarah was careful to seat Arlene next to Peter. She didn't want Peter too close.

52
SHOWTIME

The committee chairperson, Miss Ainscroft, thanked the warm-up band and welcomed everyone to the concert. The lady made a big deal out of the band's introduction, citing many of their accomplishments. Then, after a flurry of announcements about upcoming events that no one listened to, she finally introduced The Weeds with much ballyhoo.

The hall went dark except for the emergency aisle lights and a soft spot on the stage that grew gradually brighter to show a handsome Indian man sitting on a colorful, geometrically patterned Navajo blanket. After a few seconds, he started playing the flute, which no one who followed The Weeds had ever heard. The soft clear notes filled the auditorium. The music was haunting, evoking memories of ancient fires and a distant past. Then, after a couple of minutes, the chanting started along with a soft drumbeat. A melancholy harmonica added its voice to the music, and then Kathryn's bass and her clear soprano voice joined the mix, after which the stage lights came on, and the entire band joined the show.

After the introductory song, the stage lights were turned down while a spotlight focused on Roy. The crowd erupted in applause and catcalls until Roy restored calm and welcomed everyone to The Weeds' Sun Valley concert. Sitting in the front row, this close to the man in her dreams, it was all Sarah could do to control her emotions. My God, but the man was good-looking, and he had such a mesmerizing voice. He was yet to sing, but his voice, while soft, carried to the furthermost reaches of the room.

Roy noted Peter and his parents and the two lovely ladies sitting between Peter and his folks. And man was that lady in gray ever fetching. Something about her seemed familiar, but he couldn't quite dredge up the memory. Maybe she just looked like someone he met in the past.

The concert was scheduled for two hours, but everyone planned for three plus a thirty-minute intermission. The rest of the first set was typical Weeds music, with songs from all of their albums mixed in with impromptu solos by John and another Wohali flute rendition accompanied by Kathryn.

Roy announced the intermission with the promise of a major surprise in the second set. He did not know just how big the surprise would become.

When the lights went down to begin the second set, there was no vacant seat in the house. The first set was beautiful and satisfying, but Roy had yet to yodel, and the band still had several hit songs they had not played.

Roy took the microphone to open the second set.

"Ladies and gentlemen, about fifteen years ago, I stood by the train tracks with my horse Jupiter, watching a train pull up to the water tank on our ranch. This vision was no ordinary train; it was the New York Flyer. You may not have heard about this train, but it carried all the hopes and dreams of a lonely country boy. This sleek passenger train never stopped at our ranch, only the freight trains needed water from the tanks on our ranch, yet the New York Flyer stopped for water on this momentous day. I don't know why."

"Now, you have to understand; I was a young boy from the small town of Clifton. That's about four hours south of where we are now. I'm about to share a story that occurred at the height of the big war. Like most people in Clifton, we were poor, but we didn't know we were poor, since we always had food on the table and a warm roof over our heads. I remember my pants were torn and patched, yet there were still a few ragged-edged holes here and there. I was working on our barbed wire fence, and my hands were bloody. We couldn't afford gloves. I wore an old tattered straw hat, and my shoes were two sizes too big because they were hand-me-downs from my older brothers, who were away fighting in the war."

"Watching the New York Flyer go past our ranch was one of my greatest pleasures. People inside those train cars seemed to enjoy life to the fullest. They were all dressed in fancy clothes, drinking and laughing. Some people were reading a paper or a book. They were going to exotic places like Hollywood or San Francisco. It was my dream to ride that train to some beautiful place one day where it was always warm, and I didn't have to do any chores. But that was not for me."

"I felt trapped and lonely. I could never see myself leaving the ranch, so watching this train and the beautiful people inside was my escape. It was just a dream, but I lived in my fantasy for a few minutes as the train flew by."

"On one particular day, the Flyer stopped. It was the only time I remember a passenger train stopping for water at our tanks. As the train was slowing, nearly stopped, something extraordinary, something magical happened."

As Roy spoke about something magical in his monolog, a pretty young lady wearing riding breeches came on stage, leading Jupiter. And the crowd went wild. They all knew the story about the lady on the train and how a boy and his horse met a beautiful, lonely lady who had lost her husband in the war. The album and songs were legends. Roy took the lead rope from the girl leading

Jupiter, gave the fellow a big hug, and whispered something into his ear. There was a thunderous ovation as Roy introduced Jupiter to the audience

"I guess you don't need an introduction to Jupiter. I asked the good folks from Clifton to bring Jupiter to Sun Valley for a reunion, as I had not made it back home for a while. Since he was here, I thought for this next song, you might like to see my horse as he was standing there with me watching the Flyer stop at our ranch."

"You probably all know the story about what happened next, as it was in the song. But you may not know what happened to me after that incident with the train. For the next seven years, I received gifts from this unknown lady, one of which was the beautiful blond Gibson guitar I play. My whole musical career is because of a kind woman's generosity. She gave me life."

A stagehand brought out Roy's acoustic, and Roy handed the lead rope back to the girl, who remained on stage. The crowd was eerily quiet as Roy began singing *A Brief Encounter*.

He was almost at the end of the first stanza when he stopped singing. No one knew what was happening. This situation had never happened before. Roy never stopped singing in the middle of a song, especially this one, practically his signature song.

As he was singing about the woman on the train, he saw an image of the lady's eyes in his mind. When he remembered seeing the woman's eyes on the train, he finally recognized the lady in gray. Their eyes met, and he knew.

Calling the stagehand back, Roy handed him the guitar with another instruction. Then he leaped from the stage into the audience. The band and everyone present wondered what in the hell was happening.

Roy went directly to the woman in gray. "You are her, aren't you?" he asked. "The lady from the train. I know you are. Those eyes do not lie. Would you please join me on stage?" Roy held out a hand as he waited for the lady to accept his invitation.

Sarah was embarrassed, thrilled, excited, and nervous as hell. She felt hot all over, and her legs felt like lead. When Roy held out his hand for hers, Sarah was powerless to resist. Roy had to support her for a few seconds as she waited for her legs to respond.

They took a roundabout way to the stage so Sarah could climb the steps. Once back on stage, Roy held Sarah's warm hand while he took the microphone from its stand in his other.

No one knew what was happening. Apart from some jokes and references about the city they were in and local events, The Weeds were not known to have much interplay with the audience. Sarah was shaking like a leaf in a windstorm, anxious to know what Roy had in mind for her presence on the stage in the middle of a concert. Here she was, standing in front of her friends and associates without a clue, yet somehow, from somewhere deep within, Sarah knew that this was her destiny. So frightened, confused, and ecstatic, she waited for the man in her dreams to explain his actions.

"Ladies and gentlemen, I apologize for the interruption, but this beautiful lady you see standing here was the lady on that train fifteen years ago. Our eyes met then, and just now, I saw those eyes again, and... well, you know the song."

The audience began clapping and shouting. This scene was unprecedented—my God. Here was the lady on the train living in their midst, and she had never once hinted that she was the one.

The stagehand came back with a chair and Roy's guitar. Roy helped Sarah sit down on the chair, and then taking the guitar, he leaned against Jupiter and sang Sarah's love song. There was not a dry eye in the crowd or backstage. The scene was just too poignant, too full of emotion. Once the song ended and, as the audience began showing its appreciation by thunderous applause, Roy sat his guitar down on the stage, grabbed Sarah's hand, and pulled her to her feet. Before she knew what was happening, Roy took her into his arms and gave her a kiss that seemed to last forever. The audience and everyone in the band began clapping and cheering.

Taking the microphone, Roy addressed the audience. "I told you about my background and the poverty we experienced during the war. This lady gave me the Gibson guitar; she gave me money and provided me the opportunity to become who I am today. It is not an exaggeration to say that there would be no Weeds and no Roy Dalton without this lady."

Roy moved Sarah's chair over by Jupiter's head and had her sit by Jupiter for the rest of the concert. The next song was *Chime Bells*, which brought the house down, and Sarah could not stop crying. Someone brought her a box of Kleenex. Her emotions were out of control. Never in her wildest dreams had this scene ever been expected. Down in the first row, Arlene felt Peter's hand reach for hers, and she thought, *what the hell, why not? After this show, the chances for ole Peter getting in Sarah's pants did not look too good.*

After the final encore and the band left the stage for the last time, Roy finally asked, "Would you please tell me your name?"

Sarah got herself pulled together and could answer. "I'm Sarah Peroni."

When he heard these words, his heart fell to the floor as he remembered the table in the Pioneer Saloon reserved permanently only for Sarah Peroni. And he remembered Peter's sly remarks about the woman who painted the elk picture in his lobby. Roy could only think of one reason Peter would dedicate a table for Sarah's exclusive use, and the memory did not feel good.

"Mrs. Peroni, I am sorry for taking such liberties with you on stage. I did not know you were in a committed relationship. I should have known. Please forgive me. I will talk with Peter and explain my actions if I can. Truly, I cannot explain it to myself."

"Whatever are you talking about? And I am Ms. Peroni; I ditched the missus label years ago."

"Well, I saw a table reserved for you at the Pioneer, and Peter seemed to have a proprietary interest, so I assumed you were his woman."

"Oh, that. Peter gave me the table in return for the elk painting in the lobby. He felt he owed me something. I just gave him the picture because I like his restaurant and Peter as a friend."

"Sarah, now that I have finally found you, would you go with me someplace for a drink so we could talk a bit? I feel like I owe you my life."

"Yes, my master," she said with a smile. "And do not apologize for kissing me. I needed that more than you can ever know."

"Would you come with me to say hello to my parents? I need to tell them goodbye. They are waiting out by my limousine."

"Sure, and if you are comfortable, we could go to my place for a drink. That way, autograph hounds will not bother us."

"Your place sounds perfect. I'm curious about where the world's most talented decorator lives. Let us just say goodbye to my folks. They are just outside."

Roy introduced Sarah to his parents, who were delighted to finally meet the woman who owned their son's heart. Then, of course, they had already met, but they did not know who she was to their son when they met inside the concert hall. Sarah did not think Roy would recognize her after all this time. Fifteen years ago, he was an eleven-year-old boy. Who would expect him to remember someone from the past he only saw briefly on a train more than half his lifetime ago?

Roy escorted Sarah to the limousine that would take them to her house. He was a nervous wreck. Excited, anxious, and happy, yet uncertain about what might lie ahead. He could hardly wait to see her home and what the rest of his evening would be like.

Sarah could not process the tremendous emotions and thoughts flooding her body and mind. Until a few years ago, she never knew what happened to Roy Dalton, and since finding that album in New York, her life had become a roller-coaster of highs and lows, hoping, praying, and dreaming about the handsome singer. The current events were overwhelming.

The Sun Valley concert audience knew they had just experienced history unfolding. Never had such terrific emotions been experienced before. The audience left the auditorium knowing they had witnessed something extraordinary. This Sun Valley concert would be talked about for years. And as the legend grew, you could scarcely find a person who had not been there for that momentous meeting between Roy and the lady from the train.

53
SARAH'S PLACE

Roy had Sarah give his limo driver directions to her house. It seemed strange that both seemed shy and hesitant when they were alone together in the car, after the intimate kiss in front of the entire world. Two strangers with a fifteen-year-old bond created when they briefly met somewhere in time and space were brought together again by chance, they had so much to talk about, yet neither one could find the words to begin a conversation.

During the ten-minute ride to Sarah's place, Roy held Sarah's hand while searching for a way to begin a conversation. After dreaming about meeting this lonely widow for the most significant part of his life, Roy was utterly at a loss for words now that she was here. What do you say to a dream? How do you address someone who has played such a large part in making you who you are? How do you even say thanks for my life?

Sarah was an emotional wreck. The rollercoaster euphoria of Roy's recognition and the terrifying visit to the stage in front of thousands, followed by a love song written solely about and for her and that wonderful, frightening kiss. Oh my God! Sarah was also at a loss for words. What do you say to someone you have fantasized about ever since seeing his picture on an album cover?

She had painted a picture of the boy and his horse. In hindsight, after discovering his music, she had spent more time thinking about Roy than she ever did about her long-dead husband, Dean.

She had loved Dean, and while the memories of him had faded, Sarah remembered the good times they had together. Now, fifteen years later, her romance with Dean seemed like a high school fling, fun and serious as young people can take themselves, but what someone would call puppy love. What she was feeling now seemed overpowering. Sarah was not sure she could call it love. After all, the man was almost a stranger. Sure, she knew his music and the poetry of his songs, but who was the man? There was so much to talk about and no way to get started.

Likewise, Roy discovered how challenging it was to start a conversation. He was at a loss for the words to begin a dialogue.

What do you say to start a dialogue in a situation like this? Sarah's mind was running wild. *"The concert was incredible? Simply fantastic? I love your music."* Or how about, *"Wow, that was one heck of a kiss."*

And so they rode in silence, holding hands. It seemed like enough at the moment. The time for talking could come later, after a drink, to calm the nerves. Hell, make that a whole bottle to calm the nerves.

The limousine driver pulled up at Sarah's front door and waited for instructions. Roy got out first and then helped Sarah while admiring her beautiful house. Knowing that she was a successful painter, decorator, and entrepreneur with her furniture line, he did not think she would live in a hovel. Still, after seeing the simplicity of the structure and graceful, eye-catching design, he felt nervous. Sarah was accomplished in many areas, obviously intelligent, extremely beautiful, and wealthy, while he was just a country singer.

"Sarah, your house is beautiful. I learned you are also a successful decorator. Did you design your home?"

"Why thank you for noticing, and yes, I confess to helping make the house plans."

Roy dismissed their driver with instructions to take the rest of the evening for himself. Then, when he was ready to leave, he would have Sarah drop him back at the lodge.

Sarah took Roy's hand and led him inside, where her paintings and stunning décor took his breath away.

"Oh, my God. You are so incredibly talented." Roy was almost speechless. "You make me feel almost insignificant, and that isn't an easy accomplishment because my ego knows practically no bounds."

"Come on, Roy. You know you are one of Earth's most talented and loved people. Tonight, thousands of fans were thrilled to hear you perform, and I was one of them."

Roy caught sight of the painting Sarah did with him riding Jupiter. "Man oh man, I didn't realize you were such a fan."

"Let me get a bottle of wine, and let's sit down and talk," Sarah suggested. "Make yourself comfortable while I go grab a bottle or two."

"Okay, if I start a fire?" Roy asked as Sarah was leaving the room.

"Yes, that would be lovely. Everything you need should be there by the fireplace."

When Sarah returned, Roy had a blazing fire burning. He sat in her love seat and admired the room and the furnishings.

Sarah handed Roy the wine bottle and corkscrew. "Would you mind doing the favor?"

"Not at all; it will be my pleasure."

Roy pulled the cork and poured the wine while Sarah played some light classical music on the phonograph.

"For most of my life, I've been a music snob," Sarah confessed. "I always thought country music was for red-necked hillbillies. You must have realized that I kept track of you until your eighteenth birthday, and after that, I lost track of you for several years. Not being a country music fan, your success and rise to fame went completely unnoticed. I attended opera and ballet. Symphony orchestras playing classical music were my true love. I often traveled worldwide for opening nights of the world's great symphony orchestras. And then, one day, I passed a music store that had a Weed album in the window. It was the cover of Timeless, and I recognized the watch because I bought it personally. I believe that was my first gift."

Roy remembered. The gift had been a complete surprise, and he did not know who had given him such a valuable gift. It had been a year since the train experience, and Roy had never dreamed that a stranger would give him such a present. The lady on the train could not know who he was, so he never thought of her as the present giver. Years passed before he figured it out.

Sarah paused her confession and took a sip of wine. Sitting next to Roy in front of the fire and drinking wine was working wonders to relax her body's tension.

"I went inside and inquired, for I had never heard of The Weeds. I thought it was such a ridiculous name. In my mind, it was some stupid, unbearable country caterwauling, but I had to check it out. That watch took me into the store."

"The album cover interested me, and the young man running the store told me about the band and your music. He then showed me The Lady on The Train album, and for the first time, I read the words to *A Brief Encounter*. Oh my God, Roy, I bawled like a baby reading the poem. The store clerk must have thought I was a sick lady crying about a poem on an album cover. Then the young man played the album. Oh, good heavens. Such a beautiful song. I fell in love with a man named Roy Dalton and his music."

"Sarah, you know you made it all possible. Without your gifts, I would probably still be working the ranch, looking for a way out of my life. It is no exaggeration to say that you saved my life."

"I started looking for one of your concerts to attend. I wanted to experience your music live. You were touring in Europe, and I was waiting for your return when you had that terrible accident, and then I could not find out what happened to you."

"Yeah, I hit a rough spot. Fortunately, our band manager, Larry Perkins, found a physical therapist who worked with me every day for a year and helped me rebuild my body. I never expected to play or sing again, yet it all worked out. I believe my experience in Australia also helped." Roy did not mention Anita. Instead, he thought it best to let those memories remain private.

"Well, now that we've bared our souls, how about taking me to bed? I have been waiting for you long enough."

"If you show me the way, I'll help you shed that beautiful dress."

Neither one got any sleep that night.

54
THE DAY AFTER

Roy and Sarah were sitting at her kitchen counter drinking coffee and eating cinnamon rolls. Sarah looked both ravishing and ravished. Wearing a red semi-sheer silk robe, she glowed like a hundred-watt lamp. The sparkle in her eyes and the red cheeks spoke of happiness, yet her hair looked like it had been in a tornado, which wasn't far from the truth. Roy wore a black guest robe, which Sarah informed him had never been worn by another man. Sarah told Roy that he was her first formal male visitor, other than handypersons and service technicians. The smile on Roy's face said it all.

"Sarah, my love, I have waited for you all my life. I'm so happy that you spotted that album in the store window. After those first two albums, when I never heard from you, I lost hope of ever seeing you again. Since we had shared such an intimate moment, I thought maybe you were embarrassed to see me or something."

"Dear, dear, Roy. You can't know how many of your concerts I tried to attend once I heard your music. They were sold out, or I had scheduling conflicts. You can't imagine how difficult it is to find out anything about your personal life. There is plenty of information about you and the band. Where you'll be playing, information about your music, but nothing personal. I didn't know if you were married, had a steady girlfriend, or slept with every groupie that follows the band. Then you had that terrible accident, and no one knew where you were or if you would ever perform again. Then, I learned you were in Australia doing some walk-about thing, and I never thought I'd see you. Mr. Dalton, you are not an easy man to catch up with."

"Sarah, we know very little about each other, except I think we know each other intimately. I don't mean last night. Our eyes met fifteen years ago. I knew you like I know you knew me, and things haven't changed, except you're rich and famous, and I sing in a country music band."

"I know what you mean, Roy, except you are much more famous than I am and probably have more money now than I do."

Roy waited until Sarah looked up at him from the table so he could look into her eyes, "Sarah, my love, the fame, and fortune stuff doesn't mean that much unless you can share it with someone special, and Sarah, I don't want to go on through life any longer without you. I don't want to leave your side unless you drive me away."

"Oh, Roy. I've been so damned lonely waiting for you. And unless you take me right back to bed, I'm going to go crazy."

It was late in the afternoon when Sarah gave Arlene a call. "Hey friend, I need a favor. Could you come by and work on my hair, please? And then take me to go get my car?"

"What, you don't do beauty parlors anymore? Wait, don't answer that. I'm dying to hear about your evening and why you are stranded, but that can wait. I'll be there in fifteen minutes."

Arlene arrived with a bit of a glow of her own and a sparkle in her eyes. "So, where's the stud? Don't tell me he dumped you already."

"That's the friend I know and love. Always full of optimism. Roy called his limo, and I could have ridden with him to get my car, but I don't look fit to go out in public. The hairdressers are booked, and I need my hair fixed for tonight's concert." Although it would be difficult for a woman of Sarah's beauty ever to look bad, she had that look of a horse who had been ridden hard and then put up wet.

"Okay, enough foreplay. I want all the nitty-gritty. Come on, girl, give. I don't do hairdressing for free."

"My God, Arlene. I don't know where to start. I'm so damned happy. We hardly ever got out of bed except to grab something to eat and drink. I'm so sore I can hardly walk."

"So, what is he like in bed? You know I want to do him vicariously."

"Well, contrary to what you might think, I don't have much experience making love, but I could make love with Roy forever. He is the most gentle, considerate lover a woman could want. And he knows how to make a woman happy. Oh lord, does he know how to please a woman! I don't know where he learned how, but he had one hell of a teacher."

"Let's forget the vicarious part. How about taking turns?"

"Sure, and like you, share *your* lovers. Speaking of which, do I see a little sparkle in your eyes today?"

"Well, ole Peter got all worked up watching you and Roy swap spit on stage, so he wanted a little action to call his own. I was there, didn't have a date, and things happened. It was okay, except I still don't have my private table at the Pioneer, and Peter, while good in bed, is still full of himself."

"No, but you have the next best thing. The owner's interest." Sarah saw that this statement pleased her friend. Sarah didn't know how interested Peter was in any woman. Arlene herself told Sarah that Peter's only real love was himself.

"Only because Peter got the message pretty loud and clear that you are now officially off-limits," Arlene said with a bit of pout. But whether he and she were serious, it was hard to tell.

"Well, how did it happen?" Arlene pressed. "You all just came in the door and hopped into bed?"

She was half teasing but still serious. Roy was a handsome man. Sarah could imagine almost anyone wondering what he might be like in bed.

"Almost. We started drinking wine and talking. Roy built a fire, and it was pretty romantic. Then, well, it just happened."

"So, best friend. Where do you go from here? What's next?"

Sarah had to think for a minute. Everything was happening so fast, and her emotions were still not entirely under control. "The Weeds have their final concert here tonight, and then one last show is scheduled in San Francisco in three days. After that, Roy is going to take a break from the band. We don't have any plans made right now, so I guess we'll just take it one day at a time."

"Are you going to San Francisco with Roy?"

"I don't think Roy will let me out of his sight, at least not for a while. And hey, I'm not complaining. Right now, we cannot get enough of each other."

"Damn, girl, but I envy you. I might have had such a romance once, but I messed it up. That isn't a chapter in my life I want to rehash right now. Maybe never. Some things are better left unsaid."

"Says the lady who wants to sleep with my newfound love."

"Well, you can talk about some things and some things you'd rather not discuss. Screwing Roy is something we can discuss. From what I have heard, from good authority, these bands on the road share girls all the time. They might have two or more couples doing it in the same room; then, they switch partners after a while. So come on, Sarah, Roy's been on the road for years. He's probably shared hundreds of girls. Why not you and me?"

"I don't know your authority for that observation, but I'm pretty sure Roy didn't take part in that behavior. Not that it would make any difference. But from what I gathered, he is somewhat of a loner. I got the impression that in the evenings after a concert was the time Roy spent working on new compositions."

"God, Sarah. I was only joking. Well, maybe just a little serious, but don't go all righteous on me. You have to admit; the man is one hell of a hunk."

"Yeah, I know you were kidding, at least a little, but Arlene, dear, you have the reputation of an alley cat. And we both know damn well that if Roy and I were willing, you would jump in bed with us in a heartbeat."

"That might be true, but it doesn't change the fact that I love you. How's the hair looking?"

"Wonderful. Just for that, I'll ask Roy if he wants to go to bed with you."

"Don't tease me, Sarah. When it comes to sex, I don't have a funny bone."

"Yeah, we've beaten that horse beyond anything alive. Listen, are you and Peter going to tonight's concert? You have tickets for both nights."

"Funny, but that never came up last night. I'll be there. I wouldn't miss a live Weeds concert for a week in Peter's bed. I imagine Peter will be there as well, but we didn't discuss his plans."

"I thought it might be fun to go over to the Pioneer and grab a late dinner. Peter and Roy got along comfortably together yesterday, and I don't think it would be awkward, but maybe that's for you two to decide."

"Peter said he liked Roy," Arlene responded. "And, of course, we both know he loves his music. Also, since Peter is boarding Roy's horse, they may want to discuss arrangements for tomorrow."

"We have a few hours. How about a glass of wine, Arlene? Then you can take me to pick up my car."

"Sounds like a plan. Is Roy sending his limousine for you?" Arlene sounded a bit envious.

"Yes, and I'll come to pick you up unless you're riding with Peter."

"Oh, would you? I love riding in limousines. It makes one feel so important. Does Roy's have a bar and all the toys? And you know Peter. We didn't discuss transportation. We had a night of fantastic sex, and then he rolled over and went to sleep. He let me sleep in this morning but left me a note and keys to one of his cars. He had something he had to take care of early this morning."

"Well, we've talked about everything else. So, what did you and Peter think about the concert?" Sarah was eager to get her friend's appraisal of last evening's concert.

"Oh my God, Sarah. Do you even have to ask? That was probably the best concert ever performed by any band, at any time and in any place. You should hear what people are saying. Ole Peter couldn't stop talking about it until, of course, we wound up in bed, and then he had to play some of the Weed's albums while we screwed our brains out. Finally, that was the most outstanding concert those other five thousand people in the building will ever attend."

"Yeah, that was my impression, but of course, I am a little prejudiced."

"After last night, Sarah, The Weeds legend, and the name Roy Dalton and the lady on the train will live on in the minds of Sun Valley people for decades."

"Okay, let's get out of my dressing room and go have that wine," Sarah said with enthusiasm. "And because you have been so damn nice, fixing my hair and saying all those nice things about the concert, I'll even fix you a ham sandwich."

"Oh, my God, will miracles never cease?"

55
TAKE TWO

Roy met Peter at the stables to go riding. Peter had already saddled riding horses, and Roy led Jupiter with a leash, which was probably unnecessary. Jupiter seemed to want Roy's company and was happy just following along the trails. The two men swapped stories about life and living, neither mentioning the ladies in their lives. After showing Roy much of the valley from the floor, Peter took him up Baldy, one of the area's steeper ski mountains. Near the top was a level spot with several granite boulders that made perfect seats to sit and admire the view. Peter pulled a couple of water bottles from his saddlebags, and the two men sat and relaxed, enjoying the magnificent scenery while drinking water.

"Roy, that was the God-damnedest concert I have ever attended. You sing like a blooming angel, and your music is off the charts. You, sir, have one hell of a great band. I only discovered that our Sarah was your lady on the train a few days ago when I tried to seduce her. My mistake in setting the mood was playing the love song you wrote for her. That, of course, ended our evening, but I have to admit, you two seem made for each other."

"I can't blame you for wanting to get Sarah into bed. She is a beautiful lady and fun to be around. I'm happy you enjoy The Weeds. We try to play the music that appeals to a broad audience. However, I believe Sarah is the first classical music lover who converted or opened up to other possibilities besides Brahms."

"Oh, I wouldn't be too sure about that, Roy. Sun Valley has been a snobbish group of people when it comes to music. Yours is the first nonclassical musical act we've had in Sun Valley, but based on what happened last night, I believe you have several thousand new fans."

"Thanks Peter. I appreciate the kind words. What do you say we take these horses home? I need to check in with the band and see about arrangements for tonight. And I have got to spend some time with my parents."

Roy spent the next two hours having lunch with his parents at Peter's Pioneer Saloon. Peter wouldn't hear of letting Roy eat at any other place, and he admired Mr. and Mrs. Dalton.

Sarah was still fussing with her makeup and hair when Roy's limousine drove into her driveway. She had tried on a dozen different outfits to find the right one for tonight. She wanted to look sexy without being cheap. As the time for her ride to appear drew close, the nerves kicked in, and Sarah felt like a mess. Although Arlene had done a splendid job with her hair, Sarah couldn't decide if she was happy or if it needed more work. It was impossible to find the right shade of lipstick to go with her form-fitting Emerald green sheath, and the damn shoes clashed with everything. The limousine driver waited a few minutes, and when his ride didn't appear, he left the vehicle and knocked on her door.

Out of time, Sarah grabbed a white leather jacket and said to hell with it while heading for the door. She didn't need to impress anybody, and Roy would be pleased no matter how she looked. Still, as she settled into the back of the limousine, Sarah couldn't ever remember being this nervous. Hell, she had entertained Presidents, heads of state, royalty, and billionaires with hardly a quiver, yet the thought of seeing Roy again and being onstage with him had her shaking like someone riding a jackhammer.

Sarah directed the driver to Arlene's place. On the drive over, she checked out the limousine. Arlene had asked about a built-in bar and other luxurious amenities Sarah had overlooked during her earlier rides. Roy was along in her thoughts, occupying her mind and time. She was delighted to discover an open bottle of champagne with two chilled glasses. Hopefully, they could drink it all before going to the concert.

Arlene was standing outside of her house when the limousine arrived. She knew the time was getting short and was worried that perhaps Sarah had forgotten her when the big white vehicle drove into her yard. She looked fetching, wearing a short Navy blue pleated skirt and knitted white top with a silk wrap that matched her skirt. Arlene couldn't wait for the driver to open the door for her; she just grabbed the handle and jumped in before the car completely stopped.

"Oh, my God. Champagne. You beautiful girl," she said, taking the glass Sarah handed her.

"It wasn't my idea, but thanks anyway," she said. "I was a nervous wreck, but this seems to help," she added, tilting her glass in Arlene's direction.

"So, where's the music and hors d'oeuvres?" Arlene asked with a smile.

"Your hostess for this trip is out of her mind." Sarah tried to return the smile, but her face felt frozen, and the smile didn't materialize.

"You poor dear. I can see the nerves are active and alive." To distract her friend, Arlene prattled on. "That's a beautiful green dress, Sarah, and it compliments your eyes."

"Thanks, Arlene. Unfortunately, I discovered my lipstick wouldn't match after I had it on, and I didn't have the right shoes.

Last night, I wasn't expecting anything to happen, and when everything came crashing down, I was too busy and occupied with events to get nervous. Now, I feel Roy will have me on stage again, and I'm going crazy."

"Sarah, you are beautiful beyond words. You're talented, rich, and could probably have any man you wanted. Roy is a dreamboat, highly gifted, and crazy about you. Hell, girl, you have the entire world in your hand. Enjoy the ride." Arlene sat back and sipped her champagne.

Managing an embarrassed and wistful smile, Sarah responded, "I have been extremely fortunate, especially having you for a friend. Hang in there with me, and I'll pull myself together. Another bottle of this bubbly, and I won't feel a thing."

"That's a good idea, except we'll have to chug-a-lug the rest of this bottle. We're almost there."

Their driver took them to the back of the concert hall, close to the stage door. Jupiter, munching on a grass pile, was there with his handler holding his halter, and just seeing the horse had a calming effect on Sarah as she thought about her painting of Jupiter and Roy. The horse seemed calm and unaffected by the production, so why should she be different?

Sarah sat back in her seat. "I will finish this bottle like a civilized lady, not chugging. What do you say, Arlene? Are we real late?"

"No, dear friend, we have plenty of time, and I believe Roy is about to join us. I saw him duck out of the stage door just now. Do we have another glass?"

"Probably, but let's see if he wants a drink or just to coordinate our activities."

Roy opened the rear door next to Sarah and, with a big smile, said, "Welcome, ladies. Are you ready for take two?"

56
THE LAST ACT

The buzz in the audience was electric. Many of the patrons were in attendance last night when the lady on the train was revealed, and those who were not here last night knew about last night's concert. Just to think that one of the most famous ladies in music history lived right here in Sun Valley was unbelievable. One of their very own. Tonight's patrons couldn't wait for the encore to see what would happen during tonight's show. When Sarah and Arlene entered the auditorium, they could feel the audience's anticipation was at a fevered pitch.

Someone recognized Sarah as the lady on the train when she entered and shouted her name. The audience stood and applauded, whistling and shouting in appreciation and joy. Sarah was embarrassed and hurried to her seat as she brushed past hands, reaching out to touch the famous lady. Mr. and Mrs. Dalton were both seated but stood and gave their son's lady friend a big hug before she could sit down. Arlene was happy to see Peter in his seat and even happier when he leaned over and gave her a brief kiss on the cheek.

"Did Roy tell you his plans for tonight's show?" Arlene asked Sarah.

"No. We never got that far," she explained with an embarrassed grin. "It seems like everybody already knows who I am, so it cannot be the same surprise it was last night."

"Well, just hold on to your girdle because I feel he has an encore already in mind," Arlene said with a smirk.

"Oh, God, I hope not," Sarah responded. But before she had even finished speaking, she saw Roy coming across the front row towards her seat.

"Sarah, I know you don't like the attention, but everyone here wants to see the lady on the train. Maybe it would be more appropriate for you to be backstage with me and then come on stage when I introduce the song and you to the audience. Then you can return to your seat or stay on stage for the rest of the show. Your choice. What do you say?"

"You know I avoid bringing attention to myself, but this is your concert, and I know people want to hear your song and see the mysterious lady. I'll come with you, but would it be okay if I returned to my seat after the song?"

Holding out his hand for her to take, Roy said with a huge smile, "You betcha, darling, and that dress is dynamite."

Roy escorted Sarah backstage, where she was given a chair next to Jupiter, who nuzzled her like an old friend. Sarah was too nervous to notice that the horse messed up her hair. The stray hairs he worked loose made her appear even more charming, somehow more human, not so much the Japanese doll in a glass cage look.

This concert began just like the last one, with Wohali sitting on his patterned blanket, playing his flute in a soft spotlight.

Many factors contributed to a successful show. However, it was always surprising to the performers just how much effect the audience has in making a show tremendous or even spectacular. For example, there are nights when even the funniest lines delivered perfectly elicit hardly a grunt and other times when the weakest lines bring down the house. Having studied audiences for many years, Roy was still amazed at how different audiences can bring out the absolute best in a performer. Tonight's audience was a crowd performers dream. They were almost all Weeds fans and knew the music, and everyone knew the famous lady on the train was here in the auditorium. Delirious with joy while anticipating the big number, it felt like every musical note was delivered primarily to each individual in the audience.

When performing for an audience, the actor, musician, or comedian can sense how the act is being received. When an audience is exceptionally attentive and appreciative, something magical happens. It is almost like alchemy. Performers find themselves in a zone where they can do absolutely no wrong. Every single note, every word, every gesture is spot-on perfect. It is almost as though the audience pulls the very best out of the performer. And such was tonight's show.

Wohali's flute seemed to settle into the fabric of every being, reminding them of a lifetime's past, ancient stories of creation, and the beauty of life. The pure silver notes hung in the air, sparkling like diamonds, and the audience was enthralled. As Wohali played, he felt the magic; he knew something fantastic was happening, and tears of joy ran down his cheeks. When Kathryn added her bass to the flute, she felt the magic and Wohali's happiness, and it felt like her fingers hardly moved to bring out the most haunting bass counterpoint to Wohali's flute. Backstage, Roy sensed they were in for an evening to remember, so the audience gasped when he added a melancholy harmonica to Wohali's melody. The haunting song was almost too beautiful to bear.

And so, the concert went. The player's fingers never got tired. No one missed a note. Roy's voice never cracked, and the audience's expectations grew with every number, so when the girl handling Jupiter brought the horse on stage, you could hear the audience roar a mile away. Then, when Sarah walked on stage with Roy and his acoustic guitar, it was pandemonium. This scene and musical selection were the moments the audience had been waiting for all evening.

Roy held his hand up to still the crowd, but it took several minutes before the audience would let him speak.

"Thank you for such a welcome. I know Jupiter appreciates your applause." His words brought a big laugh from the audience.

"I guess everyone knows that this divine lady here by my side, Miss Sarah Peroni, is the famous lady on the train. I wrote two albums trying to get her to introduce herself to me, and it took a high school kid in New York managing a music store to finally introduce her to The Weeds and my music. Then, it still took several years before we finally met, right here, last night."

Roy was not finished speaking, but the crowd stood as one erupting in another round of applause and cheering.

When the noise died down and everyone was seated, Roy continued, "By now, everyone knows the story about how she bought my Gibson guitar and provided the money that allowed me to pursue my dreams. No words can adequately describe my love and appreciation for Sarah, so I guess this song will have to do."

With that introduction, Roy strummed the opening chords to *A Brief Encounter*, bringing the house to another standing ovation. Roy just kept strumming on the acoustic until the crowd settled down. Then he launched into the song, bringing tears to nearly every eye.

While the house was still ringing with applause, Roy escorted Sarah back to her seat, which she gratefully sank into along with the arms of her good friend, Arlene.

It would not be fair to say the rest of the concert was anticlimactic, for the band was hitting every note in perfect synch with each other, and the feeling was still electric, but clearly, the high note of the concert had been reached. The audience got to see their darling Sarah, they heard their favorite song, and their favorite singer was entertaining them.

Roy saved *Chime Bells* for the last number of their third and final curtain call. When Roy struck the last high note on the Gibson, echoing his ringing yodel, the audience went nuts. Everybody, including the band, was in awe of the evening's performance, a night to remember.

The concert lacked last night's drama, but it surpassed that performance with an exceptional evening of music and happiness. When folks attend something genuinely extraordinary, they leave feeling full, happy, and even ecstatic, and they don't want the feelings to end. As the audience left the auditorium, you could hear the pleasant buzz of satisfied, happy people. The only unhappy person was Peter because his dreams of bedding the gorgeous Sarah Peroni would never be realized. Arlene was a fabulous second choice. Maybe he would have to get serious with the lady now that Sarah was no longer in play.

Roy waited for Sarah backstage with Jupiter. Along with everyone else, he never wanted the evening to end, but finishing it with his horse and the lady of his dreams was not a bad way to close it out.

57
AFTERWORD

That night back at the Sun Valley Lodge, Roy held a short meeting with the band announcing the decision to hang up his spurs. Everyone in the band knew their days were numbered, and Roy's announcement came as no surprise, especially with the lovely Sarah Peroni by his side. San Francisco would be their last performance for this tour. Maybe there would be a future tour; no one ever knows what the winds of fate may have in store. Perhaps tomorrow's tide would wash up a new opportunity.

Roy said goodnight to the band and left to go home with Sarah. Their future seemed bright now that the brief encounter appeared to be a long-playing act. After their final concert, Roy planned to stay with Sarah in Ketchum and compose music. He already had the next album's title, *AS TIME MOVES ON, KEEP SMILING*.

AUTHOR'S NOTES

I was the young boy watching the passenger train, catching the eyes and exchanging looks with the lonely, sad lady with her tear-stained face pressed against the window. Then, a few years ago, I began a blog about life on our farm one mile long. For the blog called *The Longest Mile*, I wrote short essays about growing up in a small rural Idaho town and life on the farm. One of the essays described my brief eye encounter with the lady on the train.

Sharing my blog with others, including cousins from Clifton, I never expected much response, yet Larry Perkins fell in love with my story and wondered whatever happened to the woman. Instead, he fantasized about the lady in her old age, looking to find out what happened to the boy.

During one of our lunches, he suggested writing a novel about the boy and lady describing an event when they eventually meet. Larry wanted us to take turns writing, one chapter at a time. He wrote one chapter and then decided that writing novels was too much work. Larry died some time ago, yet his dream about the lady meeting the boy later in life kept surfacing in my mind until I had to write the story.

Since *A Soul Encounter* would have never been written without his prompting, I named one of the characters after my friend and cousin, Larry Perkins. The background is as remembered, and several of the events described in the story happened. But my horse was named Sunshine, and I played the Gibson guitar in a dance band and sang solo in nightclubs and concerts, including the Limelite. My defining act on stage was yodeling in *Chime Bells*. I was never a Roy Dalton and never met the lady on the train, but maybe someday?

Clifton, Idaho, nestled in the Rocky Mountains with the Union Pacific railroad tracks just east of town, is as the author remembers. However, sadly, the New York Flyer no longer travels the tracks, and the old water tank has been gone for ages. Diesel engines don't need water. The Chickaree happened, and there was a Smokey Joe. I am amazed at how much of my life is described in *A Soul Encounter*. I never intended the story to be my autobiography, and it isn't, but including the names of many Clifton residents and small-town incidents in the story somehow makes it seem more real. But, please remember, this is a work of fiction. None of the characters portray living people.

Sun Valley with the Pioneer Saloon and its excellent ambiance and fine food is as described, and should you visit the area, be sure and check out the Sun Valley Lodge. Their winter ice sculptures are world-class. Or go in the summer and try ice skating in July.

I had another brief encounter, but this was with the picture of the lady who is now my wife. I felt a strange and wonderful feeling looking at the photo, so I searched for her. Something magical happened when the lady saw me because I wore an eye patch, which seemed to have special significance. I think she recognized we were destined to be together. We still are, thirty-eight years later.

Thanks for reading my book. I love to hear from my readers who can leave a message and see more of my work at **clarkviehweg.com.**

ABOUT THE AUTHOR

Clark Viehweg is the author of five previous books published by Black Rose Writing. He lived as a Shaman described in the *Hokee Wolf* books and spent many years working as a contractor for the CIA developing Black Works technology. He lives in Utah with his wife, Kim, and dog, Quigley.

NOTE FROM THE AUTHOR

Word-of-mouth is crucial for any author to succeed. If you enjoyed A *Soul Encounter*, please leave a review online—anywhere you are able. Even if it's just a sentence or two. It would make all the difference and would be very much appreciated.

I would love to hear from you at **clarkviehweg07@gmail.com**

Thanks!
Clark Viehweg

We hope you enjoyed reading this title from:

www.blackrosewriting.com

Subscribe to our mailing list – *The Rosevine* – and receive **FREE** books, daily deals, and stay current with news about upcoming releases and our hottest authors.
Scan the QR code below to sign up.

Already a subscriber? Please accept a sincere thank you for being a fan of Black Rose Writing authors.

View other Black Rose Writing titles at
www.blackrosewriting.com/books and use promo code
PRINT to receive a **20% discount** when purchasing.